7/23/04

mys
FIC
Qiu

Qiu, Xiaolong

When red is black

DUE DATE

WHEN RED IS BLACK

Also by the Author

Fiction
Death of a Red Heroine
A Loyal Character Dancer

Poetry Translation
Treasury of Chinese Love Poems

Poetry
Lines Around China

WHEN RED IS BLACK

Qiu Xiaolong

SOHO

Published in the United States by

Soho Press, Inc.
853 Broadway
New York, N.Y. 10003

Library of Congress Cataloging-in-Publication Data

Qiu, Xiaolong, 1953–
When red is black / Qiu Xiaolong.
p. cm.
ISBN 1-56947-369-2 (alk. paper)
1. Chen, Inspector (Fictitious character)—Fiction. 2. Police—
China—Shanghai—Fiction. 3. Translating and interpreting—
Fiction. 4. Real estate developers—Fiction. 5. Shanghai (China)—
Fiction. I. Title.
PS3553.H537 W47 2004
813'.6—dc22   2003023436

10 9 8 7 6 5 4 3 2 1

In memory of my parents Renfu and Yuee,
who, like many Chinese people in the book,
suffered during the Cultural Revolution
because they were politically black.

Acknowledgments

I want to acknowledge the help of my friends during the writing of this book. They include Charles Turner, who simply is Ouyang, as in *Death of Red Heroine*; Staci Rohn, who has helped to shore these fragments against the wasteful days; Carole Wantz, who finds herself to be a fire dragon in harmony with the elements of the book; and of course Laura Hruska, my American editor, and Liana Levi, my French editor, who have both pushed me so positively, along with the other great assistance they have provided.

Chapter 1

Detective Yu Guangming of the Shanghai Police Bureau stood alone, still reeling from the blow. Its impact had been slow in coming, but when it came, it nearly crushed him. After months of meeting after meeting, negotiation after negotiation, he had lost the promised apartment in Tianling New Village. It was a new apartment, and had been officially assigned to him; the assignment had even been announced, to thunderous applause, at the bureau.

In the overpopulated city of Shanghai, home to more than thirteen million people, the housing shortage was grave. The assignment of an apartment was a significant event. For many years, it had been up to one's work unit—the Shanghai Police Bureau for Yu—to decide which of its employees would get a room or an apartment from the unit's annual government allotment. As recognition of his outstanding service of more than a decade, Yu had finally been awarded a two-bedroom apartment—or at least the keys to it. But before he could even make plans to move, the apartment had been unexpectedly taken back.

Yu was standing in a small courtyard, littered with dust-covered odds and ends, the discards of all the families living in this old *shikumen*-style building, which housed no fewer than twelve families, including his. The ancient courtyard looked like a junkyard, which was what his mind felt like. He lit a cigarette.

The explanation—or pretext—for the withdrawal of the apartment involved the adjustment of debts among the state-run companies. A creditor of another state-run company had seized some of the new apartments in Tianling New Village just built by the Golden Dragon Construction Corporation. Among them was the very unit assigned to Yu. This reversal of fortune was absurd; it was as if a roasted Beijing duck had flown back into the sky.

A few days earlier, when delivering the bad news, Party Secretary Li of the Shanghai Police Bureau had had a long talk with Yu before concluding, as always, on a characteristic positive note: "Economic reform is ushering in great changes. A lot of these changes would have been unimaginable two or three years ago. Our housing system is affected too. Soon, Chinese people will no longer have to depend on a government-housing quota. My brother-in-law, for example, recently bought a new apartment in the Luwan District. Of course, you are still at the top of the list here. The bureau will take your case into special consideration. Even in the event you purchase an apartment in the future, we may be able to get some housing compensation for you."

This was to be his consolation!

After more than forty years during which housing in the city had been government-assigned, a new policy made it possible for people to buy their own apartments, but, as the saying went, *Policy may change three times in a single day.* No one could foretell the future of reform in China. For Party Secretary Li's brother-in-law, owner of several expensive restaurants and bars, there had been no problem in purchasing an apartment at the price of four thousand Yuan per square foot. For Detective Yu, a low-level cop with a monthly salary of around four hundred Yuan, such an expenditure was a dream he could not dare to dream.

"But I have already been awarded the apartment," Yu had said stubbornly. "It was a formal bureau decision."

"I understand. It's not fair to you, Comrade Detective Yu. Believe me, we have tried everything possible on your behalf. We are all aware that you have done an excellent job as a police officer. But we have done all we could. We are sorry."

Li's smooth talk did not change the hard fact: Detective Yu had lost the apartment.

It was going to be a terrible loss of face too. His friends and relatives had learned about his new apartment, all of them had congratulated him, and some of them had prepared for a house-warming party. Now what?

But what worried him far more was the reaction of his wife, Peiqin. During the fifteen years of their marriage, they had always been, *Holding hands together, talking, talking, talking*, in the words of a popular song. Since their days as "educated youths" sent to Yunnan during the Cultural Revolution, and then as one of millions of ordinary couples in Shanghai, they had always been close. Of late, however, she had seemed withdrawn.

This was not hard for him to understand. All those years, he had brought little home in comparison to her. It was undeniable, and occasionally unbearable too, that Peiqin earned more as a restaurant accountant than Yu as a policeman. And this gap had increased in the last few years, as Peiqin had received many bonuses. Not to mention the free delicacies that she brought home from the restaurant.

The initial announcement about the apartment had momentarily pulled him up a peg or two, so to speak, in both their estimations. She had been ecstatic, telling everybody about the apartment he had been given "because of his excellent work."

Since they got the bad news, though, she had hardly spoken. He contemplated this, the cigarette burning down between his fingers. Just another sign that as a low-level policeman in today's society, he was going nowhere.

In his father's days, Old Hunter, a cop too, had at least enjoyed the dignity of being part of the "proletarian dictatorship" and the knowledge of being equal in material terms with everybody else in an egalitarian society. Now in the nineties, it was a changed world: one's value was one's money. Comrade Deng Xiaoping had said, "Some should be allowed to get rich first." Some did, absolutely. And in this socialist country, becoming rich now meant becoming glorious. As for those who did not become rich no matter how hard they worked, the *People's Daily* had no comment.

A conscientious cop, Detective Yu did not have so much as a room of his own, although he was already in his early forties. The one single room in which he had lived with Peiqin and their son Qinqin since their return to the city in the early eighties, had origin-ally been a dining room, in the wing of the house that had been assigned to Old Hunter in the early fifties.

Peiqin had not really complained, but after this apartment fiasco, her silence spoke volumes. She had once questioned his dedication to police work, although not directly. In this time of "economic reform," it was possible for people to make their own career choices, even if some paths involved risk. As a cop, Yu had his "iron rice bowl" which, for many years, had meant life-long job security in Chairman Mao's communist utopia. The iron—unbreakable—rice bowl was a synonym for a permanent job, with guaranteed income, medical benefits, and food ration coupons. But now having an iron rice bowl was no longer so desirable. Geng Xing, one of Peiqin's former colleagues, had quit to run a private restaurant, and, according to Peiqin, made five or six times more than at the state-run restaurant. Peiqin had talked about Geng's choice as if expecting some response from Yu, he remembered.

This was a crisis, Detective Yu concluded somberly, grinding out his cigarette butt on the concrete sink in the courtyard, before he went back to their room.

Peiqin was washing her feet in a green plastic basin. She remained seated, hunched over on the bamboo stool, without looking up. There were puddles of water on the floor. Inevitable. The basin was too small. She could hardly flex her toes in it.

In their "educated youth" days in Yunnan, now almost like another life, Peiqin, sitting beside him, had dabbled her feet in a brook, a clear, peaceful brook that ran behind their bamboo hut. At that time, their one and only dream was of coming back to Shanghai, as if everything would then unfurl before them like the rainbow against the blue sky. A flash of light on a blue jay's wings. Then a shrimp in the water had seized her toe, and she had fallen against him in panic. They had returned to the city in the early eighties, but only to this single twelve-square-meter room, to the realities of life. Few of their hopes had been fulfilled except for the birth of their son Qinqin, who had grown into a tall boy. For them, the rainbow over that distant brook had long since disappeared.

In that new apartment in Tianling, there was a small bathroom, where he had planned to install a shower head. Shaking his head, Detective Yu caught himself crying over spilled milk once again.

On the table behind Peiqin, he noticed a bag of steamed barbequed pork buns, from Geng's restaurant, presumably. Business
there was brisk. Peiqin had been helping Geng with his accounting work, and he paid her with food to take home.

Was it possible for Yu, too, to do some work on the side in his
spare time?

Then the phone rang. It would be the police bureau, he
guessed, and he was right.

Party Secretary Li could not find Chief Inspector Chen Cao, Yu's
boss on the special case squad, at this late hour. There was an
urgent new case—a murder—so he was calling Yu.

"Yin Lige," Yu repeated the name of the murder victim after
putting down the phone. Li had not explained much except that it
was politically imperative to solve the case. Yin must have been
well known, Yu assumed, or the case would not have been assigned
to their squad, which dealt with crimes with political implications.
However, he could not think of anything in association with that
name. Yin was not a common Chinese surname, and if she had been
famous, he should have heard of her.

"Yin Lige!" Peiqin spoke for the first time, repeating Yu's words.

"Yes. Do you know anything about her?"

"The author of *Death of a Chinese Professor*. The name of the professor was Yang Bing." She added, drying her feet with the towel,
"What happened to her?"

"She was murdered in her home."

"Is the government involved?" Peiqin asked, cynically.

He was taken aback by her response. "The bureau wants us to
solve the case in the shortest time possible. Party Secretary Li said so."

"Everything may be *political* for your Party Secretary Li."

She might be referring to the way some investigations were

conducted under Li, but also, possibly, to the withdrawn housing assignment. Peiqin suspected that the state-run corporation three-way-debt explanation Li had given was only as an excuse to take back the apartment. Yu had no political clout at the bureau.

Yu himself had suspected this, but he did not want to discuss it now. "What was Yin's book about?"

"The book was based on her personal experience. It's about an old professor falling in love during the Cultural Revolution. It received a lot of media attention, and was controversial for a while." Peiqin got up, holding the basin in her hand. "Shortly after its publication, it was banned."

"Let me help you," Yu said, carrying the basin out to the court-yard sink. She followed him outside in her slippers. "There are a lot of books about the Cultural Revolution. What made hers so special?"

"People say that some descriptions in the book are too realistic, too full of bloody details for the Party authorities to swallow," she said. "The novel attracted critical notice abroad, too. So the official critics called her a dissident."

"A dissident, I see. But the book is about the Cultural Revolution, about the past. If she's not involved in today's freedom-and-democracy movement, I cannot see why the government would have had to get rid of her."

"Well, you have not read the book."

Maybe Peiqin was still reluctant to talk, he thought, after this curt reply. Or maybe she didn't want to talk to him about books. That was one difference between them. She read, he didn't—usually.

"I'll read it," he said.

"What about Chief Inspector Chen?"

"I don't know. Li cannot find him."

"So you will investigate this case."

"I think so."

"If you have questions about Yang—sorry, about Yin—I may be able to help," she offered. "I mean, if you want to know more about the book. I will have to read it again, I think."

He was surprised by this offer. As a rule, he did not discuss his cases at home, nor did she show much interest in them.

This evening she was volunteering to help, after having said practically nothing to him for days. Well, it was progress.

Chapter 2

An offer he can't refuse.

Chief Inspector Chen Cao, of the Shanghai Police Bureau, knew nothing about the case assignment Detective Yu had just been given by Party Secretary Li, when a line from *The Godfather* came into his mind. He was sitting in an elegant bar, opposite Gu, CEO of the Shanghai New World Group, a startup with both government and triad connections. Taking a leisurely sip of the French red wine in his glass, which scintillated under the dazzling crystal chandelier, he reflected on the irony of the situation. Their table by the window commanded a superb view of the Bund, the embankment that runs along the harbor south of the Customs House. The water of the river shimmered under the ceaselessly changing neon lights. At the table next to them sat a European man with a Chinese girl, talking in a language foreign to Chen. And Gu was making him an offer he could hardly decline.

But the similarities ended there, the chief inspector hastened to remind himself, as Gu added wine to his glass. He had been offered an enormous sum to undertake a translation project, which Gu said would be a favor he was asking of Chen, rather than the other way around.

"You have to translate this business proposal for me, Chief Inspector Chen. Not simply for my sake, but for that of the city of Shanghai. Mr. John Holt, my American partner, said that he would pay in accordance with American rates. Fifty cents per Chinese word, U.S. currency."

"That's quite a lot," Chen said. Having translated several mysteries in his spare time, he knew the going rate. A publishing house would normally pay a translator a one-time fee of ten cents per word, Chinese currency. Ten cents Chinese was equivalent to about one cent American.

"The proposal is about New World, our group's newest project, a huge shopping, entertainment, office, and residential complex to be built in the center of the city, with all the architectural splendor of the thirties," Gu declared. "All the houses will be designed in the *shikumen* style: gray brick walls, black doors, brown stone door frames, small courtyards, various wings, and winding wooden staircases. The buildings will be arranged along lanes that crisscross each other, exactly the same as in the original design of the foreign concessions. In short, you will walk right into the middle of those good old days, as if you were stepping back into a dream."

"I'm confused, Mr. Gu. A modern complex in the center of Shanghai, yet with all outdated, old-fashioned buildings—Why?"

"Let me tell you something. I was in Italy last year, in Rome, where I stumbled on a number of those worldwide brand-name stores located in tiny side streets, just like our lanes. Streets paved with cobblestones, not wide enough for a truck. Yet all the finest stores were located in those ancient sixteenth or seventeenth century buildings. Moss-covered, ivy-mantled, but alive with fashionable men and women shopping inside, drinking coffee outside, modern or postmodern music rippling in the air. I was simply overwhelmed, as if I had been struck by a Zen master's stick dealing the blow that enlightens. I have been to many places. Shopping here or dining there does not make much difference to me. But in Rome I really felt astonished. It was a unique experience, like being immersed in ancient memories juxtaposed with modern luxuries."

"It sounds fabulous, Mr. Gu. Only Shanghai is not Rome."

"We have *shikumen* houses in Shanghai. I'll have the whole complex designed in the *shikumen* style. In fact, a lot of houses already there are *shikumen* houses. And there will be lanes too. Some of the houses will be thoroughly restored and redecorated. If necessary, the old houses will be torn down, and new houses will be rebuilt in the same style. All new materials in the same old style, the outside unchanged, but the inside with air conditioners, heating, whatever modern conveniences you can think of."

"*Shikumen* used to be one of the dominant residential architectural styles in Shanghai in the Foreign Concession era," Chen said.

"It will also work for stores, bars, restaurants, and nightclubs. It will be an attraction for foreigners—exotic, strange, colonial, postcolonial, what they do not have at home. And it will attract Shanghainese too. I have done some market research. Nowadays people are becoming nostalgic, you know. What was the city called then? 'The Paris of the East.' 'An Oriental Pearl.' Books about Shanghai in the golden days sell like hotcakes. Why? A middle class is rising up fast here. Now that they have money, they long for a tradition, or a history, they can claim as their own."

"It is a grand project," Chen said. "Have you gotten the approval of the city government?"

Gu was a shrewd businessman, Chen knew. There was no need to worry about the New World Group's business strategy. But the price he had been offered to make a translation of their proposal was out of all proportion to the task. It was as if a moon cake had fallen from the skies; it was too good an offer for Chen not to be suspicious. He had better find out whether there were any strings attached.

"Of course, the city government is all for the project. When the New World goes up, it will not only enhance the image of our great city, but also bring in huge tax revenues." Gu lit a cigarette before he added, "Well, I'll let you in on a secret. I applied for the use of the land for cultural preservation. After all, *shikumen*-style architecture is an integral part of Shanghai's history. One or two small museums may be included in the concept as well. A museum for ancient coins is one idea; I have already been contacted by someone. But most of the new *shikumen* houses will be for commercial use. Really high-end, luxury premises."

"Like those in Rome?"

"Exactly. In my proposal to the city government, I did not dwell on those details, or the land price would have soared. From another perspective, however, you can say that it really is for the preservation of Shanghai's culture."

"How true," Chen said. "There are so many perspectives from which one may examine one and the same thing, and you can choose the perspective you like."

"The city government has approved the plan. The next step is to get loans from investment banks abroad. Large loans. It is a huge gamble, I admit, but I'm betting on it. China's entry into the World Trade Organization will open its doors even wider. No one can turn the clock back. Several American venture-capital companies are interested in the New World, but none of them knows anything about Shanghai's culture. So I want to give them a detailed business proposal, fifty pages long in English. Everything depends on the translation. You alone are up to the task, Chief Inspector Chen."

"Thank you, General Manager Gu." Indeed, it was a high compliment. Chen had majored in English in college, but, through a combination of circumstances, had been assigned to a job at the Shanghai Police Bureau. Over the years, he had only done translations in his spare time, and he felt flattered by Gu's choosing him.

"But there are many qualified translators in Shanghai," Chen protested. "Professors at Fudan or East China universities. I don't think you need me to introduce one of them to you."

"No, they are not really up to the task. That's not just my own opinion. As a matter of fact, I asked a retired professor from Fudan University for help, and faxed his sample translation to an American associate. No good. 'Too old-fashioned, too literal' was his conclusion."

"Well, I studied under those old-fashioned professors."

"But for the government's college-graduate-assignment policy at the time, you would have been a well-known professor by now. Of course, things have worked out very well for you. An emerging Party cadre, a published poet, a renowned translator; you are the envy of those professors. And you are different. As a government representative, you have been in frequent contact with American visitors. Your American friend, Catherine—I remember her name—says your English is absolutely wonderful."

"American exaggeration. You cannot take her word for it," Chen said. "Besides, I have served only as a representative of the Shanghai Writers' Association. Nor have I done that often."

"Yes, that's another reason I need your help. This business proposal has a lot to do with Shanghai's culture and history. The Chinese text is written in quite poetic language. And you are a poet. That's no exaggeration, right? I honestly cannot think of a better candidate for the job."

"Thank you," Chen said, as he studied Gu over the rim of his glass. Gu must have given this offer some serious thought. "It is just that I'm overwhelmed with work at the bureau."

"I'm asking a lot, I know. Take a week's leave for me. Rush service! We'll pay one and half times the rate I offered for rush service: seventy-five cents a word. I'll tell my American partner. I know it will not be a problem."

This was a small fortune, Chen calculated quickly. At the rate of seventy-five cents per word, at about a thousand Chinese characters per page, for a total of fifty pages, this would be over thirty thousand American dollars, equivalent to three hundred thousand Yuan, an amount that it would take him thirty years to earn as a chief inspector, including all the bonuses he might get.

As he had attained the rank of chief inspector in his mid-thirties, Chen was generally viewed as a success: an emerging Party cadre with a promising future, with a bureau car at his disposal, a new apartment in his own name, and an occasional photo appearance in local newspapers. As an iron-rice-bowl holder, however, his monthly income of around five hundred Yuan was sometimes barely enough to cover his needs. But for the extra money from his translations of foreign mysteries and the occasional short technical translation, as well as the "gray area" perquisites of his position, he didn't know how he could have managed.

And, as an emerging Party cadre, he also felt the need to live up to certain unwritten standards. When he met with connections like Gu, for instance, he considered himself obliged to offer to pay occasionally, even though those businessmen would invariably insist on picking up the check.

Of late he'd also had sizable expenses due to the increasing cost of medical treatment for his mother, whose former employer, a state-run factory, had fallen into terrible shape and was unable to reimburse its retirees for their medical bills. She had talked to the factory director a number of times without success. The company was on the brink of bankruptcy. So Chen had taken it upon himself to pay. The money from the translation of the New World business plan would be like timely rain in the dry season.

"You have to help me," Gu pleaded with utter sincerity. "I cannot turn in an unreadable proposal to an American banker. The translation must be first-class."

"I cannot guarantee anything. To translate a total of fifty pages will take time. I doubt I will be able to manage in just one or even two weeks, even if I take a leave from the bureau."

"Oh, I forgot. For such a large project, you will surely need help. What about White Cloud? That girl you danced with in the Dynasty Club, remember her? She's a college student. Bright, capable, and understanding. She will be a little secretary for you."

A "little secretary"—*xiaomi*—another current term, which actually meant a "little mistress." Newly rich businessmen—Mr.Big Bucks—like Gu made a point of having young, beautiful "little secretaries" in their company. A necessary sign of one's social status, if not of something else. Chen had met White Cloud—a "K girl"— in the private karaoke room at Gu's Dynasty Club while pursuing an earlier investigation with triad ramifications.

"How I can afford secretarial assistance, General Manager Gu?"

"It's in the interest of the New World that you have help. I will take care of it."

The fragrance from her red sleeves accompanies your writing deep in the night . . . a Tang dynasty line rose from the recesses of his mind, but Chen pulled himself back to the present. A free little secretary. Like a bottle of Maotai in addition to the moon cake falling from the skies.

So far, there had been no strings attached, Chen thought. A shrewd businessman like Gu might not play all his cards too obviously, so early, but the chief inspector believed he did not have to worry yet. It seemed that he was being offered a straight business proposition, albeit a very favorable one. If something came up later, he would then decide how to deal with it.

There are things a man can do, and things a man cannot do. That was one of the Confucian dictums his father, a Neo-Confucian scholar, had taught him at the time of the Cultural Revolution, when the old man refused to write a dictated "confession" incriminating his colleagues.

"Let me to talk to Party Secretary Li," Chen said. "I'll call you back tomorrow."

"He won't refuse you, I know. You are a rising star, with a most promising future. Here is part of the advance." Gu took a bulging envelope out of his brief case. "Ten thousand Yuan. I'll have the rest delivered to you tomorrow."

Chen took the envelope, making up his mind not to worry about it. There were other things to concern him. He would buy a box of red ginseng for his mother. That's the least he could do as her only son. Perhaps he should also engage an hourly maid for her; she lived alone in an ancient attic, and was in poor health. He drained his cup, saying, *"Drinking with you, we talk to our hearts' content, my horse tied to a willow tree, by a high building."*

"What is the allusion? You have to enlighten me, my poetic chief inspector."

"It's just a quote from Wang Wei," Chen said without further explanation. The couplet referred to a promise given by a gallant knight in the Tang dynasty, but he and Gu had merely concluded a business deal, which was anything but heroic. "I will try my best."

Chapter 3

The bus, full of people packed like sardines, was stuck fast in an early-morning traffic jam. As a low-level cop, Detective Yu had no access to a bureau car, unlike his boss Chief Inspector Chen. This morning, Yu considered himself lucky when he obtained a seat in the overcrowded bus shortly after he boarded. Now, unbuttoning the top button of his uniform, he had plenty of time to think about the new murder case.

Party Secretary Li had called earlier in the morning, informing him that Chief Inspector Chen was on vacation, and that Yu would be in charge of the Yin case. Chen had also phoned, explaining that he was too busy translating a business proposal at home to come to work. Yu would have to investigate the Yin murder by himself.

Information had been gathered about Yin Lige already. He had been given a fat folder full of material from the Shanghai Archives Bureau, as well as from other sources. Detective Yu was not surprised at this evidence of bureaucratic efficiency. A dissident writer like Yin must have been the subject of secret police surveillance for a long time.

The folder contained a picture of Yin, a bamboo-thin, tallish woman in her mid-fifties, her high forehead and oval face deeply lined, sad eyes looking out through a pair of silver-framed eyeglasses. She wore a black Mao jacket and matching black pants. Her photo was like an image copied from an old postcard.

Yin had been a Shanghai College graduate, class of 1964. Because of the enthusiasm she displayed in student political activities, she had been admitted to the Party and, after graduation, assigned a job as a political instructor at the college. Instead of teaching classes, she gave political talks to students. It was then considered a promising assignment; she might rise quickly as a Party official working with intellectuals who forever needed to be reformed ideologically.

When the Cultural Revolution broke out, like other young people she joined a Red Guard organization, following Chairman Mao's call to sweep away everything old and rotten. She threw herself into criticism of counterrevolutionary or revisionist "monsters," and emerged as a leading member of the College Revolutionary Committee. Powerful in this new position, she pledged herself to carry on "the continuous revolution under the proletarian dictatorship." Little did she suspect that she herself was soon to become a target of the continuous revolution.

Toward the end of the sixties, with his former political rivals out of the way, Chairman Mao found that the rebellious Red Guards were blocking the consolidation of his power. So those Red Guards, much to their bewilderment, found themselves in trouble. Yin, too, was criticized and removed from her position on the College Revolutionary Committee. She was sent to a cadre school in the countryside, a new institution invented by Chairman Mao on an early May morning, after which May 7th Cadre Schools appeared throughout the country. For Mao, one of their purposes was to keep politically unreliable elements under control or, at least, out of the way.

The cadre students consisted of two main groups. The first was composed of ex-Party cadres. With their positions now filled by the even more left-wing Maoists, they had to be contained somewhere. The other was made up of intellectuals, such as university professors, writers, and artists, who were included in the cadre rank system. The cadre students were supposed to reform themselves through hard labor in the fields and group political studies.

Yin, a college instructor, and also a Party cadre for a short while, fit into both categories. In the cadre school, she became the head of a group, and there Yin and Yang met for the first time.

Yang, much older than Yin, had been a professor at East China University. He had been in the United States and had returned in the early fifties, but soon he was put on the "use under control" list, labeled a Rightist in the mid-fifties, and a "black monster" in the sixties.

Yin and Yang fell in love despite their age difference, despite the "revolutionary times," despite the warnings of the cadre school authorities. Because of their untimely affair, they suffered persecution. Yang died not too long afterward.

After the Cultural Revolution, Yin returned to her college, and wrote *Death of a Chinese Professor*, which was published by Shanghai Literature Publishing House. Although described as a novel, it was largely autobiographical. Initially, as there was nothing really new or unusually tragic in the book, it failed to sell. So many people had died in those years. And some people did not think it was up to her—as an ex-Red Guard—to denounce the Cultural Revolution. It was not until it was translated into English by an exchange scholar at the college that it attracted government attention.

Officially, there was nothing wrong with denouncing the Cultural Revolution. The *People's Daily* did so, too. It had been, as the *People's Daily* declared, a mistake by Chairman Mao, who had meant well. The atrocities committed were like a national skeleton in the closet.

To be aware of the skeleton, at home, was one thing, but it was quite another matter to drag it out for Westerners to see. So Party critics labeled her a "dissident," which worked like a magical word. The novel was then seen to be a deliberate attack on the Party authorities. The book was secretly banned. To discredit her, what she had done as a Red Guard was "uncovered" in reviews and reminiscences. It was a battle she could not win, and she fell silent.

But all that had happened several years earlier. Her novel, filled with too many specific details, did not attract a large audience abroad. Nor had she produced anything else, except for a collection of Yang's poetry she had earlier helped edit. Then she was selected for membership in the Chinese Writers' Association, which was interpreted as a sign of the government's relenting. Last year, she had been allowed to visit Hong Kong as a novelist. She did not say or do anything too radical there, according to the files.

Closing the folder, Detective Yu failed to see why the government might be implicated in her murder. He could see, however, why the Party authorities were anxious to have the case solved quickly. Anything to do with a dissident writer might attract attention, unpleasant attention, both at home and overseas.

When the bus finally arrived at his destination, Detective Yu found that Treasure Garden Lane, where Yin had lived, was only half a block from the bus stop. It was an old-fashioned, medium-sized lane accessed through a black iron grillwork gate, possibly a leftover from the French Concession years. Its location was unfashionable, and the neighborhood had been going downhill in the last few years. As new buildings appeared elsewhere, the lane had become something of an eyesore.

Yu decided to take a walk around the area first. He would be working with a neighborhood cop, Old Liang, who had been stationed nearby for many years. Old Liang was to meet him at nine thirty in the neighborhood committee office, close to the back entrance of the lane. Yu was fifteen minutes early for their appointment.

The front entrance to the lane was on Jinling Road. At the intersection of Jinling and Fujian Roads, two or three blocks away, he could see the Zhonghui Mansion—the high-rise once owned by Big Brother Du of the Blue Triad—standing on the corner. The back entrance of the lane led into a large food market. There were also two side entrances along Fujian Road, lined with tiny shops and stalls. In addition to the main lane, he saw several sub-lanes crisscrossing each other. Most of the houses were built in the *shikumen* style, like his own home, a typical Shanghai two-storied house with a stone door frame and a small interior courtyard.

Looking into the lane from the front entrance, Yu saw an elderly woman pushing open the black-painted door of a *shikumen* house with one hand, carrying a chamber pot in the other. It was an eerily familiar sight, as if he had been transported back to his own lane, except that Treasure Garden Lane was even shabbier, its winding tributary lanes more full of twists and turns. More full of noises too. Near the front entrance, a green-onion-cake peddler hawked his wares loudly, clanging on the large flat pan with a steel ladle. A little girl of five or six stood alone in the middle of the lane crying her heart out, for reasons Yu would never discover. Conducting an investigation here would be difficult, he realized. With the constant flow of people, and all sorts of ceaseless lane activities too, a criminal could have easily sneaked in and out without being noticed.

As Yu turned in the direction of the neighborhood committee office, he saw a short, white-haired man stepping through the doorway, waving his hand energetically.

"Comrade Detective Yu?"

"Comrade Liang?"

"Yes, that's me. People here just call me Old Liang," he said in a booming voice. "I am just a residential policeman. We really have to depend on you to investigate, Comrade Detective Yu."

"Don't say that, Old Liang," Yu said. "You have worked here for so many years, it is *I* who must rely on *your* help."

Old Liang was in charge of residential registrations and records for the area. At times, his job was to provide liaison between the neighborhood committee and the district police station. So he had been assigned to work with Detective Yu.

"Things are not like in the past, you know, when the registration rules were really effective." As he spoke, Old Liang led Yu into a small office, which looked like it must have been partitioned off from the original hallway, and offered him a cup of tea.

Old Liang had seen better days, in the sixties and seventies, when residential registration was a matter of survival in a city with a strict food-ration-coupon policy. Coupons were needed for staples, such as rice, coal, meat, fish, cooking oil, and even cigarettes. What's more, Chairman Mao's class-struggle theory was applied to all walks of life. According to Mao, throughout the long period of socialism, class enemies would never stop attempting to sabotage the proletarian dictatorship. So a residential cop had to stay alert at all times. Everyone in the neighborhood had to be viewed as a hidden potential class enemy. Neighborhood security was extremely effective. If someone moved into the lane in the morning without reporting to local authorities, a residential cop would knock at his door the same night.

But things changed, gradually in the eighties, and dramatically in the nineties. The food-ration-coupon system had been largely shelved, so people no longer depended so much on residential registration cards. Nor was there strict enforcement of the regulation regarding residential permits. Thousands of provincial workers swarmed into Shanghai. The city government was well aware of the problem, but cheap labor was much needed by the construction and service sectors.

Still, Old Liang must have done a conscientious job. Some of the information Yu had reviewed on the bus undoubtedly had come from this veteran residential cop.

"Let me give you some general information about Yin, Detective Yu," Old Liang said, "and about the neighborhood too."

"That would be great."

"Yin moved into the lane from her college dorm sometime in the mid-eighties. I do not know the exact reasons for the move. Some said that she did not get along with her roommates. Some said that because of the publicity for her novel, the college decided to improve her living conditions. Not much of an improvement, a *tingzijian*, a tiny cubicle partitioned off from the staircase on the landing, but at least a room for herself, in which she could read and write in privacy. It seemed to be enough for her."

"Nobody in the police bureau contacted you about her move into the lane?"

"I was informed of her political background, but no one gave me any specific instructions. Dealing with a dissident can be sensitive. As a residence cop, all I could do was to maintain high vigilance and collect whatever information I could about her from her neighbors. The neighborhood committee did not try to do anything in particular. Things pertaining to a political dissident would have been too complicated for us. We treated her just like any other resident in the lane."

"What was her relationship with her neighbors?"

"Not good. When she first moved in, her neighbors did not notice anything unusual about her except that, as a university teacher, she had written a book about the Cultural Revolution. Everyone had his or her own experience in that national disaster. No one really wanted to talk about it.

"As details of her book became known, some people took a sort of interest in her. A heart-breaking story, for she remained single after all these years. Some neighbors were compassionate, but she did not get along well with them. She seemed bent on shutting herself up in the *tingzijian* room, licking her wounds in secret."

"I would say that's understandable. Her woes were personal, and perhaps too painful for her to talk about."

"Yet what is special about living in a *shikumen* house is the constant contact with your neighbors, every hour, every day," Old Liang said, taking a sip of his tea. "Some describe Shanghainese as born wheelers and dealers. That's not true, but people here have always lived in such miniature societies, and learned from this ongoing education in relationship management. As an old saying goes, *Close neighbors are more important than distant relatives.* But Yin seemed to have purposely distanced herself from her neighbors. As a result, they resented her and treated her as an outsider. Lanlan, one of her neighbors, said something to the point: 'Her world's not here.'"

"Perhaps she was too busy writing to make friends," Yu said, stealing a glance at his watch. Old Liang resembled his father, Old Hunter, in one aspect: both of them were tireless talkers, and at times wandered from the point. "Did you have any direct contact with her?"

"Well, I did when she came to register her residence. She was rather unfriendly, even a little hostile, as if I were one of those who had beaten up Yang in those days."

"Have you read her novel?"

"Not the whole book by any means, only some paragraphs quoted in the newspapers and magazines. You know what?" Old Liang went on without waiting for an answer. "Some readers were really pissed off by what she wrote about having been a Red Guard out of proletarian fervor, and doing what she referred to only as 'some too passionate deeds' in the name of the revolution."

"Was that the reaction of her neighbors too?"

"Oh, no. I don't think too many here have read her book. They may have heard of the book. What I know is from the research I have done."

"You have done a lot of work, Old Liang," Yu said. "Let's go to her place now."

Chapter 4

Detective Yu stood before the black-painted front door of solid oak and touched the shining brass knocker, which must have been there since the *shikumen* house had been built.

"There are two entrances to the house," Old Liang explained. "The front door can be latched from inside. Normally, it is closed after nine o'clock. There is also a back door opening to the little back lane."

The explanation was hardly necessary for Detective Yu, who had not mentioned the fact that he had lived in a similar building for many years, but he was willing to listen. Crossing the courtyard, he stepped into the common kitchen area. Squeezed into that space were the coal stoves of a dozen or more families, as well as their pots and pans, rows of coal briquettes, and pigeonhole cabinets hung on the wall. Yu counted fifteen stoves in all. At the end of the kitchen area was the staircase, which differed from the one in his own house, as an additional room had been partitioned off at the curve in the staircase. A *tingzijian*, at the landing above the kitchen, between the first and second floors, was commonly regarded as one of the worst rooms in a *shikumen* building.

"Let's climb up to Yin's room. Be careful, Detective Yu, the steps are very narrow here. Isn't it a coincidence," Old Liang continued, "that a number of writers lived in *tingzijians* in the thirties? 'Tingzijian literature,' I remember, referred to the writers working in poverty. There was a well-known '*tingzijian* writer' in this area before 1949, but I cannot recall his name."

Yu, too, failed to recall the name, although he believed he had heard the term. How could those writers have concentrated with people moving up and down all the time, he wondered.

"You have read quite a lot," Yu said, convinced the elderly residence cop was not only an energetic talker, but also a digressive one.

There was a seal on the door. Old Liang was going to tear the paper off when one of the residents called in a wailing voice, "Comrade Old Liang, you have to come and help us. That heartless man has not given a single penny to his family for more than two months."

It was a family squabble, Yu guessed. It would furnish him with a timely excuse. "You don't have to accompany me, Old Liang," Yu said. "You have so many things to deal with. It may take me some time here. Afterward, it will be important for us to have a meeting with the neighborhood committee. Can you arrange one?"

"What about twelve o'clock at the office?" Old Liang asked. "Before I leave you, Detective Yu, here is a more detailed report for you, about the crime scene. Three pages in all."

Detective Yu started glancing through it as he stood on the

landing, watching Old Liang disappear into the midst of the stoves in the common kitchen area.

In the earlier information he had reviewed on the bus, the crime scene was described in one sentence as "practically destroyed." Hardly anything had been left untouched in Yin's room, due to the way the body had been discovered. An assistant who worked with Doctor Xia had come to collect fingerprints, but he said not much could be isolated from the multiple prints and smears on every surface.

The report read:

> On the morning of February 7, Lanlan, a resident at the end of the eastern wing on the second floor, returned from the food market at around six forty-five A.M. She went upstairs and passed by Yin's door. Normally, the door was shut tight. It was known that Yin usually went out to practice tai chi early in the morning, in People's Park, and she would not come back until after eight. The door was slightly ajar that morning. It was none of her business, but, as it was unusual, Lanlan noticed this. She bent to tie her shoelace, and peeping through the door, she saw something like an overturned chair. She knocked on the door, waited for a minute or two before pushing it open, and found Yin lying on the floor. A white pillow lay beside her face. *Sick, passed out, fell from the bed*—Lanlan guessed. She rushed in and pressed the indentation above Yin's upper lip,* and started shouting for help. Immediately, seven or eight people ran in. One sprinkled cold water on Yin's face, one felt her pulse, one dashed out to call for an

*CPR in traditional Chinese medicine.

ambulance, before they realized that Yin was not breathing, and noticed that several drawers had been pulled out, and their contents ransacked. Soon more people came crowding into the room. Before anyone suspected foul play, nothing in the room was left untouched.

Then Old Liang arrived with the neighborhood committee members, but this hardly contributed to the preservation of the scene. One member went so far as to put the pillow back on the bed and push in all the drawers.

One thing was not mentioned in the report. According to Party Secretary Li, shortly after Old Liang got there, Internal Security also arrived at the scene. They conducted a thorough search of the room. They should have observed the proper procedure and worn gloves, but Li had not asked about this. He knew nothing about the objective of their search. With a dissident writer like Yin, however, the involvement of Internal Security was not surprising. Internal Security had requested that the bureau keep them informed about the progress of the investigation.

Stroking his chin, Yu put the report back in the folder, tore the seal off the door, and entered the room. It was a barren, shabby cubicle. As indicated in the report, there was no sign of a struggle—or, more accurately, no sign of one remained. After a day, and in light of the description he had just read, Detective Yu did not really expect to find much.

The furniture appeared to be what she had bought when she had moved out of the dorm; it was typical of the eighties, plain, dark brown, utilitarian, but still in usable condition, consisting of a single bed, a desk, a chair, a wardrobe with a tall mirror over it, a sofa with a faded red cover, and a stool that might have served as a nightstand.

In an ashtray on the desk, he saw several cigarette butts. Brown cigarette butts. An American brand, More. There was also something like a typewriter on the desk. It was not a computer, Yu was sure. Perhaps it was an electric typewriter.

In a tiny cupboard fastened to the wall, there were several cans of tea leaves, a bottle of Nestle's instant coffee, a few rough bowls, a small bunch of bamboo chopsticks in a tree root container, one cup, and one glass. Apparently, she entertained few visitors here.

The bed had been made, probably by one of her neighbors. There was no mattress under the sheet; she'd slept on the plain hardboard. The faded cotton-padded quilt must have been four or five years old, and had plenty of patches. As he touched the quilt, he felt its stiffness. The pillow, without a cover, was relatively white in contrast to the quilt.

He turned to the desk drawers. The top drawer contained receipts from various stores, blank envelopes, and a travel magazine. The second drawer held notebooks, a notepad, a pile of paper, and a bunch of letters, several of them bearing addresses in English. The contents of the third appeared more mixed: a small assortment of costume jewelry—perhaps souvenirs from her Hong Kong trip; a Shanghai watch with a leather strap; and a necklace of some exotic animal bone.

The contents of the wardrobe confirmed his expectation. The clothes were dull in color, conventional in design, and most of them inexpensive, out of fashion. There was a new wool dress, however, that might not have been expensive but was of quite decent quality.

On the bookshelf were Chinese and English dictionaries; a set of *Han History*; *Selected Works of Deng Xiaoping*; copies of *Death of a Chinese Professor*; and copies of *Selected Poems of Yang Bing*. In addition, he saw a pile of old magazines, some from the forties and fifties, with bookmarks sticking out of their pages.

He also found an old-fashioned album with black paper pages bearing tiny aluminum photo holders shaped like stars. On the first few pages, most of the pictures were black and white. A couple of them showed Yin as a little girl with a ponytail. Then color photos appeared showing Yin with a red scarf—a Young Pioneer saluting the five-starred flag on her school campus. In a hand-colored picture, she stood happily in People's Square, between a white-haired man and a small thin woman: her parents, presumably.

He turned to a large picture, which must have been taken in 1967 or 1968, in the early years of the Cultural Revolution. Wearing a red armband, Yin stood on a stage delivering a speech, with high-ranking government officials seated in a row behind her in front of a red velvet curtain. She was a Red Guard representative at a national conference of college students but, despite her political importance, she looked more like an inexperienced girl. Hers was not exactly a young face, though animated with youthful passion. She bore a striking resemblance to a Red Guard poster he had seen. The next few pages recorded the most glorious moments of her political career. One photo showed her sitting together with top Party leaders at a conference held within the Forbidden City.

Then there seemed to be a blank. It was not that pictures were missing from the pages, but that there was an abrupt change from a young Red Guard to a middle-aged woman framed in the doorway of a cadre school. It was as if she had aged twenty years with the turning of a single page.

Closing the album, Detective Yu realized that it was time for his appointment with the neighborhood committee.

That committee had once functioned as an extension of the district police office, responsible for everything outside people's "work units": arranging weekly political study, checking the number of the people living in a house, running day-care centers, allocating birth quotas, arbitrating disputes among neighbors and, most important, keeping close watch over the residents. The committee was authorized to report on each and every individual, and that report would be included with the confidential information in a police dossier, enabling the state to maintain effective background surveillance on every person.

In recent years, the neighborhood committee, like other institutions, had undergone dramatic changes, but neighborhood security remained one of its main concerns. The committee must have kept a close eye on someone like Yin. It might also have information about other suspicious people in the house.

To Detective Yu's surprise, when he reached the office, he saw that a working lunch had been arranged by Old Liang. Six plastic lunch boxes containing three-yellow-chicken meals had been arranged down the center of the long desk; in addition to Yu and Old Liang, there were four committee members present, holding their chopsticks.

"The three-yellow-chicken is not bad—yellow feathers, yellow beak, yellow feet. Pudong-bred, home-raised, a world of difference from those in the modern chicken farms," Old Liang said, raising his chopsticks.

Comrade Zhong Hanmin, the neighborhood security head, proposed a theory about the murder. It seemed to him that the ransacked drawers in her room pointed to one possibility. "The criminal must have intended to steal from her, but when Yin came back unexpectedly, he panicked," Zhong said. "I don't think he is a resident in the building, or even in the lane. Surely he was a stranger who picked her room to rob at random. As an old saying puts it, *A rabbit does not browse too close to its den.*"

Such a possibility was not without supporting circumstances. Provincial workers had been seen wandering about the area for months, but this was not uncommon in the city, as more and more laborers poured in from other provinces.

It was understandable that Zhong was trying to keep him from focusing on the lane, Detective Yu thought. If the criminal turned out to be one of the lane residents, the local committee would bear some responsibility.

Comrade Qiao Lianyun, the general director of the committee, was the second to speak. Qiao provided a piece of information that seemed to contradict Zhong's theory. He based it on information obtained from Peng Ping, nicknamed the "shrimp woman," as she made a living by peeling shrimp in front of her door, which faced the back door of Yin's *shikumen* building and was only three or four feet away from it. The shrimp woman had an arrangement with the food market. The peeled shrimp had to be delivered before eight A.M. Shanghai wives preferred to visit the market early in the morning. As a rule, she started working around six fifteen. She did not remember seeing Yin return from tai chi practice that morning, but she had chatted with Lanlan at around six thirty. Peng insisted that she had never budged that morning until she heard the commotion in Yin's building and went inside to take a look. Qiao considered her statement reliable because the shrimp woman was known to be honest. Besides, she could hardly have gone anywhere, with her hands covered in shrimp slime. Qiao concluded, "Anyone sneaking out of the back door, however quickly and stealthily, would have been noticed by Peng, especially if it was a stranger scurrying out at an early hour. As for the front door, there were several people in the courtyard that morning who would have seen anyone leaving."

Qiao's argument was backed up by Old Liang, who started by making an analysis of lane security as well as building security. Because of recent cases of theft in the area, the neighborhood committee had taken preventive measures. All lane entrances had been secured with wrought-iron gates, which were locked at eleven thirty at night and opened at five thirty in the morning. Lane residents had to carry their keys.

In addition, there were rules about the *shikumen* building doors. Both the front and back doors of Yin's building were locked during the night. The front door, latched from inside, did not open until around seven, and then at around nine thirty in the evening it was closed again. As for the back door, people who went in and out through it, either early in the morning or late in the evening, were supposed to lock it behind them.

Yu listened, jotting down notes in his notebook, without making any comment. After an hour and a half, the events of the previous morning could be reconstructed as follows:

Yin was one of the early birds. She left the building on the morning of February 7, at around five fifteen, through the back door. She went to People's Park to practice tai chi. No one saw her going out that morning, but there was no reason to suspect that she had changed her routine. She had practiced tai chi every morning since she had moved in, and she was known to be punctual.

On that morning, Lanlan went out at around five thirty. She found the back door locked. She opened and locked it again, and headed for the food market earlier than usual for some fresh seafood because she was expecting a guest from Suzhou that afternoon.

Shortly afterward, two other *shikumen* residents went out the back door. One was Mr. Ren, who went to a restaurant for an early breakfast. The other was Wan, who went to perform tai chi on the Bund. Each of them was positive that his departure was between five forty-five and six.

Around six fifteen, Xiong, a milkwoman who was sitting with her milk bottles by the front entrance, saw Yin coming back. The milkwoman looked at her watch, as Yin usually did not return that early.

Lanlan arrived with her purchases at around six thirty. This time she left the back door unlocked, as she chatted for a few minutes with the shrimp woman sitting on the corner, and went across the courtyard to unlatch the front door, which was her habit. Around that time, other *shikumen* residents got up. Some of them came out to wash up in the courtyard sink. There were at least three or four people there that morning, Lanlan remembered.

The times fit. According to Doctor Xia, Yin had been suffocated to death by some soft object between six fifteen and six thirty. In other words, she had been killed shortly before Lanlan's discovery of the body.

Yu started putting some thoughts together in his notebook. There seemed to be two possibilities. In the first scenario, in accordance with Zhong's theory that the murderer was an outsider, the criminal had followed Yin into her room and committed the crime. But that left several points unaccounted for. The milkwoman saw Yin walking back into the lane by herself. Of course, the criminal might have approached her somewhere in the shadows of the lane unobserved. But then, the murderer had to get out of the building.

A stranger would have been noticed by those in the courtyard if he left through the front door, and, if he went out through the back door, someone happening to look in that direction from the courtyard might have seen him, and the shrimp woman sitting outside the back door could not have missed him. But no one had reported having seen a stranger during that period of time.

Alternatively, Yin might have been murdered by one of the *shikumen* residents. If so, the doors, as well as the lane gates, presented no problem. Afterward, the murderer simply sneaked back to his own room. As long as he was not seen in the act of entering or leaving Yin's room, no one would suspect him. This narrowed down the range of possibilities. It seemed Yu need only focus on the building's residents.

"I have made a list of possible suspects within the building," Old Liang whispered in his ear. "And I have also started collecting their fingerprints."

"I'm going to study the list," Yu said, glancing at his watch at the end of the meeting. "Thank you, Old Liang. We'll start doing interviews tomorrow."

If the villain lived in the *shikumen*, Yu had to find a motive for the crime. Old Liang had hinted at the poor relationship between Yin and her neighbors, but that would not have been enough reason to commit murder. What could have caused a woman to be killed by one of her next-door neighbors?

When the neighborhood committee meeting was over, Detective Yu decided to walk back to the bureau. It was a long walk. It would take him about forty-five minutes, and he wanted to do some solid thinking on the way. He was not in a hurry to decide on a course of action. He wanted to exclude other possibilities before focusing on the building's residents.

He came to a stop at the sight of a public phone near the foreign language bookstore. Stepping into the booth, he made a phone call to the Shanghai Literature Publishing House. He wanted to find how much Yin had earned from publication of her novel. After spending ten minutes searching for the editor responsible for Yin's book, and almost emptying his pockets of change, he finally located Wei, the editor of *Death of a Chinese Professor.*

"I took a huge risk in accepting the manuscript; we might have lost money by publishing it. At the time, no one expected that the book would turn out to be so controversial. Yin made about three thousand Yuan," Wei said.

That was not a large sum, even several years ago. Nowadays an eggroll peddler could have earned that much in a couple of months.

Wei did not know the exact amount of money Yin had received for the English translation, but according to the information he had, it was not a large sum. The novel had been of interest to sinologists, but it was not a popular seller.

"Besides," Wei explained, "in the early eighties, China had not entered the international copyright agreement. The American publisher only paid a small one-time fee."

But Yu remembered those letters with English addresses, whose dates were much more recent.

He dialed Chief Inspector Chen's number.

Chapter 5

Chen looked out of the window at the dull gray apartment complex in the morning light, and then down at the file on his desk, the New World proposal, and started typing on his electric typewriter. The project was ambitious. The document was not easy to translate, as it contained many architectural terms interspersed throughout the text. He had done a few technical translations for money, although none had been as lucrative as this one. Normally it took him hours to become familiar with the relevant technical terms before the translation could even begin.

Chen had obtained two weeks' leave from the Shanghai Police Bureau. Party Secretary Li had agreed, although reluctantly. The Party boss had been promising Chen a vacation for quite a long time, but, for one reason or another, his vacation had never come through. Li was hardly in a position to say no to Chen's request now, in spite of the urgency of the Yin case.

Chen had not mentioned the translation when he requested leave. There had been other reasons for him to seek time off. He had been quite upset with the way a recent case had been concluded. He had done what he could as a cop, but all his efforts, while "in the interests of the Party," seemed to have plunged a poor woman further into misery. Public Security Minister Huang had made a long-distance phone call to him, praising his "excellent work under the leadership of the ministry," and encouraging him to "make larger strides as an emerging cadre of the new Chinese police force." Party Secretary Li had not been pleased at this praise for his protégé. Minister Huang's call to Chen, rather than to Li, might have signified something. Li was quick to read the possible message. The too-swift rise of Chen—at Li's expense—was unacceptable. Tension rose between the two men.

There were other things in the bureau that were irritants to Chen. Mountains of political meetings and seas of Party documents. Several cops, including one in his special case squad, had been suspended because of their involvement in a smuggling case. An old Party cadre had raised issues about Chen's poetry writing once again. It was ironic, as his literary inspiration had almost run dry over the last few months. He'd had neither the time nor the energy. All he had produced were some fragmentary lines. He did not know when he would ever be able to put them together.

On top of all that, after a long process of meetings and negotiations, had come the withdrawal of the offer to Yu of a modern apartment. Chen took the blow personally. He, too, suspected that the reneging on what had been agreed might have been more complicated than it appeared on the surface. Everybody knew that Detective Yu was Chief Inspector Chen's man. This was a terrible loss of face for Chen. As the proverb said, *You have to think about its master's face before you kick a dog*. It was Chen who had handed the apartment key over to Yu. Party Secretary Li might have been at work behind the scenes, to get back at Chen. Whatever the correct interpretation of these events might be, Chen had concluded that he did not have sufficient authority at the Shanghai Police Bureau yet.

To take his mind off police work, it would be best to do something different. He was not a man who could relax by doing nothing, as in Laozi's *Tao Te Ching*. In a way, Gu's translation job offered just what he needed, not to mention the monetary incentive.

The New World project proposal on his desk started with an introduction detailing Shanghai's architectural history from the beginning of the century. It did not take him long to realize that the success of the project would depend on a myth—on nostalgia for the glitter and glamour of the thirties, or, to be exact, on the recreation of that myth—blending the past into a delicious brew, a cup of cappuccino, to delight customers in the nineties.

But then, much about business success had proven mysterious to him. When Kentucky Fried Chicken had first come to Shanghai, he had laughed at the idea. The prices alone would scare away most Shanghainese, he believed, but he had been wrong. Kentucky Fried Chicken enjoyed a huge success. Several branch stores had opened in the city. Last summer, he had wanted to talk with his cousin Shan about his mother's health problems, and Shan suggested that they meet in "Kentucky": "It's cool there. So clean and air-conditioned."

An advantage of translating rather than writing was that he could keep working on a text mechanically even if its meaning was beyond him, putting words together, like pieces of a jigsaw puzzle, without worrying about the whole picture for the moment. He had barely finished a half page when there was a light knock at the door. Opening it, he saw a girl standing there, her long hair hanging over her shoulders, a college badge on her scarlet jacket. He recognized her as White Cloud, the "little secretary" promised by Gu.

"Chief Inspector Chen, I am reporting for work," she said, in a voice as tender and sweet as freshly peeled litchi.

She was a delicious girl with a watermelon-seed-shaped face, almond eyes, and cherry lips.

"General Manager Gu did not have to send you here. He shouldn't have done so." Chen did not know what else to say, but he felt he had to make some protest.

"He is paying me to come here," she said in mock dismay. "You surely don't want me to lose my job, do you?"

She could hardly help with the translation, as her major was Chinese literature, he remembered. What else was there for her to do? There might be phone calls, which a secretary could answer for him. But he thought better of this. He didn't receive many calls at home, for one thing. And then, a female secretary in his room—what would others imagine? Afterward, he would have to spend more time making explanations than she could possibly save him.

But she seemed to be quite at ease already, almost at home. Taking off her jacket, she started to wash up the cups and the ashtray on the desk without waiting for his orders.

Perhaps Gu had given her *his* orders.

"What about your schoolwork?"

"I have only one class this evening."

"I cannot think of anything for you to do at this moment. There are magazines on the shelf. You may pick one to read if you like."

"That's very considerate of you, Chief Inspector Chen."

He did not feel comfortable with someone moving about in back of him. She had started to straighten the books on the shelf. It was hard to drive the associations he had with the phrase *a little secretary* out of his subconscious. She had on a white sweater with an extraordinarily large collar and sleeves. Very fashionable. He wondered whether there was a special name for the style. Then an idea came to him. He was not that familiar with the architectural styles of the thirties. If she could take a few pictures of a *shikumen* house, of a lane from the thirties, in the former concession area, it would help him visualize. He asked if she could do that for him.

"Sure. Can I have your door key?" She added, "In case you are out when I come back."

"Okay."

She left with a key ring dangling from her finger, apparently quite clear as to where she would take those pictures he had requested. Her retreating figure reminded him of "a traveling cloud," an image with various connotations in Chinese poetry, but at this moment, he thought of *A traveling cloud / that forgets to come back / unaware of the spring drawing to an end,* from a poem by Feng Yansi that he had read not too long ago.

In classical literature, more often than not, the word "cloud" was accompanied by "rain," evoking sexual love.

Once again he tried to settle down to his work.

It was not easy. He had to use a Chinese–English dictionary, and a picture dictionary as well. After an hour or so, he had another idea. Instead of typing on, doggedly, he took out an extra copy of the proposal, and, with a highlighter, underlined the words he was not sure about. That was not difficult, but it was time-consuming, requiring a close reading. Still, he was getting a more general—yet at the same time more concrete—picture of the New World.

He stopped only once, to make himself a cup of instant coffee, which he drank absentmindedly.

White Cloud came back around one thirty, with a dozen color pictures she had taken and had developed. One-hour service, perhaps. She also carried a plastic bag in her other hand filled with boxes of barbequed pork, and smoked eel, and a bag of mini-soup buns.

"Have you had your lunch, Chief Inspector Chen?"

"No, I haven't been hungry."

"I'm so sorry, I had no time to prepare lunch for you today. This is something I bought from a restaurant."

"Thank you! How much do I owe you?"

"Nothing, Mr. Gu will reimburse me."

He did not really like it, the way Gu had given her instructions—and money too.

"He does not have to pay for my lunch."

"Mr. Gu pays me quite handsomely, as you know. Please, help me keep my job."

He examined the pictures with approval. They appeared clear, well focused. He picked up the first soup bun. "Well, I can't complain."

"Please eat now," she said. "The buns are warm."

They looked as dainty as quail eggs, almost transparent, the minced pork stuffing mixed with minced crab meat, combining the flavors of land and river. The soup inside burst out at the touch of his lips, hot, and delicious.

"Be careful," she said with a giggle, hastily wiping his chin with a pink paper napkin.

Her fingers wiping the soup from his chin embarrassed him, and he felt obliged to say something. "According to a recipe book I read, the soup bun is special because its stuffing is mixed with pork skin jelly. When steamed, the jelly turns into hot liquid. You have to bite into it very carefully, or the soup will splash out, or even scald your tongue."

In spite of his book knowledge, he had made a small soup mess on the desk, and she brought a towel to clean it up with.

He changed the subject. "You are really helping a lot. But you are a college student, White Cloud. I do not think—"

"I have to earn my college tuition. Both my parents have been laid off. I have to work, if not as a little secretary for you, then as a K girl at the Dynasty Club, or somewhere else."

"It takes somebody like Gu to invent such a position," he said as he put a chunk of smoked eel into his mouth. The eel was at once crisp and juicy.

"He can't get credit for this invention," she said, as she sucked the soup out of a dainty bun. "Little secretary or *xiaomi*. Surely you've heard the term? Those Mr. Big Bucks must have little secretaries; we are symbols, just like a Mercedes."

He was surprised that she spoke so casually, as if the words had no relevance to herself.

"There's another new job invention: 'passion companion.' A full-page advertisement for this work appeared in *Wenhui Daily*. I don't need to explain what it means. Believe it or not, there are high qualifications required for the position. At least a university degree. Able to talk intelligently. Presentable for social occasions, and, of course, for private occasions, too."

"I'm too old-fashioned, I'm afraid."

"You are special." She stood up and began to put the leftovers into the refrigerator. "Well, I'd better do something to make sure Mr. Gu gets his money's worth."

"I do have something for you to do: Can you check the definitions of these words for me? It will save me a lot of time. You don't have to do it right now. In the evening, if you have time, after your class, will be fine. "

"Sure. I can learn quite a few new words for myself."

The telephone started ringing. She picked it up instantly like a secretary. "Chen Residence."

"Oh." There was a pause. "I'm Detective Yu. I want to speak to Chief Inspector Chen."

"Hold on." She turned toward Chen, the receiver covered by her hand, whispering in his ear, "Detective Yu. Do you want to speak to him?"

"Of course," he said.

"Sorry to bother you, boss," Yu said in a hesitant voice.

"Come on, Yu. What can I do for you?" He said to White Cloud in a low voice, "You may leave now. I will call you tomorrow."

"You don't have to. I'll be here to make breakfast for you," she said. "See you."

"See you. Don't worry about breakfast."

"You've got company?" Yu asked, delicately.

"A little secretary." Chen added, "I'm working on a difficult translation. She will help me."

"A *xiaomi!*" Yu did not try to disguise the surprise in his voice.

"Gu insisted on sending her over to help," he said. Yu might be the only one for whom he did not have to go into detail. "Have you examined the murder scene?"

"Yes, I did. But there was not much I could see, as I told you. Judging from the time of the murder and the fact that no stranger was seen entering or leaving the building around that time, it looks like the murderer might be one of the *shikumen* residents. That's Old Liang's opinion too."

"Have you ruled out every other possibility?"

"Not yet."

"Well, regarding the residents of the building, what possible motives are there?"

"I've been thinking about that too," Yu said. "I have checked with Shanghai Literature Publishing House. She did not earn much from her novel. I found a little money in her desk drawers, but also some correspondence with people abroad. I'm not sure whether she was working on another project. Perhaps another controversial book."

That would really make this a political case. Was she working on something the government—or someone in the government—might have tried to keep from coming out?

"As for her contacts abroad, Internal Security must have a file. They can be quite effective in their own way." Chen would not say more over the phone.

"They surely can. They beat me to the crime scene and searched her room, but they haven't told us what they were looking for."

"It could be just routine practice for Internal Security if a dissident has been killed. If they left those letters in the drawer, there probably was nothing in them to worry about."

"Another thing. I did not find a checkbook in her room," Yu said. "If the murderer took it, he would have withdrawn the money from her account immediately. So far, there's no report of an account in her name from which there have been withdrawals."

"The murderer might have been too scared to go to the bank, or Yin may have kept all her valuables in a safe deposit box."

"Safe deposit?" Yu said. "I've only read about them in one of the English mysteries you translated."

"Well, you can find everything in Shanghai now. Pay a certain amount, and the bank will keep valuables in a small safe for you."

"I'll check into it. But first I will go to her college this afternoon; there is nothing unusual in her college file though." Yu added, "I'll let you know as soon as I find out anything. Thanks, Chief."

The rest of Chen's afternoon was uneventful except for several more phone calls. The first was from Gu.

"How is everything, Chief Inspector Chen?"

"It's going slowly, but steadily. I mean the progress of the translation, if that's what you are asking about."

"Oh, I'm not worried about that. The project is in good hands, I know." Gu said with a chuckle, "What about White Cloud?"

"Quite helpful," Chen said, "but she should concentrate on her studies. I don't think it's a good idea for her to come here every day."

"If you don't need her, send her back. I just thought it might be a good idea for her to help you. As for her, she should consider herself lucky to have the opportunity to work with you. There's a lot she can learn."

It was not such a bad idea to have a temporary assistant, Chen thought, in spite of his protestations. A young pretty one too. There was no point in his being too prudish about it. *If the water is too clear, there will be no fish left in the pond.*

"By the way, what about having dinner with me at the Dynasty this weekend?" Gu asked. "You may have heard of our sauna room. Now we have a new dish—sauna shrimp. Live river shrimp, of course."

"Sauna shrimp! My food finger is already throbbing, but let's wait until I've finished the translation." For some minutes after Gu's phone call, Chen tried but failed to figure out what kind of dish sauna shrimp might be.

The next caller was a surprise. It was Peiqin, Yu's wife, a wonderful hostess with excellent cooking skills, and equally good taste in classical Chinese literature. Chen had not spoken to her since the apartment had been denied to them. He felt he had let the couple down terribly.

"Yu is working on the Yin case, as you know. He does not have much time for reading. So I am going to read *Death of a Chinese Professor* on his behalf. Not just the novel, but other material related to it as well, like interviews or reviews. It may take time to find these things in libraries. I'm wondering whether you know of a shortcut to getting that material."

"I have not read *Death of a Chinese Professor*." He had heard of it, but, after reading a review, he had not bothered to obtain the book. Those stories of persecuted intellectuals were nothing new. Chen's father, a Neo-Confucian scholar, had also died a miserable death during the Cultural Revolution. "I'm afraid I cannot help."

"Yin, too, belonged to the Chinese Writers' Association, Shanghai Branch. Were you ever introduced to her at one of those meetings?"

"I don't remember having met her there." He said, after considering further, "There's a small library at the Shanghai Writers' Association. It's on Julu Road. Members are supposed to bring their works and related reviews to the library. Sometimes the writers forget to do so, and the librarian has to collect them. At the least, there should be a catalog of her publications. The librarian's name is Kuang Ming. I'll give him a call. He should be able to help."

There was one thing Chief Inspector Chen did not say on the phone. A secret archive would certainly have been kept there with respect to a dissident writer. Peiqin should have no problems finding what she needed.

"Thank you, Chief Inspector Chen. Come to our restaurant

when you have time. Now we have a new chef, Sichuan style. He is quite good."

"Thank you, Peiqin, for helping with our work," he said.

Afterwards, he thought about the fact that Peiqin had invited him to the restaurant, but not to their home. He had done his best as a member of the bureau housing committee, he thought, but those who had failed to get an apartment would never believe he had done enough, perhaps including Peiqin.

The third phone call he received was from Overseas Chinese Lu, who had earned his nickname in high school from his enthusiasm for foreign things. He was an old friend who called regularly from his restaurant, Moscow Suburb. Not for the first time, Chen received a passionate invitation to have dinner at the newly expanded restaurant.

"I phoned your office. They told me you are on vacation. Now you surely have time to dine at our restaurant."

"Not this week, Lu. I have to finish a rush translation project for Mr. Gu, of the Dynasty Club, now also the founder of the New World Group. You know him, I think."

"Oh, Mr. Gu. He asked you to do a translation for him?"

"Yes, for a business project of his," Chen said. "How is your business?"

"Great. We have unearthed a number of old pictures and posters of Russian girls in old Shanghai. Now they are all over the walls. Impressive pictures. Crowded nightclubs with half-naked Russian girls performing on the stage. It's like walking back in time into old Shanghai."

"That's exciting."

"I'm thinking of putting a stage in our restaurant, too. Peace Hotel has a band. Old men playing jazz, you know. We'll do much better. A young men's band, and Russian girls on stage," Lu added proudly. "Girls both in old pictures, and in real life."

"So Moscow Suburb is no longer merely a restaurant, just for gourmets like you."

"It still is. But people have money now. They want something more than food. Atmosphere. Culture. History. Added value, whatever it may mean. And only in the middle of all this do they think they are really enjoying their money's worth."

"It must be quite expensive, then."

"Well, people are willing to pay the price. There's a new term—conspicuous consumption. And there's a new group of people—the middle class. Moscow Suburb has become a status-conscious restaurant. Some come here for that very reason."

"Good for you, Overseas Chinese Lu."

"So come, my Chief Inspector. I've just got some caviar, genuine Russian caviar. An acquired taste, I'm beginning to like it. You remember, I read about it for the first time in a Russian novel. My mouth literally watered. Black pearls indeed. Oh, vodka too. We'll eat and drink to our hearts' content."

"I have to get back to my work, Overseas Chinese Lu." Chen had to cut him short. Lu could gush on for hours whenever he spoke on the topic of food. "I will try to make it to your restaurant next week."

These phone calls had some things in common, Chen thought afterward. Culinary delight was one. Not just that, either. Lu had also spoken about a nostalgic cultural ambiance for his restaurant. As a result of this conversation, Chen felt hungry but he decided to work on, doggedly, for two or three hours more. It seemed as if he had to prove the truth of what he had told Lu on the phone.

After a while, he looked once more at the pictures White Cloud had taken for him. He failed to see the glitter and glamour of the thirties. Perhaps that was due to the dirt and dust accumulated through the years of the construction of socialism. It might be too cynical of him, as a Party cadre, to think so, but that's what he thought.

Finally, he took the remaining food, put it into the microwave, and finished it without really tasting it.

Perhaps he ought to consult some books about old Shanghai. Not books written in the sixties, which he had read as a child, but those from an earlier time. He took out a piece of paper and wrote something down before he brewed himself a pot of coffee. Not a good idea at this hour, he knew. Inhaling the fragrance, he realized that he had been becoming more dependent on caffeine. For the moment, however, he did not want to worry about it. He had to pull himself together.

He worked late that night.

He felt tired, yet all of a sudden, more than anything else, lonely.

Several lines a friend had once quoted to him came to mind. *Trying each of the chilly boughs, / the wild goose chooses not to perch, / with the maple leaves falling, freezing, / over the Wu River.* These were lines from a poem by Su Dongpo. It was said to be a political commentary, but it was often read as a metaphor about the difficulty of choosing a bough to perch upon, whatever the reason might be. In fact, the friend had quoted it in defense of her personal life.

And then his thought jumped to a familiar sound, like the wild goose amidst falling maple leaves. A cricket was screeching outside the window.

There was no accounting for a cricket scraping its wings so

energetically, unless, as he had learned as a boy, the cricket was singing in triumph over a beaten opponent.

But what was the good of being a cricket, victorious or not, if you were always goaded by a golden rush in a boy's hand, circling round and round the world of a small earthen pot?

Chapter 6

After consulting Old Liang's list of the suspects who lived in the *shikumen* building, Yu started his investigation early the next morning at the neighborhood committee office. On the desk was a new folder that contained information about each suspect, probably derived from the records maintained by the veteran residence cop.

The first person on the list was Lanlan, the discoverer of the murder. Technically, she had had the opportunity and means to commit the crime and it appeared to Old Liang that she had a motive too.

Lanlan was a woman who liked nothing better than to mix with her neighbors; she was capable of becoming intimate with people she had known for only three minutes. She had suffered a terrible loss of face with Yin, who rejected her repeated attempts at friendship. Lanlan finally gave up with a bitter statement to the neighbors: "It was like pressing your hot face to her cold ass. What's the point?"

But this would not have been sufficient to cause an explosion unless a fuse had been lit, which, in a *shikumen* house, more often than not came from the constant squabbles about the common space. Because of overcrowded living conditions, each of the families tried hard to occupy as much space as possible—"in a fair way." Old Liang provided an example. Yin had a coal briquette stove as well as a small table in the common kitchen area. It was her space, inherited from the previous *tingzijian* occupant; she took it even though she hardly cooked. Like her predecessor, she also kept a smaller gasoline stove outside her door on the staircase landing. Like all the others, she would not give up an inch she could claim as hers. This must have vexed some of her neighbors.

One night, Lanlan came home in a hurry and stumbled over the gasoline stove. There was a kettle of hot water on the stove; the hot water spilled and scalded her ankle. It was not exactly Yin's fault. The stove had been there for years. Lanlan should have turned on the light, or moved less rapidly. Anyway, accidents happen, but she cursed like a fury outside Yin's door.

"What a white tiger star you are! You bring misfortune to everyone close to you. Heaven has eyes, and you will bring bad luck down upon yourself, too."

Yin must have been aware of the reference—white tiger star—but she knew better than to emerge from her room to shout back.

Lanlan, however, was even more enraged to be ignored like that. She voiced her complaints in neighborhood resident meetings. A lot of people heard them, and some were astonished by the animosity she had displayed toward Yin. But that was still far from being a murder motive, in Yu's estimation. Besides, the incident had happened a couple of years earlier.

He decided to move on to the second name on the list. Wan

Qianshen was a retired worker who lived alone in the attic. Wan had not been in the *shikumen* house that morning. It was his habit, too, to perform tai chi exercises on the Bund at that hour.

Old Liang's file provided a brief biography of Wan. He had been a steel factory worker "dedicated to the construction of the socialist revolution." During the Cultural Revolution, Wan had become a member of the prestigious Mao Zedong Thought Propaganda Worker Team. At the end of the sixties, when the Red Guard students clamored for more power, Chairman Mao managed to contain these young rebels by sending Worker Teams into the colleges with a new revolutionary theory. According to Mao, the students, having been exposed to western bourgeois ideas, needed reeducation. They were urged to learn from the workers—the most revolutionary proletariat. It was a high political honor to be a Thought Propaganda Worker Team Member in those days. All the students and teachers were required to listen to whatever Wan said. He was a Comrade-Always-Politically-Correct, a model for them.

With the death of Chairman Mao and the end of the Cultural Revolution in 1976, everything changed, of course. The propaganda teams withdrew from college campuses. Wan, too, came back to the lane toward the end of the seventies. Later, he retired, like any ordinary old man, and in time, like a piece of tarnished silverware, his days of stardom gleamed only in his memory.

In an increasingly materialistic society, Wan must have come to the belated realization that he had not benefited at all from all his revolutionary activities. Too busy, and too dedicated even to think about himself, he ended up alone, in an attic room. His pension did not catch up with inflation, and the state-run company where he had worked barely covered his medical insurance. So Wan complained constantly, darkly, like his steel-factory chimney, about what the world was coming to. Then fate brought Wan into Yin's path. According to an ancient proverb, *The path where enemies meet one another must be narrow indeed.* In their case, it was in this same building, as they climbed up and down the same narrow staircase every day.

In *Death of a Chinese Professor*, there were harsh descriptions of the propaganda worker teams. Wan heard about this and bought a copy of the novel. To his outrage, he found the university in question to be the very one where Wan had been stationed, although Yin named no names in the book. Wan flew into a rage and tore the book to pieces in front of her door. Yin fought back, shouting, from behind her closed door, "If you were not a thief, you wouldn't have to be nervous."

Bursting with anger, on the staircase just outside her door, Wan cursed her loudly: "What a stinking bitch! You think China is a country for bourgeois intellectuals. You should go to your grave now with that stubborn granite brain of yours! Heaven be my witness: I will make sure of it."

Several neighbors heard him, but no one took him seriously at the time.

People might say anything in a fit of anger, and soon forget about it. Not so with Wan, Old Liang pointed out. Wan had never since spoken to Yin. He bore a profound hatred for her, one in which, in Wan's words, "Two cannot share the same piece of sky."

What made Wan an even more serious suspect was his unconfirmed alibi for the morning of February 7. He said that he performed tai chi on the Bund that morning, but he could have sneaked downstairs, killed Yin, and either gone back to his room or on to the Bund without having been seen. And he could certainly use any money taken from her drawers, as the state-run steel factory had fallen several months behind in paying pensions to its former employees.

An interview was arranged between Yu and Wan at the office.

Wan did not look like a man in his mid-sixties. He had a medium build. He might even be considered tall for his generation. He wore a black wool Mao jacket with matching pants. In a movie from the sixties, Wan would have looked like a mid-rank Party cadre, with his collar buttoned high to his throat and his hair combed back. He appeared to have suffered a minor stroke, as his lips were slightly slanted downward at one corner, which added an impression of inner tension to his expression.

Wan turned out to be more ready to talk than Yu had expected. Holding a cup of hot tea tightly in his hands, he said "The world is turned upside down, Detective Yu. What the hell are those rotten private enterprisers or entrepreneurs? Black-hearted, black-handed capitalists, making obscene amounts of money at the expense of working-class people. That's why all the state-run companies are going to the dogs. What has happened to the benefits of our socialist system? Pensions, free medical care. All gone. If Chairman Mao were still alive, he would never have allowed this to happen to our country."

A passionate statement, purely proletarian, although not so loyal to present Party policy. Yu thought he could understand the old man's frustration. For years, the working class had enjoyed political privileges, and at least had felt a sense of pride in their status, based on Chairman Mao's theory of class struggle in socialist China which deemed the working class to be the most important because it was the most revolutionary. Now the tide had completely turned.

"Our society is currently in a transitional period, and some temporary phenomena cannot be avoided. You must have read all the Party documents and newspapers, and you don't need me to explain," Yu said, before coming to the point. "You must be aware of the purpose of our talk today. Tell me, Comrade Wan, what was your relationship with Yin?"

"She is dead. I should not say anything against her, but if you think my opinion matters to your investigation, I will not mince my words."

"Please go ahead, Comrade Wan. It will be very helpful to our investigation."

"She was part of the evil black force that has tried to turn back history, back to the twenties, the thirties, to the miserable years when China was downtrodden by imperialists and capitalists, while those bourgeois intellectuals enjoyed the pathetic bones thrown to them by their masters. In her book—you must have read it—working-class people are all described as clowns or thugs, without acknowledging the vital fact that it is we who overthrew the Three Big Mountains—imperialism, feudalism, and capital-ism—and built a new socialist China."

Yu could see why Wan was even more embittered than most other retirees. Wan must have given many political lectures at the college, and made himself at home with the political terms pop-ular in the seventies. Now, in the nineties, his views had become obsolete.

"She, too, suffered a lot during the Cultural Revolution," Yu observed.

"Anybody else may complain about the Cultural Revolution. Not Yin Lige. What was she? A notorious Red Guard! Why were the propaganda worker teams sent into the schools? To deal with the disastrous mess they left."

"Well, the past is past," Yu said. "Let me ask you another

question, Comrade Wan. Did you notice anything unusual about her of late?"

"No, I didn't pay any attention to her."

"Anything unusual about the building?"

"No, not that I can remember. I'm a retired old man. It's up to the neighborhood committee to notice things."

"Now, you were not at home the morning Yin was murdered, were you?"

"No, I was practicing tai chi on the Bund," Wan said. "The state-run company I worked for can no longer pay our medical bills. We have no choice but to take care of ourselves."

"I see. Do you practice tai chi with others?"

"Oh, yes, with a large number of people. Some practice tai chi with swords, and some practice tai chi with knives, too."

"Do you have their names and addresses?" Yu added, "It's just a formality. I may have to ask one of them to corroborate your presence."

"Come on, Comrade Detective Yu," Wan said. "People practice tai chi on the Bund for twenty or thirty minutes in the morning, and then go home. There's no point asking each other's names or addresses. Some people nod to me, but they don't know my name, and I don't know theirs. That's it."

What Wan said seemed to make sense, but Yu thought he caught a slight hesitancy in the old man's words. "Well, if you can locate a few tomorrow—one or two names will be enough—please let me know."

"I will, if I go to the Bund tomorrow. Now, I have something else to do this morning, if you have no more questions, Comrade Detective Yu."

"I'll talk to you later, then."

Yu lit a cigarette, tapped his finger on the desk, checked Wan's name off, and moved on to the next name. Glancing through the information about Mr. Ren, the third on Old Liang's list, Yu was about to cross his name off when he thought better of it. Mr. Ren was a "capitalist" in his class status. Before 1949, the *shikumen* building had been owned by Ren's father, who was executed as a counterrevolutionary in the early fifties, when the house was confiscated. The Rens then had to squeeze into a small room partitioned off at the end of the south wing. For the Ren family, the following years became a tale of continuous misfortune and mistrust by one political movement after another. During the Cultural Revolution, Mr. Ren was marched through the lane by a group of Red Guards, his head weighed low by a blackboard declaring "Down with the Black Capitalist Ren!" But as in the Taoist classic *Tao Te Ching*, when one's fortune hits bottom, it begins to change. With the whole society caught up in a gigantic reform, there was a reshuffling of cards among the residents. Mr. Ren's son went to study in the United States and started a high-tech company there. On a recent visit back to Treasure Garden Lane, he offered to buy his father an apartment in the best neighborhood in the city, but Mr. Ren declined.

It seemed to Old Liang, however, that there was something suspicious about Mr. Ren's choosing to stay in the building. Mr. Ren might have harbored a secret resentment for all he had suffered in those years. As the proverb says, *A gentleman may seek revenge even after waiting ten years*. So maybe Mr. Ren was trying now to create trouble for the Party authorities, acting out of long-suppressed anger.

If that were the case, Yin turned out to be a well-chosen target. The murder of a dissident writer might easily bring embarrassing pressure on the government. If the case was not solved, it could tarnish the image of the Party authorities. And then, too, Yin had been a former Red Guard. Symbolically, her death would also provide him with revenge for all his personal miseries.

Like Wan, Mr. Ren had only an unconfirmed alibi. That morning he had gone to a noodle restaurant called Old Half Place. He had breakfasted in the company of several other customers, he said, although he could not produce a receipt for that particular morning nor the address of these breakfast-mates.

The theory advanced by Old Liang was an elaborate one, perhaps inspired by the *Harbor*, one of the revolutionary Beijing operas written in the early seventies, in which a capitalist performed every possible sabotage activity out of his deep hatred for socialist society. But it appeared to Yu that this was stretching too far for a motive in the reality of the nineties.

Yu decided to interview Mr. Ren, but for a quite different reason. In the material concerning Mr. Ren, there was no mention of any unusual contact or confrontation between him and Yin. Nothing was noted of his relations with his neighbors either. Mr. Ren was like another outsider in the house, which might make him a more objective witness. In fact, the "Mr." before his surname indicated his marginal status in the *shikumen*. In the revolutionary years, the most common address had been "Comrade," although, in recent years, "Mr." had staged a comeback. It seemed his previous black status had been transmuted into an outmoded honorific title. Political fashions changed; still, people's memories were long.

Mr. Ren was a man in his early seventies who looked rather-spirited for his age. He wore a Western-style suit with a scarlet silk tie, like a capitalist image from those modern Beijing operas.

Suprisingly, he reminded Yu of Peiqin's father, whom he had seen only in a black-framed photograph.

"I know why you want to talk with me today, Comrade Detective Yu," Mr. Ren said in a cultured voice. "Comrade Old Liang has already approached me."

"Comrade Old Liang has been a residence cop for many years. Perhaps he is too familiar with Chairman Mao's words about class struggle and all that. I'm just a cop in charge of the investigation, Comrade Ren. I have to talk to everybody in the building. Any information you can give me about Yin will be really helpful to my work. I appreciate your cooperation."

"I can guess what Old Liang has told you," Mr. Ren said, studying him through his glasses. "In years past, I wore a 'Black Capitalist' blackboard around my neck, and Yin wore a Red Guard armband on her arm. So he imagines I must have harbored resentment all these years, until now. But that's nonsense. For me, a lot of things are long gone—with the wind, the political wind. A man of my age cannot afford to live in the past. She was a Red Guard, but there were millions of them. Most of them suffered too, as she did. There's no point singling her out."

"Let me tell you something, Mr. Ren. I totally understand your point. My wife's father was also a capitalist. Things were not fair for him in those years, or for her either," Yu said. "But that does not mean she's resentful today."

"Thank you for telling me this, Comrade Detective Yu."

"Now let me ask you a question, the same question I ask everyone in the building. What was your impression of Yin?"

"There's not a lot I can tell you, I am afraid. Our paths hardly ever crossed, even though we lived in the same *shikumen* building."

"Never crossed?"

"In a *shikumen* house, you either mix with your neighbors all the time, or barely at all. In my case, I used to be so black, politically black, that people avoided me like the plague. I do not blame them. No one wanted to bring down trouble upon themselves. Now that I'm no longer so black, I've gotten used to being alone," Mr. Ren said with a bitter smile. "She kept apart too, for her own reasons. It could not have been easy for her, a single woman, only in her late-forties, to have shut herself up in her memories, like a clam. No light ever came through."

"Like a clam; that's interesting."

"Yin was different because she hid herself in a shell of the past, or, to be more exact, like a snail, because her hiding place might have been her unbearable burden too. Most of the neighbors are biased against her because of her standoffishness."

"Did you ever talk to her, Mr. Ren?"

"I did not have anything against her, but I did not go out of my way to talk to her. She did not talk to others either." Mr. Ren added, after a pause, "If there's another thing in common between us, neither of us cooked much in the common kitchen. She might have been too busy writing. As for me, I am something of a frugal gourmet."

"A frugal gourmet?" Yu said. "Please tell me more."

"Well, the Red Guards took away all my personal property at the beginning of the Cultural Revolution. This must have happened to your wife's family too. A few years ago, the government gave me some compensation for my loss. Not much, as the compensation was based on values at the time of confiscation. My children do not need the money, and I can't take the compensation to my coffin.

I have a weakness—I have to confess—for good food, especially for inexpensive Shanghai specialties. So I eat out as much as I can. Besides, it's too much for an old man, to start a fire in a coal briquette stove every morning."

"My wife also starts a fire in a coal briquette stove every morning; I know what you mean. I am curious, Mr. Ren. About a year ago, you could have moved out, but you declined your son's offer to buy you a new apartment in an upper-class area. Why?"

"Why should I move? All my life I have lived here, and everything here is tinged with memories. A leaf must fall where its roots lie. My roots are here."

"But the new apartment building would be far more comfortable, with gas, bathrooms, and all the other modern conveniences."

"I am quite comfortable in my way. For a frugal gourmet, this is a super location, close to a number of wonderful restaurants. In walking distance. Perhaps that's something you have already learned. The morning Yin was murdered, I was at a noodle restaurant called Old Half Place. I go there two or three times a week. There is a group of old customers like me. Some go there every morning. Old Half Place is one of the few remaining state-run restaurants that has kept up food quality without raising prices. Delicious and yet inexpensive. You really should go there."

"Thanks for the suggestion, Comrade Ren. If you think of anything to tell me about Yin, call me."

"I will. Try the noodles there if you have time this weekend."

As the old man left the office, Yu looked at his watch and was thinking about telephoning Chief Inspector Chen, another gourmet, though not necessarily a "frugal" one, when Old Liang burst into the office. "The main office of Shanghai People's Bank has called. Yin Lige had a safe deposit box in the branch in the Huangpu District."

That could be important. Yu forgot about his lunch and headed for the bank.

Chapter 7

The morning brought with it consciousness of the scent of toasted bread, of fresh coffee, the sound of the telephone ringing, and then of a slender hand reaching for the receiver on the nightstand—

"No!" Chen jumped out of bed, snatching the receiver as he rubbed his sleepy eyes. "I'll take it."

It was Party Secretary Li. But for his quick reaction, Chen might have had some explanations to make to his Party boss. White Cloud must have arrived and prepared breakfast while he was still asleep.

Li wanted Chen to take a look at the Yin case.

"I'm on vacation," he said. "Why am I needed, Party Secretary Li?"

"Some people claim it is a political case, saying that our government has gotten rid of a dissident writer in an underhanded way. That's just bullshit, you know."

"Yes, of course. People may make irresponsible remarks, but we do not have to pay attention to them."

"Foreign correspondents have also joined in the vicious chorus.

The government held a memorial service for her, but one American newspaper described it as a cover-up," Li said indignantly. "The mayor has spoken to me about it. We have to solve the case in the shortest time possible."

"Detective Yu is an experienced police officer. I discussed the matter with him over the phone yesterday. He is doing all that can be done. I don't think I can make any difference."

"This is an extremely complicated, sensitive matter," Li said. "We have to employ our best people."

"But this is my first vacation in three years. I've already made my plans," Chen said, having decided not to mention the translation project he had undertaken. "It may not be a good idea for Detective Yu, or for the special squad's morale, for me to have a finger in every pie."

"Come on. Everybody knows Detective Yu is your man," Li said. "Moreover, you are a writer yourself and, as such, you may understand Yin better. Some aspects of the case will be familiar to you, but not to Detective Yu."

"Well, I wish I could help," Chen said. That part of Li's argument made sense. Had it not been for the lucrative translation project Chen might have been willing to cut short his vacation.

"The mayor will call me again next week, Chief Inspector Chen," Party Secretary Li went on. "If the case remains unsolved, what shall I tell him? He understands the case is being investigated by your special case squad."

Chief Inspector Chen bristled at the implication. "Don't worry so much, Party Secretary Li. Surely the case will be solved under your leadership."

"We cannot overestimate the political significance of the case.

You have to help Detective Yu in whatever way you can, Chief Inspector Chen."

"You are right, Party Secretary Li." It was not unusual for Li to harp on the political significance of a case and Chen decided to compromise. "I'll go there to take a look as soon as I have time. Today or tomorrow."

Putting down the phone, he saw a sly smile on White Cloud's lips. Then he observed something like a briefcase on the desk.

"Oh, what's that?"

"A laptop. It may save you some time. You won't have to type and retype on your typewriter. I told Gu about your work and he asked me to bring this computer to you today."

"Thank you. I have a PC in the office but it's too heavy for me to bring home."

"I know. I have also installed the software for a Chinese/English dictionary. It will be quicker for you to look up words on the computer."

She also took out the list of words he had given her. She had printed it out both in English and Chinese.

A clever girl. Gu had been right in sending her to help him. As Confucius said, *You tell her one thing, she will know three things,* Chen thought. But then he grew unsure if Confucius had really said that.

"You are helping a lot, White Cloud."

"It's a pleasure working with you, Chief Inspector Chen."

She started toward the kitchen area. She was wearing a pair of soft-soled cotton slippers which she must have brought with her. Quite a considerate girl too: she'd realized it would be best to walk about without making noise.

He started working on the laptop. The keyboard action was much lighter than the typewriter's, like her soft-footed step.

Every movement of hers seemed still to be registering on his subconscious, even when she was busy in the kitchen area. It was hard for him not to think of her as the K girl he had met in the private karaoke room at the Dynasty Club, or to remember the way Gu had referred to her as a little secretary—though, in a different environment, people could appear to be very different.

She's a temporary assistant for a project, he reminded himself.

In one of the Zen lessons he had read, the master said solemnly, *It is not the banner moving, nor the wind blowing, but your own heart jumping.*

As he reentered into the computer what he had previously translated on the typewriter, he took a sip of the coffee, which was fragrant, strong, though now lukewarm. She brought over the coffee pot again to refill his cup.

"I have something else for you to do today," he said, giving her the list he had prepared the previous night. "Please go to the Shanghai Library and borrow these books for me."

It was not exactly an excuse to send her away. These books should be able to tell him something about the splendors of old Shanghai. He needed to know more about the history of the city.

"I'll be back in a couple of hours," she said, "just in time to make lunch for you."

"I'm afraid you are doing too much for me. It reminds me of a line by Daifu," he said, trying to be ironic since he did not know what other pose to strike. *"It's the hardest thing to receive favors from a beauty."*

"Oh, Chief Inspector Chen, you are as romantic as Daifu!"

"I'm joking," he said. "A pack of Chef Kang instant noodles will do for me."

"No, that won't do," she said, pulling on her street shoes. "Not for Mr. Gu. He will fire me."

There appeared to be a small tattoo, like a colorful butterfly, above her slender ankle. He did not remember having seen that in the Dynasty Club. He tried to get back to his translation work. After Li's phone call, however, there was something else on his mind. He did not agree with Li, yet he kept thinking of the fact that Detective Yu, alone, was handling the murder case of a dissident writer. It seemed to Chen that a number of Chinese writers had been labeled as "dissidents" for reasons that were hardly plausible.

For example, there were the so-called "misty" poets, a group of young people that had come to the fore in the late seventies. They did not really write about politics; what made them different from the others was their preference for difficult or "misty" images. For one reason or another, they had a hard time having their poems published in the official magazines, so they started publishing an underground magazine. That got the attention of Western sinologists, who praised their works to the skies, focusing on any conceivable political interpretation. Soon the misty poets became internationally known, which was a slap in the face for the Chinese government. As a result, the misty poets were labeled "dissident" poets.

Might he himself have become a dissident writer had he not been assigned, upon graduation from Beijing Foreign Language University, to a job in the Shanghai Police Bureau? At that time, he had published some poems, and a few critics even described his work as modernist. Police work was a career he had never dreamed of. His mother had termed it fate although, in the Buddhist religion she believed in, there was no particular deity in charge of fate.

It was almost like a surrealistic poem he had read, in which a boy picked up a stone at random and threw it carelessly into the valley of red dust. There the stone had turned into . . . Chief Inspector Chen?

Around one o'clock, he received a phone call from Detective Yu.

"What's the news?"

"We have found her safe deposit box. Two thousand Yuan, and about the same amount in American dollars, were all that was in it."

"Well, that's not very much for a lockbox."

"And a manuscript," Yu said, "that is, something like a manuscript."

"What do you mean? Another book?"

"Perhaps. It is in English."

"Is it the translation of her novel?" Chen went on, after a pause, "I don't see the point of locking it up when the book has already been published."

"I don't know what it is for sure. You know that my command of English is not good. It appears to me to be a poetry translation."

"That's interesting. Had she done any translations from Chinese into English?"

"I really don't know. Do you want to take a look at it?" Yu said. "The only words I understand in it are some names, like Li Bai or Du Fu. I don't think Li Bai and Du Fu are related to the case."

"There might be something in it," Chen said. "You never know." Poetry had once given him some insight into the complexities of a case involving a missing person.

"The bank is not far from your place. Let me buy you lunch,

Chief. You need to take a break. How about meeting me at the restaurant across the street? Small Family—that's its name."

"Fine," Chen said. "I know the restaurant."

As he had promised Party Secretary Li, he was going to take a look at the Yin investigation.

Would White Cloud, who had offered to make lunch for him, be disappointed? She's only here for business reasons, Chen reflected as he got ready to go out. He left a note for her.

The restaurant opposite the bank seemed to enjoy good business. Yu was in his uniform, so they were able to get a table in the corner that offered some privacy. They each had a bowl of noodles covered with soy-sauce-braised tripe. At the suggestion of the amiable hostess, they also had two appetizers, one of river shrimp fried with red pepper and bread crumbs, and one of soya beans boiled in salt water, plus a bottle of Qingdao beer each, which the hostess offered them with the compliments of the house.

There were a couple of young waitresses flitting around like butterflies. From their accents, Chen judged them to be non-Shanghainese. During the ongoing economic reform, provincial girls too had come pouring into the city. Private entrepreneurs hired them at low wages. Shanghai had been a city of immigrants as early as the turn of the twentieth century. History was repeating itself.

The manuscript Yu brought to the restaurant consisted of two folders. In one the manuscript was handwritten; in the other, it was neatly typed. There were no signs of whiteout corrections or of mistakes in the typed manuscript. Apparently it had been done by a computer. The two were practically identical in their content.

Detective Yu was right. The manuscript consisted of a selection of classical Chinese love poems, including poets like Li Bai, Du Fu,

Li Shangyin, Liu Yong, Su Shi, and Li Yu, with focus on the Tang and Song dynasties. The translation appeared fluent as Chen glanced through the first few pages.

Something else was noticeable: the original form—either a four- or eight-line stanza—disappeared in the English renditions, some of which were informed with a surprisingly modern sensibility:

> A spring silkworm may not stop spinning
> silk until death. A candle's tears dry
> only when it is burned down to ashes.

In the Chinese original, Chen remembered, this was a well-known couplet about a lover's self-consuming passion. This was not the time, however, for him to study the manuscript at length. Nevertheless, he did not think this translation could have been Yin's work.

"Yes, it's a poetry translation."

"I don't know why she valued it so much."

"It must have been done by somebody else—by Yang, probably," Chen said. "Hold on—yes, I have found an Afterword here, written by Yin. Yes, it is Yang's work, it says. She only edited the collection."

"Please take it. Read it when you have time. Maybe you will spot something. Please, boss?"

Chen agreed, then asked "Have any new leads turned up in your interviews?"

"No, not really. I have been interviewing the residents of the building all morning. That hypothesis is not very convincing."

"You mean the theory that she was murdered by one of the *shikumen* residents?"

"Yes. I've studied the list of suspects prepared by Old Liang. Yin was not popular there, either because of some trivial dispute in some cases, or because of her conduct long ago in the Cultural Revolution, but neither of these is a strong enough motive for murder."

"Alternatively, the murderer could have intended to burglarize her room, but panicked when she came back early and interrupted him. You discussed this with Old Liang, I remember."

"That's possible. But was she a likely burglary target? Everybody knew she was not a rich businesswoman. And the contents of her safe deposit box have proven that."

"Well, she had made a trip to Hong Kong. Someone might have imagined she was wealthy just on the basis of that."

"As for her Hong Kong visit," Yu said, "I contacted Internal Security, hoping they could give me some information. You know what? They shut the door right in my face."

"Well, Internal Security. What can I possibly say?" Chen commented as he peeled the shrimp with his fingers. "It's not easy for anyone to get them to cooperate. "

"They are the cops of the cops. I understand. But in such a case, they should help—in the interests of the Party or whatever. Their attitude does not make sense," Yu said, as he put a green soya bean into his mouth, "unless they have something to hide from us."

"I hope not, but what they do often makes sense only to themselves. You never know; they may have their own interests in the case," Chen said. "Have I ever told you about my earliest encounter with them?"

"No, you haven't."

"It was in my college years in Beijing. I published a few poems, and made several pen pals. One day, one of them invited me to his home, and a guest there brought an American poet with him.

On that day we talked of nothing but poetry, but the next day Party Secretary Fuyan of the English department summoned me to his office."

"What did he say to you, Chief?"

"'You are young and inexperienced, and we trust you, but you have to be more careful. Don't be so naive as to believe that the Americans like our literature for literature's sake,'" Chen repeated. "I was confounded. Then I realized he must be referring to the poetry discussion the day before. How could people have reported it so quickly? Years later, I found out that it was the work of Internal Security. I was lucky because the university dean did not want the image of the university tarnished by having one of his students put on the blacklist, so he worked out a deal with Internal Security."

"That's outrageous! Their arms reach everywhere."

"So don't worry about their refusal to cooperate. We may still be able to find out something indirectly. Let me make a couple of phone calls."

"That would be great."

The noodles arrived, the soup almost red with dried pepper, strewn with chopped green onion, the tripe done to just the right degree, quite chewy, a welcome contrast to the crisp texture of the noodles. It was a pleasant surprise for such a small family restaurant. The hostess stood beside their table, beaming, as if waiting for their approval.

"Wonderful food," Chen said, "and wonderful service, too."

"We hope you will come back, Boss," the hostess said with a bright smile, bowing slightly before she moved on to another table.

That was another new term of address. Not *that* new, perhaps. Before 1949, people had used this term, and it was staging a comeback.

"It's their own business," Yu said, "a private business. Of course they want to please their customers, who are their bosses."

"That's true."

"By the way," Yu asked, the noodles hanging like a waterfall from his chopsticks, "is Old Half Place also a good restaurant?"

"A very good one, especially known for the noodles they serve early in the morning. Why?"

"Mr. Ren, a resident who is on the suspect list, told me that he goes there two or three times a week, and he calls himself a 'frugal gourmet.'"

"Frugal gourmet. Great, I like it," Chen said. "Yes, Old Half Place has a lot of regular customers early in the morning, every morning. It's almost like their ritual."

"Why?"

"You have asked the right man. I happen to have read about this restaurant. The chef there plunges noodles into boiling water in an extremely large pot, so the noodles acquire a special crisp texture. But the water soon turns thick with starch and then the noodles lose this texture. It's not easy to change the water in such a large pot. Instead, the chef just adds more cold water, but that's not really good. Gourmets believe that the noodles boiled in the early morning taste much better."

"Heavens, can there be so much to learn about a bowl of noodles?"

Chen was amused at the shocked expression on his partner's face. "And the xiao pork is a must too. The pork sort of melts in the noodle soup, and then on your tongue. It comes in a separate side dish. Very special, and inexpensive too. You ought to go there this weekend."

"You should have interviewed Mr. Ren, Chief. There would have been a lot for you to say to each other."

"A frugal gourmet," Chen repeated, putting the last shrimp into his mouth. "I don't know what sort of man Mr. Ren is, but, according to your description, he no longer lives in the shadow of the Cultural Revolution."

When Chen reached his home, he found a short note from White Cloud on the table. "Sorry, I have to leave for school. Lunch is in the refrigerator. If you need me this afternoon, please call me."

The meal she had prepared was simple but good. The pork marinated in wine might have come from some deli, but the hot and sour cucumber slices mixed with transparent green bean noodles looked fresh and tasty. There was also an electric pot of rice, still quite warm. That would make a good dinner, Chen decided. Closing the refrigerator door, he tried not to think about the Yin case. At this stage, it was a matter of routine to go on interviewing her neighbors, which was what Yu had been doing, and which, if he had been working on the case, he would be doing too.

What else could he possibly do?

He stared at the New World business proposal, and the business proposal stared back at him.

Chapter 8

Qinqin had called home, saying that he would sleep over at the apartment of a schoolmate. It was not that often that Yu and Peiqin had a night by themselves. In spite of his frustration with the day's investigation, Yu decided to turn in early with Peiqin.

It was a cold night. They sat under the quilt, leaning against the pillows propped up against the hard headboard. It took quite a while for the warmth of their bodies beneath the old cotton-padded quilt to make the cold of the room endurable. His feet brushed hers; her toes were soft, still slightly chilled. He put his arm around her shoulders.

In the soft light, she looked like the same girl she had been the first time with him in Yunnan, on that cool creaking bamboo bed, in the shadow of the flickering candlelight—except for those tiny fishtail-like lines around her eyes.

But Peiqin had something else in mind this evening. She wanted to tell him the story of *Death of a Chinese Professor*. She put the novel on top of the quilt; a bamboo butterfly bookmark stuck out of it.

Yu did not read much. He had tried several times to get into *The Dream of the Red Chamber,* Peiqin's favorite, but he gave up, invariably, after three or four pages. There was no way for him to relate to those characters who had lived in a grand mansion hundreds of years ago. In fact, the only reason that he had made the attempt was because of Peiqin's passion for the book. As for the books about the Cultural Revolution, he had read only two or three short stories, all of which struck him as totally untrue. If there had been such foresighted heroes to question or challenge Chairman Mao in the early sixties, Yu reflected, the national disaster would not have started in the first place.

With Yin's case on his hands, he had thought he had no choice but to read *Death of a Chinese Professor* from beginning to the end. Fortunately, Peiqin had already undertaken the assignment. She had told him a little about the book and this evening wished to give him a detailed account.

"What I'm going to recount," Peiqin said, folding her legs, "is perhaps influenced by my own point of view. I will focus on the role of Yang, since you are familiar with Yin's history, and then I will dwell on the love affair between the two."

"Wherever you want to start, Peiqin," Yu said, taking her hand in his.

"Yang was born into a wealthy family in Shanghai. He went to study in the United States in the forties, where he got a Ph.D. in literature, and started publishing his poems in English. In 1949, he hurried home, full of passionate dreams for a new China. He taught English at Eastern China University, translated English novels, and wrote poems in Chinese before he suffered a major setback during the Anti-Rightist Movement in the mid-fifties. Suddenly condemned as a reactionary Rightist, and deserted by his friends and relatives because of his Rightist status, he stopped writing poems, although he continued translating such books as were approved by government, like the works of Charles Dickens and Thackeray, about whom Karl Marx had made favorable comments, or those of Mark Twain and Jack London, some of whose works showed an anti-capitalist tendency. He was then transferred to the Chinese department, in an effort to prevent him from disseminating 'decadent Western ideas' in English at a time when most of the Party officials did not understand a single word of English.

"At the outbreak of the Cultural Revolution, Yang turned overnight into a target of revolutionary mass criticism. He was forced to denounce himself. His college years in the States were described as years of espionage training, and his translations of English and American literature as attacks on proletarian literature and art in socialist China. In the early seventies, with more and more new class enemies being discovered in the course of the unprecedented revolution, Yang became a 'dead tiger'—it was no longer so much fun for revolutionary people to beat him up. Like other 'bourgeois intellectuals,' he was then sent to a cadre school in the countryside. It was there that he met Yin.

"They were both cadre students, but there was a marked difference in their political status. Yang, a Rightist with serious problems in his past, was at the bottom. Yin, a Red Guard who was charged with 'minor mistakes' in the Great Revolution, was made a group leader, responsible for supervising members of the group to which Yang belonged.

"At this time, some still believed in everything Chairman Mao said, even there at the cadre school. A well-known poet wrote in ecstasy about the cure of his insomnia through physical labor in the fields, as a result of following Chairman Mao's instruction. Some were disillusioned, however, in spite of Mao's 'newest and highest directions' set forth in those endless Party documents. After a day's hard labor, a few of them started thinking. Theoretically, after having successfully reformed themselves through hard physical labor and political studies, the cadre students should have been able to 'graduate' and have new jobs assigned to them. After a couple of years, however, they knew they had been pretty much forgotten. It seemed they were never going to be allowed to go back to the city, even though they were no longer at the center of the revolution.

"Yin, too, found reason to reflect. No longer so sure about the correctness of her actions as a Red Guard, she realized that she had been used by Mao. She tried to think about her future. As an ex-Red Guard, her prospects were bleak, she admitted to herself. If she were ever to return to her college, it would not be as a political instructor. She was no longer in any position to give political talks.

"Then she began to notice Yang. He worked as a kitchen helper. It was not considered a burdensome job; he gathered firewood, prepared rice and vegetables, and washed dishes. There was a local peasant chef responsible for the cooking. So between meals, Yang had time to read books in the kitchen—English books—and to write, too.

"The cadre students were not supposed to read anything except Chairman Mao's work or political pamphlets. But there had been an unusual event the previous year: Chairman Mao had published two new poems in the *People's Daily,* and an English translation was required. Mao's Poetry Translation Office under the Central Party Committee in Beijing, or someone in the office, remembered Yang and consulted him with respect to a few words. There was one especially difficult phrase—'Don't fart.' That was exactly what Mao had written, but the official translators were worried about its vulgarity. Yang was able to find some reference to that word in Shakespeare, which put their minds at ease. Thereafter, Yang was allowed as a special case to read English books, for the school authorities anticipated that there might be other important political assignments in the future.

"Yang suddenly fell sick. Due to ill nourishment and hard work, not to mention the effects of the persecution he had suffered for many years, what began as flu soon turned into acute pneumonia.

"Most people in the group were old and weak. They were experts on physics or philosophy, but were hardly able to take care of themselves. There was no hospital nearby, only a clinic with a 'barefoot doctor.' Her class status was that of a full-time farmer working in the rice paddy, still barefoot, with no medical training in 'bourgeois colleges.' So, as the group leader, Yin took it upon herself to take care of him. She worked in his place in the kitchen, made food for everybody, and prepared special meals for him. She managed to have antibiotics sent from Beijing. As he gradually recovered, she continued to help him in every way possible, exercising the little power she still possessed in the cadre school on his behalf.

"In the meantime, she started to study English on her own, and to consult him with questions from time to time. President Nixon's visit to China had already taken place. On one of the official radio stations, an English study program started. It was no longer politically incorrect for people to learn English, although it was rather unusual for students in a cadre school where people were supposed to keep washing their brains as their top priority.

"Yin's visits to Yang gave rise to gossip. She visited him frequently, to the great inconvenience of his roommates. Their dorm room was small and cramped, with three bunk beds in it. When she sat talking with Yang, the other five roommates felt obliged to leave, to walk around outside in the cold. It did not take long for people to see that their 'English study' was a pretext. They talked about much more than her English problems. While looking at an English book on the table, it was noticed, they held hands under the table.

"She may have started with a vague notion that knowledge of English might come in handy some day, even for a downtrodden man like Yang, but in her studies with him, she soon started to see a new prospect.

"They covered not only language, but literature as well, for there were no textbooks available in the cadre school. Yang had to use novels and poems as teaching materials. Yin had filled her college years with political activities; she had learned little in the classroom. From him, she now absorbed the knowledge she had not gotten previously. Reading an English novel, *Random Harvest*, she picked out one sentence, 'My life began with you, and my future goes on with you—there's nothing else.' She repeated it to Yang with tears trembling in her eyes.

"On the epigraph page of *For Whom the Bell Tolls*, which Yang had translated, she read a passage, 'No man is an Island, entire of itself; every man is a piece of the Continent, a part of the main . . . any man's death diminishes me, because I am involved in Mankind. And therefore never send to know for whom the bell tolls; It tolls for thee.' Yang told her that it was a quote from John Donne, who had compared separated lovers to the two points of a compass in a celebrated love poem. Having read 'A River Merchant's Wife,' she understood the Chinese poem 'Changgan Song' for the first time. In a short story by O. Henry, she found the significance of life in a solitary leaf painted on the wall, and when Yang compared himself to that leaf, she stopped him with her hand over his mouth.

"That was the point of no return for her: she found all the meanings unknown to her before, with him—it was *him*. This was a passion she had never experienced before, a passion that gave a new meaning to her existence.

"And for him, the affair came as a vindication of humanity despite all the political calamities that had befallen him. In his bookish way, he fought for love as one of those ideals he had striven for all these years. At one point of his life, he had been dis-illusioned but now he was filled with conviction.

"Love might have come late, but its arrival made all the difference.

"The cadre school was located in a marshland in Qingpu. There was no library nor any movie theaters nearby. Instead of staying in the dorm room, they started to walk out, openly, arm in arm. For lovers, to be is to be with each other.

"Yang was in his mid-fifties. Except for a pair of broken eye-glasses, he looked like an old farmer, weather-beaten, white-haired like an owl, and with a pronounced suggestion of a stoop. As for Yin, she was still in her early thirties. Though not a beauty, she was animated with passion, blossoming beside him. To people's con-fusion, it was she who clung to him with abandon.

"*His white hair shone against her rosy cheeks,* just as described in a well-known proverb. But that proverb was commonly considered to be negative, with an implication that such a couple was unsuit-able. What the lovers saw in each other was, of course, a matter of opinion. They were both single. There was nothing legally against them being together, but that was the least of it since, at the very beginning of the Cultural Revolution, Chairman Mao had called for the demolition of the bourgeois legal system.

"Still, it should have been no one else's business. But it turned out to be.

"She was not popular. Some of the people in the school had suffered mistreatment by her when she was a Red Guard. Also, the cadre school authorities were upset. A political scandal might develop. Instead of reforming themselves in the cadre school, they had fallen in love. It was politically outrageous, for the concept of romantic love was a political taboo in the early seventies. It implied a decadent detraction from one's dedication to Chairman Mao and the Party.

"They did not try to keep their love affair a secret, which proved to be too naive of them."

As Peiqin started leafing through the book, Yu said, "Yes, there's not a married couple in the eight modern revolutionary Beijing operas—with the exception of Madame Aqin, whose husband is conveniently away on business. It is all political fervor, there are no personal feelings in those operas."

"Here is what I was looking for," Peiqin said, shifting to a more comfortable position. "Let me read a few paragraphs to you."

They were in a world where there was nothing they could take for granted. No certitude. No reliability. No conviction.

Except him in her, and her in him.

After a day's labor, he would sometimes read poems to her, in Chinese, and then in English, behind the cadre school pigsty, or on a ridge in the rice paddy, their hands soil-covered, a broken loudspeaker repeating Chairman Mao's quotations in the air, black crows hovering over the deserted field.

The Cultural Revolution was a national disaster, they realized, in which each and every individual was smashed to pieces, "burned to ashes," as in a revolutionary slogan. For them, however, it was as if they had been reborn out of the ashes.

"A terrible beauty is born," he said. "There will be a new future for the people, for the country."

He especially liked a poem entitled "You and I," written by a woman poet named Guan Daosheng in the thirteenth century. The passion was expressed quite directly, as was seldom seen, according to him, in classical Chinese poetry.

> *You and I are so crazy*
> *about each other,*
> *as hot as a potter's fire.*
> *Out of the same chunk*
> *of clay, the shape of you,*
> *the shape of me. Crush us*
> *both into clay again, mix*
> *it with water, reshape*
> *you, reshape me.*
> *So I have you in my body,*
> *and you'll have me forever in yours too.*

After having finished reading the long quote in an emotion-suffused voice, Peiqin said "But such a passion was hardly comprehensible in the cadre school. What's worse, it was a passion viewed by one of the school leaders as a brazen challenge to the Party authorities.

"So a mass criticism meeting was held. Yang was marched onto a temporary stage and denounced as a negative example of the reactionary intellectual who resisted ideological reform by falling in love. Yin's lot was hardly better: in addition to a serious inner-Party warning, she was ordered to stand barefoot beside him on the stage. She did not wear a blackboard; she bore a halter of ragged shoes around her neck, a time-honored symbol of shame, of being worn out after being used by numerous men, like the dirty shoes.

"There is a famous quotation by Chairman Mao, *There is no groundless love or hatred in this world*. There must have been a reason for the two 'black elements' embracing each other, their revolutionary critics said. It must have been out of their common hatred of the Cultural Revolution, the critics concluded.

"Yin and Yang remained defiant, continuing to meet each other, whenever and wherever possible, despite the repeated warnings of the cadre school authorities.

"He was then put into an 'isolation room,' deprived of all contact with the outside world and Yin. He was ordered to write confessions and self-criticisms all day long. He refused to do so, declaring that there was nothing wrong in one human being loving another. After a week, he was marched out to work for extralong hours in the rice paddy during the day, then sent back to the isolation room to write in the evening.

"She, too, suffered terribly. Half her hair was shaved off down to the scalp—in a special style called the Yin–Yang haircut, designed for class enemies—a cruel play on the coincidence of their family names. She did not even bother to wear a hat, as if proud of the price she had had to pay for her passion.

"What's worse, she was not allowed to see Yang. After a day's work, she could only wander, alone, around the hut in which he was kept, hoping to catch a glimpse of his silhouette against the window. She kept repeating the lines he had taught her, 'What a starry night this, / but not that night, long ago, lost. / For whom do I find myself standing here, / against the wind and the frost / deep in the night?'

"Not long afterward, Yang fell sick again. Because of his lack of cooperation with the school authorities, they made it hard for him to get proper treatment. The barefoot doctor believed that a silver acupuncture needle could cure any illness, because Chairman Mao said that traditional Chinese medicine could perform miracles. Yin was denied the right to visit him until the very last day of his life, when everybody could see that he was beyond hope. It was a cold day, and his hands in hers were even colder. All his roommates left the room, making one excuse or another, leaving the two of them together. Holding her hand, he remained conscious to the end, even though he was no longer able to speak. He died in his dorm room, in her arms. As a poem Yang had translated says: *'If only your body, cold as ice, as snow, / could be brought back life / by the warmth of mine. . . .'*

"Two years later, the Cultural Revolution came to an end. The cadre school dissolved. She went back to her college. Because of the English she had learned from him, she was assigned to teach English.

"As for Yang, it was officially declared that he had died a natural death. He had not been executed or beaten to death like some intellectuals, so there was no need to look into the specific circumstances of his last days. So many had died during those years. No one bothered. Nothing was done about him in the first few years after the Cultural Revolution.

"In the early eighties, the Party authorities issued a document entitled 'Correction of the Anti-Rightist movement in the Fifties,' in which having labeled such a large number of intellectuals as Rightists was acknowledged as a mistake, although 'at the time, there might have been a few of them who harbored malicious intentions against the government.' Anyway, the survivors were no longer Rightists, and they shot off firecrackers in celebration. There was a movie about such a Rightist who had been lucky enough to find his love during his Rightist years, and survived miraculously, of course, to make new contributions to the construction of socialism.

"Not so Yang. In a belated memorial service for him, Yang was posthumously de-Rightisted and called 'Comrade Yang' once again. A few of his colleagues attended the service. Some of them were actually summoned to it because the school authorities were worried that people might have already forgotten about him. At the memorial service, Yang's death was declared a 'sad and serious loss to modern Chinese literature.' The event was reported in the local newspaper.

"There was a small incident not covered in the report though. Qiao Ming, one of the former cadre school leaders, also came to the service. Yin angrily spat in his face. People separated them in a hurry. 'The past is past,' people said to her, and to Qiao too.

"Life went on as usual. She remained single and edited a poetry manuscript left by him. A collection of his poems was then published by Shanghai Literature Publishing House. But it was not until after the publication of *Death of a Chinese Professor* that anyone began to talk about Yang again. Or, to be exact, about the romantic affair between Yin and Yang.

"That's the gist of the story," Peiqin said at the end of her narrative. "What I have told you is also based on information I obtained from the library, from reviews, or from people's reminiscences."

"Isn't there anything else?"

"Well, there have been various responses to the book."

"Tell me about those responses."

"Some believed that this must be a true story of their love affair. A few even blamed her for his death. But for their affair, Yang would not have ruffled the feathers of the authorities and suffered persecution. He might have survived." Peiqin shifted to a new position, nestling against Yu's shoulder. "Some discredited the story totally. For one thing, a cadre school was no place for romantic love. The dorm rooms were so cramped. They would not have been able to find any place to meet, even if they had the desire and the energy. Not to mention the political atmosphere. The officials of the cadre school would have been too vigilant."

"So what do you think of the book?"

"When I read it for the first time, I had mixed feelings about it. I liked some parts, but not others. And to tell the truth, I used to be such a fan of Yang's work, so I was more or less disappointed."

"Really! You have not told me about that."

"I read most of his poetry in the early seventies, and it was not that safe, you know, to discuss such writing."

"But I still don't see why you were disappointed. It's her book, not his."

"Well, don't laugh at me, but I thought he deserved someone better, and my first reading could have been affected by my bias."

"You mean someone better than the woman in the picture on the back cover of the book—a withered, middle-aged, bespectacled woman?" Yu asked.

"Not exactly. It could also have been a better book," Peiqin said. "I did not like the overly detailed introduction about Red Guard organizations. It's almost irrelevant. And then some of the descriptions of the affair put me off."

"What was wrong with them?"

"Some parts were really touching but some were a bit too melodramatic. It was almost like a teenage infatuation. It's hard to imagine that a scholar of his age and caliber would have been so naive."

"Well, in those years, people clung to anything," he said. "They would grasp at any straw to preserve some semblance of humanity. This might have been true for her—and for him too."

"That might be so," she agreed. "Perhaps I was too much of a fan of his writing. This time, after having gone into their backgrounds, and having read the book more closely for a second time, I realize that she must have really cared for him. Too strong an emotion might have not been good for her writing. She was such a pitiable woman."

"I think so, too," he said, reaching for a pack of cigarettes on the nightstand.

"Please don't," she said, turning to look at the alarm clock on the nightstand. "We have talked such a long time about others."

Under the quilt, he felt her toes touching his shin. It was just like in their Yunnan years, with the brook gurgling behind their hut.

He saw the message in her eyes and removed the pillow propped against the headboard. It was one of those rare nights of privacy on which they did not have to try to hold their breath, or to make as little sound and movement as possible, as they clasped each other tightly.

Afterwards, he still held her hand, peacefully, for a long while.

To his surprise, Peiqin started snoring a little, though ever so lightly. It happened sometimes when she was overtired. She must have stayed up late reading for the last few nights. For his sake.

After all these years, he still found Peiqin full of surprises.

He sometimes wondered whether she should have lived a different life. Pretty, talented, she might not have crossed his path but for the Cultural Revolution, to which Yu actually had a reason to be grateful. So many years after the national disaster, she was still with him, even joining him now in an investigation.

Despite all his disappointments, Yu considered himself a lucky guy.

But all of a sudden, he also felt disturbed. It was not just about Yin and Yang; it was something more vague, yet personal. He realized that there was no telling whether another Cultural Revolution might befall China.

In the moment before he went to sleep, strange ideas came crowding into his mind. *Fortunately, Peiqin is not a writer*—that was one of his half-formed thoughts as he finally fell asleep that night.

Chapter 9

Chief Inspector Chen woke up with an unpleasant thought, as annoying as the shrill ringing of the alarm o'clock on the nightstand. He was going to give in, although he was still too disoriented to tell what he was conceding.

He got up, rubbing his eyes. It still appeared gray outside the window.

It was not his case, he told himself one more time. Yu had been doing all that could be done. Any interference by him would not make a difference, not at this stage. His priority must be the translation of the New World proposal sitting on his desk.

Gu had not pressed him for the translation the way Party Secretary Li had urged him to head the investigation, at least not as directly, although it occurred to him that White Cloud might have been assigned to him not just as a helper but also as a subtle reminder that he was to concentrate on the translation.

Still, Chen felt that he had to do something with respect to the investigation. There were a number of reasons for him to do so. He ought to pitch in for the sake of Yang, if for nothing else, a writer whose career had been tragically cut short, and whose works Chen should have read earlier.

In his middle school years, Chen had read *Martin Eden,* a novel translated by Yang, and knew Yang was one of the best-regarded translators of English fiction, but then Chen started studying English and reading books in their original language. When he himself started writing poetry, Chen did not read any of Yang's poems—they were not easily available at that time. By the time Yang's poetry collection came out, Chen was already busy as an emerging Party cadre, too busy to do as much reading as he wanted.

In fact, his own writing career had now reached a critical stage, Chen knew. There were too many books waiting to be read. In the middle of one homicide investigation after another, however, he did not know how he could ever manage to keep up.

He felt an affinity to Yang, a poet as well as a translator. But for the dramatic reversal of politics, what had happened to Yang could have happened to Chen.

Chen did not know that Yang had translated from Chinese into English, an attempt Chen had never made before, except for a few fragmented lines for a friend from the United States. He started to brew a pot of coffee, a Brazilian brand, a gift from her, that faraway friend.

He took out Yang's poetry translation manuscripts that Yu had given him. Instead of studying the computer printout, he focused on the handwritten manuscript. The two were practically identical. In his research for a paper he had written years earlier about *The Waste Land,* he had learned that a handwritten manuscript might be a useful entree into the mind of a creative writer.

A general impression he had gotten of Yang's manuscript was

that he had made a conscientious effort to make the text readable to contemporary English readers, but what caught Chen's attention were some abbreviated notes left in the margins.

"Chapter 3," "C 11," "C 8 or C26," "C 12 if not C 15," "For the conclusion."

Apparently, these references had meaning for Yang alone.

Perhaps they indicated the books consulted for the purpose of the translation, Chen speculated. Classical Chinese poems could be open to endless interpretations. As a renowned scholar, Yang might have done a lot of research before settling upon one particular rendition.

But that did not make much sense. For that purpose, Yang should have jotted down page numbers, not chapters. It would have been much easier for him to check his citations afterward.

The collection included a number of poems Chen recognized immediately, even in English, but a few of them offered no clue as to what the original might have been. It was possible that Yang had selected these poems from earlier or less-known collections. That might be an explanation for the abbreviated references. But then, why all the "Cs" instead of editors' names?

The lack of an introduction or conclusion gave Chen a different idea. He, too, had written conclusions for different projects, in which he sometimes quoted a line or two. Yang might have been in the process of writing a conclusion for his poetry translation, but had died without having finished it.

In spite of his failure to see any relevance to the murder case, Chen did not put the manuscript down. He could see why Yin had cherished the manuscript. It contained wonderful love poems, as Yin had said in the Afterword, which also evoked the most memorable days of their lives. In the cadre school, they would have pored over those poems together, in English and in Chinese, holding hands. On such a night, they might have felt as if the poem of Su Dongpo had been written for them, and that they themselves were united forever through its lines:

The night watchman struck the third watch.
Golden waves of the moonlight fading,
a jade handle of the Dipper lowering,
we calculate with our fingers
when the west wind will come,
unaware of time flowing away like a river in the dark.

The Afterword was written in a clever way. Yin did not try to say too much, but merely presented the scenes in which she and Yang had read and discussed those poems at the cadre school. She ended, however, with a scene in which she stood alone, reading a poem written by Li Yu, which had once been recited to her by Yang, deep in the night:

When will the endless cycle
of the spring flower and the autumn moon
come to an end?
How much remembrance of things past
does a heart know?
Last night, in the attic revisited
by the eastern wind,
it was unbearable to look
toward home in the fair moonlight.

The carved rails and the marble steps must remain
unchanged, but not her beauty.
How much sorrow do I have?

It is like the spring flood of a long river flowing east!

The manuscript had enormous sentimental value. Chen touched it gently. No wonder Yin had kept it in a bank safety deposit box.

Now he stood up and moved to the window, looking out at the street waking under his gaze. Across the road, he saw a Young Pioneer hurrying out the door, tying his red scarf with one hand, holding a fried rice cake in the other, a heavy satchel on his back—it appeared, for a fleeting moment, as if he was Chen himself, hurrying to school, thirty years ago. The chief inspector collected himself and turned back to the desk littered with dictionaries and papers.

Now he had something else for White Cloud to do in the Shanghai Library. Some of the poems translated by Yang might have appeared in English study journals, although Chen was not sure when that might have occurred—perhaps before the Anti-Rightist movement in the mid-fifties. If so, some annotation there might throw light on the mysterious abbreviations in the manuscript. They might not turn out to be important or relevant, but he was curious. In addition, the library must have some catalogs from Chinese and foreign publishers. He could try to contact some of them, to see whether they might be interested in publishing the collection. There was no hurry, but it gave him comfort to think that he was attempting to do something for the dead.

In that way, Chen could also keep White Cloud busy, and away from his room. Then he felt he would be able to settle down to working on his translation. And he did just that, productively, for a couple of hours, before she arrived for the day. The laptop helped.

When sunlight came streaming through the window, and White

Cloud entered the room, carrying a paper bag of fried mini-buns, he had already finished several pages. He explained her new assignment: To find poems in magazines translated by Yang, and to identify publishers that might be interested in publishing a collection of such poems. Also, he had an elusive feeling this might uncover something else, even though he did not know what. It was a long shot. He himself would probably not go to the library on the basis of that sort of hunch, but having White Cloud available made it possible.

"I have to assist Detective Yu, as you know, anyway I can," Chen explained to her, "but I do not have time to do so and to work on the translation for Mr. Gu too. So you are really helping a lot."

"A little secretary is supposed to do whatever her boss wants her to," she said with a sly smile. "Anything. You don't have to explain. Mr. Gu has emphasized it many times. But what about your lunch?"

"Don't worry about that," he said. "It may take you several hours. Take your time at the library."

Surprisingly, he received no phone calls that morning. The translation progressed smoothly. A sparrow twittered outside his window in the cold wind despite the barrenness of the twigs. He forgot about his lunch, for he was transported back into the glitter and glamour of the city in the thirties. Like visitors to the New World would someday be, he was "drunk with money, dazzled with gold."

When the phone finally rang, waking him from the scene of a French girl dancing a modern dance, her bare feet flashing like snow on a red-carpeted stage inside a postmodern *shikumen* house, he felt disoriented as he abruptly returned to reality. The caller was Yu. He had not made much progress in the investigation, he reported. Chen was not surprised. Not that he did not have a high opinion of Yu's ability. Investigations took time.

"I don't know if the interviews will lead to anything," Yu said.

"We may at least learn something more about Yin."

"That's another thing. Her neighbors seem to have known very little about her. She was a writer, she had published a book about the Cultural Revolution. That's about it. Otherwise, she was an outsider in the building."

"What about her colleagues?"

"I've talked to her department head. I got nothing really informative from him. As for the file provided by her school authorities, it contains little except a bunch of official clichés."

"Anybody would be nervous discussing a dissident writer," Chen said. *The less said, the better.* It's understandable."

"But to substantiate the insider-murderer theory, and to rule out people who knew her at the college, I would have liked to have interviewed some of her colleagues."

"My guess is that they will not say much either, but it's too early to exclude any possibilities."

At the end of the conversation, the clock said one thirty.

But for the translation project, Chen thought as he made a cup of soybean milk for himself, it might have been a good idea for him to visit some of the scholars who had known Yin or Yang. Instead, he picked up the phone and dialed Professor Zhou Longxiang, who had worked at the same college as Yin. Chen had once consulted Zhou about classical Chinese poetry, and had since kept in touch.

Professor Zhou, apparently lonesome after his retirement, was glad of Chen's call. He launched into a lecture about the death of poetry for fifteen minutes before Chen was able to bring the conversation to the subject of Yin. At once Zhou's voice showed irritation. "She was a shameless opportunist, that Yin Lige. I should not speak ill of the dead, I know, but when she was a Red Guard, she showed no mercy at all toward others."

"Perhaps she was too young then."

"That's no excuse. What a disaster of a woman! She brought nothing but trouble to people close to her. Including Yang, who was a fine scholar."

"That's a very interesting point, Professor Zhou," Chen said. "As you are not superstitious, please enlighten me."

"It's simple. But for the affair with her, he would not have been subject of criticism meetings at the cadre school," Zhou said. "Karma. By her actions during the Cultural Revolution, she brought her troubles upon herself."

It was a cruel thing to say, whether one was Buddhist or not. The old professor's opinion must have been fixed there and then in the furnace of the Cultural Revolution. It did not throw much light on the investigation, but it reconfirmed the impression of her unpopularity even among her colleagues.

Looking at his watch, Chen told himself he could not afford to make many phone calls like that. Then he had an idea: he might try an approach of a different sort. It would be something else for White Cloud to do. It was surprising that she kept floating into his mind like a cloud that hovered over his work, and not just the translation work. He was not without a touch of self-satisfaction as he thought a little more about it. He could send her to talk to Yin's former colleagues. He was, as in the proverb, *A general who makes plans in his tent, and determines the outcome of a battle thousands of miles away.* Even on his vacation, he was still able to contribute to the investigation.

A few minutes before four, White Cloud returned carrying two plastic bags. She had changed her clothes, and wore jeans and a leather jacket over a low-cut white sweater. On her feet were a pair of short, shiny black boots.

"I've got something for you." She put one of the plastic bags on the desk.

"You've been really quick. Thank you so much. I know I can count on you, White Cloud."

"I have photocopies of Yang's poetry translations. You may read them for yourself." Still carrying the other bag, she added, "I'll fix something for you in the kitchen."

"What do you have in your hand?"

"A surprise."

He had no clue as to what the plastic bag contained. It was large and black, and there seemed to be a faint, indistinct sound coming out of it.

He started reading the photocopied pages. Yang's poetry translations had been published in a number of English study journals, mostly in the last few years. Such journals had an enormous circulation in China, where so many people were now engaged in learning English.

In most cases, to Chen's surprise, the editors had put in a few words as to why people should read Yang's poetry today. According to one magazine editor, it would be a good way to impress Americans. According to another, it would become fashionable, especially among lovers, to quote these translated poems on Valentine's Day, which was being introduced into China. There were also several short introductions by Yin, about the techniques employed in the translation of these poems, which might be helpful to beginners. However, he failed to find any clue to the mysterious abbreviations.

White Cloud was making noises in the kitchen area. She must be cooking, even though it was still a bit early for dinner.

She finally emerged, carrying a large tray with a broad smile. "From the Dynasty Club," she announced, placing on the folding table an impressive dinner that included some delicacies he had never seen before. One was a small dish of fried sparrow gizzards, golden crisp. How many sparrows had gone into the making of that dish, he wondered. The other dish, of duck, was also original—it was duck heads with the skulls removed, so people could easily reach the tongues, or suck out the brains. It was the sauna shrimp, however, that really impressed him. River shrimp were brought to the table in a glass bowl, live, still jumping and wriggling. She also provided a small wooden pail whose bottom was covered with red hot stones. She poured some wine into the bowl of shrimp, then took the drunken shrimp from the bowl and put them into the pail. There was a shrill hiss, and, in two or three minutes, a plate of sauna shrimp appeared.

Gu must have given her many instructions, including how to prepare the sauna shrimp. She might not be an excellent cook, but she knew how to procure delicious food, and that was good enough for him.

"Is that what you wanted?" she said, picking up one copied page of the poetry translation.

"It may be a piece of the puzzle. I will have to try to fit it in."

"You will," she said. "I hope you like the shrimp too."

"Thanks. You are spoiling me."

"Not at all. It's a great honor to work with you, as Mr. Gu tells me."

To Chen, however, it sounded somewhat like a reminder to concentrate on the translation lying on the desk, and to remember that theirs was a business relationship.

He recalled their first meeting in a private room in the Dynasty Club. She, too, had been quite professional—as a K girl. The least he could do now was to show his appreciation. He picked up another shrimp with his fingers.

Chapter 10

Detective Yu arrived at the neighborhood committee office early. He wanted to do some reading, even after Peiqin had told him the story of Yin's novel. Peiqin had also underlined some parts for him to study more closely. The first few pages he turned to described Yang reading to Yin at night behind the pigsty, with piglets grunting off and on as a chorus.

The cloud seems to be changing its shape. / Insubstantial, soft, wrapping itself against the other, / curling up. Then comes the rain. . . . It took Yu a minute to figure out the metaphor. It was clever of Yin to write in such highly suggestive language, without being explicit. He wondered, however, if Yin and Yang could have really done anything while they were at the cadre school. They both lived in the dorm, with many roommates in their respective rooms. Even if their roommates were out of the way for an hour or two, it would have been too risky for the two to attempt anything. In those years, if people were caught having extramarital sex, they could be sentenced to years of imprisonment. He read the lines one more time. After close study, it was even more provocative. Chief Inspector Chen, who wrote his own poetry more or less like that, might appreciate it.

The few other underlined sections were largely about politics. There was one long paragraph about the head of the cadre school, another about the worker propaganda team. Yu could imagine how some people might feel uncomfortable about this book. It would be easy for them to believe that the characters in the book were based on themselves.

He did not know why Peiqin wanted him to read those parts. And he was not able to read for long. He was rung up by Party Secretary Li, who had traced him to the neighborhood committee office. This phone call had been provoked by a fairly long article in the latest issue of a popular magazine, published under the pretext of commemorating Yin's death, but actually more about the death of Yang. It also contained several long quotes from *Death of a Chinese Professor*. One was a statement, made at the professor's deathbed, toward the end of the novel: "From this moment on, she would live for him, and die for him too."

That was a subtle insinuation that Yin's death might be politically complicated.

The magazine had sold out immediately, which served as yet another reminder of the mounting popular interest in this murder case. Such interest was far from pleasant to the Party authorities.

"The case has to be solved as quickly as possible," Party Secretary Li declared once again.

In a non-political case, it might not matter much if the investigation took a few weeks longer. Some of them remained dormant, with no clues and no solution in sight, for many months, or longer, sometimes forever. But this particular case needed a quick resolution. As a member of the special case squad, Detective Yu was not unfamiliar with the usual arguments.

"If unsolved, the case may keep on feeding wild speculation," Li continued sternly, "and that will bring too much pressure to bear on the city government, and the bureau too."

"I understand, Comrade Party Secretary Li," Detective Yu said. "I will do my best."

"What is Chief Inspector Chen up to? It's hard to understand. He insists on taking his vacation in spite of the urgency of solving this important case. And I don't know how long his vacation will last."

"Nor do I," Yu said, knowing that Chen had not told the Party boss about his translation project. But he did not like the implication—whether Party Secretary Li really meant it or not—that he would not be able to handle a "special case" without Chief Inspector Chen supervising him.

In the special case squad, the spotlight usually was on Chen, and the credit went to him too. It was little wonder since Chen was an emerging Party cadre with connections stretching as far as Beijing. It was plain that he was being groomed to succeed Party Secretary Li and it would be good for the bureau to have a party secretary who actually knew something about policework, even if he had not been trained for it. And to be fair, Chen did a good job. It did not matter to Yu how much credit he personally received for an investigation he conducted together with Chen. It was all the work of their special case squad. Yu had not complained about staying in Chen's shadow. Not too many bosses like Chen were left in the police force. Yu sometimes considered himself lucky to be Chen's partner. Nevertheless, this did not mean that only Chief Inspector Chen was up to the job.

Yu did not care much what others might think, or say, behind his back, but he could not help feeling upset when his colleagues, and now Party Secretary Li, brought the issue up to his face, as if the special case squad was nothing but Chen, as if Yu deserved no recognition.

Even Peiqin had once mentioned something to that effect, he remembered.

What Party Secretary Li said hurt him, Yu realized somberly. It was as if the earth stopped moving with the absence of Chief Inspector Chen.

But what else could Chen possibly have done if he had been involved with the investigation? In fact, Yu and Chen had discussed every aspect of the case.

"Don't worry, Party Secretary Li. I'll take care of it," Yu said. "The case will be solved shortly."

"I have given my *junlingzhuang* to the city government, Comrade Detective Yu." *Junlingzhuang* was a pledge an ancient Chinese general gave: something would be done or he would be removed from his position.

"Then I give mine to you, Party Secretary Li."

Afterward, Yu regretted his impulsive response. Perhaps something had been going on in his subconscious for a long time. Perhaps it was the time for him to think about a career change. For him, the case of Yin Lige was taking on a new dimension. It was no longer simply that he was determined to solve it all on his own, with Chief Inspector Chen on leave. It was also an investigation that might testify to the meaning of his profession, his career. He had believed that, even though only a bottom-level cop, he could make a meaningful difference to society. In addition, his was a meaningful task because it was significant to Peiqin, as Yang's writing had meant such a lot to her.

The political aspect of this investigation was not his concern. If anything, it only highlighted the fact that nothing was free from politics in China, a fact he had known for a long time. The problem was how to make a breakthrough at the *shikumen* house. Instead of continuing the interviews of the *shikumen* residents, he decided to review his strategy with Old Liang first.

They had concentrated on the possibility that someone who lived in the building had killed Yin. They seemed to have excluded the possibility that an outsider had committed the crime because no stranger had been seen entering or exiting, either through the front or the back door. But what about the possibility of a cover-up? What if one witness, or more than one, was not telling the truth?

A problem immediately presented itself. There were three people in the courtyard who came from three different families. While the neighbors' relationships—with the exception of those with Yin—might have been as wonderful as Old Liang declared, it was hard to imagine that three different families were involved in a conspiracy to commit or cover up a murder. That someone had left through the front door was therefore practically impossible. As for the back door, the shrimp woman was positive about her statement: she had never budged. But was she telling the truth?

While Detective Yu made this analysis, Old Liang clung to his insider theory.

"You should keep interviewing the *shikumen* residents," Old Liang maintained. "If you want me to participate in the interviews here with you, that's fine, but I think it's worthwhile for me to continue making background checks."

"Your background checks are important, but we really need to speed it up. There are more than fifteen families in the building. Party Secretary Li is pushing me for results."

"So we are running out of time."

"We have to be more selective in choosing our interviewees. Let's take a look at the next name on the list."

Lei Xueguang was the fifth suspect listed.

"Oh, that Lei! Believe it or not, Yin helped him, in her way," Old Liang began, in a most dramatic tone that reminded Yu of his father, Old Hunter. "But you know what they say, *No good deed goes unpunished.*"

In the early seventies, Lei, then a high school student, had been caught in the act of stealing from a district government van and sentenced to ten years. It was his hard luck that this particular year there was a "strike-hard-against-crime campaign." As a result, those caught were punished much more severely than in other years. When Lei was released, he was jobless. There was no possibility of his finding work in a state-run company. Private business was then just beginning to be allowed, but only in a very limited way, as a "nonessential supplement to the socialist economy." If Lei had a first-floor room with a door opening onto the street, he might have been able to turn it into a tiny store or eatery. Several people in the area had done that, converting most of their living space to business use. Lei did not have such a room. Nor any connections. His attempt to obtain a business license proved to be fruitless.

To the surprise of everyone in the lane, Yin mentioned Lei in an essay published in *Wenhui Daily*, as an example of the insensitivity of the neighborhood committees. "A young man has to find some way to support himself, or he may get into trouble again," she wrote. The local committee members must have read the newspaper; Lei was granted a business license to run a green-onion-cake booth at the head of the lane. Nobody had any real objection, except those reckless bike riders who tore in and out of the lane all the time. The new onion-cake maker must have heard about the newspaper column. The first time Yin came to the booth to buy food, he refused to accept any money from her.

Business was not bad. Lei soon had a local girl working with him, and she became his girlfriend. Nor did it take long for him to begin to plan to expand. In addition to the onion cakes, he began a lunchbox service, offering a variety of popular specialties such as pork steak, beef in oyster sauce, dry-fried belt fish, or Aunt Ma's spicy tofu, each choice served on top of steamed rice, plus a small cup of hot and sour soup. Since his space was rent-free, Lei was able to provide fairly good food at low prices. The plastic boxes and disposable chopsticks especially appealed to white-collar workers from the new office buildings nearby. The fame of Lei's lunch boxes spread. Customers had to stand waiting in long lines to order. He set up a second big coal stove at the lane entrance, and hired two provincial girls to help him.

"*In misfortune, there is a fortune; in fortune, there is a misfortune.* That's exactly what Laozi said in *Tao Te Ching* thousands of years ago," Old Liang commented. "How true it is, even today, even for Lei in our lane."

"Someone with a new girlfriend and a fresh business plan," Yu said, interrupting Old Liang's narrative, "is unlikely to have murdered a neighbor."

Old Liang argued, "But he needs money more than ever for business expansion. Where can he get capital? Judging by his tax return, Lei hardly breaks even."

"Oh, his tax form. Have you talked to him about that?"

"Yes, I have. He denied having anything to do with the murder, of course, but he offered no explanation about where he plans to get capital for expansion."

"What about his alibi?"

"Lei starts the coal stove fires around five thirty every morning. Several people recall seeing him at work at the stoves that morning."

"So his alibi is solid."

"Still, I don't think we can rule him out. He could have dashed back home for a minute or two. No one would have noticed. He keeps most of his supplies in the courtyard, or in his room, so he often goes back and forth."

"It's possible," Yu said. "Still, I think he must be grateful for Yin's help. Her comment changed the course of his life."

"Gratitude from such a man? No, no way." Old Liang shook his head vigorously. "In fact, there's something else about him. Of all her neighbors, Lei alone has entered Yin's room a couple of times to deliver lunch boxes. Heaven alone knows what he might have noticed there."

"You have a point, Old Liang. I'll talk to him," Yu said. "Now, the next one?"

"As for the next one, his name is Cai. Not exactly a resident here, at least not registered as a resident. So you see, we have not excluded other possibilities."

"Okay, but why have you picked him out?"

"It's another long story." Old Liang lit a cigarette for Yu, and then another for himself. "Cai is Xiuzhen's husband. She and her mother, Lindi, and her brother Zhengming live in a room at the end of the north wing. When Cai and Xiuzhen got married, he ran one of the few private hotels in Jinan District and talked a lot about buying a high-class apartment."

"So he was a Mr. Big Bucks," Yu said.

"Perhaps, at the time. Xiuzhen was then only nineteen years old. Most people believed that she had made the right choice, even though Cai was eighteen years older, and had served several years in prison for gambling. On their honeymoon, they stayed in a suite in the hotel because he was registered at home with his mother in the slums in the Yangpu District. Cai did not have time to look for a new apartment, Xiuzhen explained to her neighbors.

"But things with him were not as rose-colored as he had described them, she soon found out. The hotel business was in terrible shape, running into debt, and she was already pregnant. *The rice is cooked, nothing that is done can be undone.* When her baby was born, the prospect of moving into a nice apartment totally disappeared. Not long afterward, the hotel went out of business.

"His slum home is in an area designated for a new housing project, where most the buildings had already been torn down. A few families have refused to move out unless their demands are met, and they are still there. They are called 'nail' families, in the sense that they have to be forcefully pulled out, like nails. The district government has made it hard for those nails to stay there, cutting off their water or electricity from time to time, and when that happens, Cai comes to stay with Xiuzhen in Treasure Garden Lane."

"That's a different love story," Yu said, anxious to bring Old Liang to the point. "So what does Cai do now?"

"Nothing. In the summer, he makes money as a cricket fighter. A cricket gambler, to be more exact, betting on the cricket fights.

People say he has triad ties, which must help him greatly in this kind of business. For the rest of the year, heaven alone knows what he is really up to. He does not appear to be unemployed, like his brother-in-law Zhengming, who loiters about all day in the lane. As for Xiuzhen, still a young, pretty girl, she is like a fresh flower growing on top of a dung heap."

"You can say that again," Yu said, wondering at the appropriateness of the ancient proverb, for manure would be nutritious to a flower. "Does Cai gamble on crickets in the lane?"

"No, he does not fight crickets in the neighborhood. To make a living out of this, he has to mix with those nouveau-riches who will bet thousands of Yuan on a tiny cricket," Old Liang said. "Once a Mr. Big Bucks, always a Mr. Big Bucks. People believe he still earns more than most of the others in the lane."

"What about Zhengming?"

"He is good for nothing. He has not worked at any real job since high school. I don't know how he manages to muddle along. Now he actually has a live-in girlfriend, and she doesn't work either."

"Does he depend on his mother?"

"Yes. I cannot make out these young people. The world is really going to the dogs." Old Liang added "But we don't have to worry about him. He broke a leg ten days ago, and can hardly move out of the attic."

"Then what about Cai—apart from his history?"

"*History is like a mirror, capable of showing what a man really is.* Once a criminal, always a criminal."

"That is another quote from Chairman Mao," Yu observed in a matter-of-fact way.

"Cai says he was not here that morning, but with his mother in that 'nail' room. That's just what he says, of course."

"Yes, we will check on that."

But he was not so sure whether the interview of either of these two suspects would lead to anything. When Old Liang left to pursue background checks, Yu decided to do something different. He made a telephone call to Qiao Ming, the ex-dean of the cadre school, upon whom Yin had spat at the memorial service.

Peiqin and he had discussed the possibility that Qiao might have had a motive to murder Yin. In view of the autobiographical nature of the novel, even though Yin had named no names, many people might have been nervous or indignant. Wan, the upstairs neighbor, was only one example. Those who had been at the cadre school must have been panic-stricken. Furthermore, no one could predict whether Yin might produce a second book, containing even more embarrassing realistic details. Anything was possible.

"Don't believe anything you read in *Death of a Chinese Professor*," Qiao began. "It's a pack of lies."

"*Death of a Chinese Professor* is a novel, I understand. But I'm working on a homicide case, Comrade Qiao, so I have to investigate every possible aspect."

"Comrade Detective Yu, I know why you want to talk to me, but let me make one point first. With respect to what happened during the Cultural Revolution, we must have a historical perspective. No one was a fortune-teller, capable of foretelling all the changes in the future. At that time, we simply believed in Chairman Mao!"

"Yes, everyone believed in Chairman Mao, I have no question about that, Comrade Qiao."

"The book makes a selling point of the persecution they suffered in the cadre school. Now, that was no place for people to fall in love—not at the time. The top priority was, according to Chairman Mao, for people to reform themselves there. Because of that phone call from Beijing about Mao's poems, the cadre school actually made a point of allowing Yang books and dictionaries. That was a real privilege at the time. Someone reported he was writing a book, and we did not even try to interfere at first. You see, for Yang, those years were not totally wasted."

"Did you find out what kind of book he was writing?"

"Later, when we put him into the isolation room, we searched his dorm room, but we did not find anything. It might have been a manuscript in English."

"Please tell me about the circumstances of Yang's death."

"It was a sweltering hot summer. We all worked in the rice paddy, just like the local farmers. It was not Yang alone who had to work there. In fact, a lot of people were sick. As for any possible negligence, now by hindsight, if we had known he was so seriously ill. . . . But perhaps he was not aware of it either. The cadre school was located in Qingpu. Transportation then was not like it is today. There wasn't a single taxi in the area in those years. How could the cadre school be possibly held responsible for his tragic death?"

"It may be too much to say that he was persecuted to death, but we can understand Yin's reaction. She suffered a lot those years."

"So did I!" Qiao snapped. "All those years, I stayed at the cadre school, working there. Have I gained anything? No, nothing. At the end of the Cultural Revolution, I was subjected to 'political examination' for two years. And my wife divorced me, discarded me like a dirty sock."

"Just one more question. Where were you on the morning of February seventh?"

"I was in Anhui, collecting debts for my company. A number of people, including those at the hotel, can testify to that."

"Thanks, Comrade Qiao. I don't think I have any more questions for you today. 'Look to the future,' as the *People's Daily* always says."

The telephone interview had been unhelpful, although not a total waste. For one thing, Yu learned that in his last few years, Yang had kept on working, which could have resulted in the translation of classical Chinese love poems they had found in Yin's safety deposit box. Also, it reconfirmed Old Hunter's maxim, that the past is always present. Almost twenty years later, people still looked at the Cultural Revolution from their own perspective forged at the time.

He removed the cassette on which he had taped the phone call. Chief Inspector Chen might be interested in it, Yu thought. He dialed the home number of his boss.

"You may suspect everyone in the building," Chen said after having listened to Yu's short briefing, "but when everyone is a suspect, nobody is a suspect."

"Exactly," Yu said. "Old Liang sees only what he wants to see."

"Old Liang has been a residence cop for too many years. The job of a residence cop, however important in the years of class struggle, is hardly relevant nowadays. But he still cannot help seeing the world from his outdated angle," Chen said. "Su Dongpu has put it so well: *You cannot see the true face of the Lu mountains, / When you are still inside the mountains.*"

That was just like his boss, quoting some long-dead poet in the middle of an investigation. This penchant of Chen's could occasionally be annoying.

Then Detective Yu went over to the *shikumen* building.

Cai was not at home. Lindi, a fine-featured woman in her late forties, was in the courtyard, cutting open a pile of river scallop spiral shells with a pair of rusted scissors. Wan was also there, seated on a bamboo stool, drinking from a purple stone teapot. At this time of the year, people normally did not sit outside doing nothing. At the sight of Detective Yu, Wan mumbled a few words and left.

After Yu introduced himself to her, Lindi led him upstairs to a small room. It would be difficult for a medium-sized family to squeeze into such an all-purpose room, let alone three families. But she lived in it with her son and his "wife," her daughter, a crying baby and, most of the time, her son-in-law, Cai. Fortunately, it was a room with a relatively high ceiling, which made possible the construction of two added make-shift lofts, with a common ladder leading to both of them. In comparison, Detective Yu reflected with deep sarcasm, his living conditions could be considered great.

According to Lindi, Cai was not at home this morning. Nor had he been here on the morning of February 7. "No one can tell what he's really up to," Lindi said with a sigh. "I warned Xiuzhen about her choice, but she would not listen."

"I have heard about it. How about your son Zhenming?"

"Home for him is like a free hotel, and a free restaurant too. He comes whenever he wants. Now he brings another person with him as well."

"Please tell me what you know about Yin, Comrade Lindi."

"She was different."

"How?"

"She had a room all for herself, whereas in our one single room there are three families. *She* suffered during the Cultural Revolution? Who didn't? My husband died in the 'armed struggle' among worker organizations, believing he was fighting for Chairman Mao to the last drop of his blood. After his death, there was not even a memorial service for him." She went on after a pause. "One of the reasons Xiuzhen married Cai was not because of his money—he did not have such a lot to begin with—but because she had lost her father when she was only four years old."

"I see," Yu said. He was surprised by her thoughtful analysis of her daughter's reason for marrying the much older Cai.

"I'm sorry, I can't tell you much about Yin. The Cultural Revolution has left so many tragedies in its wake. Yin was a writer, and had published a book about it, but she was not willing to talk about it to us."

Detective Yu thanked her at the end of the conversation. As he moved downstairs, he felt totally depressed. People here still seemed to be covered with the dust of the past, just like the *shikumen* building itself. To be more exact, they were still living in the shadow of the Cultural Revolution. The government called on the people to look forward, never turning their head heads back, but this was extremely hard for some, including Yin, Lindi, Wan, almost everyone he had interviewed here except Mr. Ren. Now Yu wondered whether Mr. Ren really could forget, drowning his memories in a bowl of steaming noodles.

As he walked out of the *shikumen* building, he caught sight of Lei's booth at the front lane entrance. Detective Yu was not in a great hurry to interview Lei. Looking at his watch, he decided to buy a lunch box for himself. There was a line of customers stretching toward the booth, and he stood in it patiently. He watched. In spite of the help he had recently hired, Lei himself was busy, constantly stirring the contents of a heavy wok. Several rough, unpainted wooden tables and benches stood clustered around the lane entrance. Some customers walked away with lunchboxes in their hands, but some chose to eat there. Yu also took a seat.

The meal was quite good. A large portion of rice paddy eel slice fried with green onion and sesame oil on top of steamed white rice, plus a soup of pickled vegetable and shredded pork, for only five Yuan.

Afterwards, he phoned Peiqin with a question. "Do you think we can rely on Yu's tax form?"

"No, I don't think so," Peiqin replied. "Private restaurants make lots of money by not paying tax. It's an open secret. All business is done for cash. No one asks for a receipt for four or five Yuan. His tax form is not something you can trust. Nor does he put all his money in the bank either. This is a common practice among restaurant owners."

"That's true," Yu said. "I did not ask for a receipt this afternoon."

"I have done some spreadsheets for Geng. I know what I am talking about."

Yu believed Peiqin.

Chapter 11

Sitting in her cubicle at the Four Seas restaurant, Peiqin finished the accounting work for the month. It was hardly the middle of February. Still, she would come to her so-called office every day to sit with the books and papers spread out on the long desk, even though there was no work left to do. Originally a *tingzijian*, it was not much of a room, but it served as an office separated from the business downstairs. She shared the office with Hua Shan, the restaurant manager, who had an all-day-long meeting somewhere else. Slipping off her shoes, she placed her feet on a chair, then put them down again. There were two small holes in her socks.

"Peiqin, it's time for lunch," Luo, the new chef shouted from the kitchen located below the office. His voice boomed up through the cracks of the old worn floor, the air was filled with swirling dust making weird patterns in the light. "We'll have fish-head soup with red pepper today."

"Great. I'll come as soon as I finish here."

In the first year she had worked there, Peiqin had occasionally come downstairs to help. Soon she stopped doing so. In a state-run company, employees were paid the same amount regardless of how long or how hard they worked. As an accountant, she needed only to finish her bookkeeping, which normally took her a week, instead of a month. If she sat there afterward, doing nothing for the rest of the time, no one would care. So for the last few years, she had read Qinqin's textbooks under the cover of her accounting books. Qinqin would not let *his* school years slip away, unlike hers. To help him with his homework, she started learning English too, so as to be able to practice with him at home. Qinqin had to get a good education, at a top university. A college education could make a world of difference in China's fast-changing society. In fact, Chief Inspector Chen had obtained his position—in part at least—because of his superior educational background, although she acknowledged Chen was one of the few Party cadres who deserved his position on his own merit.

Sometimes she read novels in the office. Like many people of her generation, Peiqin had more or less educated herself by reading novels. The manager must have been aware of her reading, but he had not said anything. He, too, was busy doing something for himself. Peiqin did not have a clue what it was.

Sometimes, when she put down her book, she could not help being momentarily bewildered. How had she ended up here, she wondered, in this tiny office, reading novels simply because she had nothing better to do? Was she going to spend the rest of her life just like this? In her elementary school, Peiqin had been a straight-A student, even though not a popular one, because of her "black" family background. Her father had owned a small import/export company, hence he was declared a "capitalist" in his class status after

1949, which cast his whole family under a dark cloud. The dark cloud turned into a violent storm during the Cultural Revolution.

As an educated youth—a beginning high school student—in the late sixties, she had had to leave Shanghai for Yunnan. Her path had crossed Yu's then. Their relatives had introduced them, hoping that they could take care of each other in that distant place. Far away in the countryside, with her girlish dreams shattered, she learned to appreciate the man in Yu. Then after they were allowed to return to Shanghai in the late seventies, she considered herself lucky to have a family like hers. Yu was a good husband, and Qinqin a wonderful son, in spite of the fact that they all had to huddle together in that one single all-purpose room. Monotonous as her restaurant job was, she managed to see herself, literally, as one level above those working in the kitchen. She had long since accepted the truism that happiness comes only in contentment.

The lackluster, unchallenging work actually suited her well if she chose to look at it from another angle. For she could devote herself more to her family. The best years of her youth had been wasted during the Cultural Revolution, but she saw no point blaming fate, or crying, like so many others. She had been content to play the traditional role of good wife and mother.

Of late, however, she had become less at peace with the status quo. The world around her was changing. Some of the values, or meanings, which she used to think she had found in her life seemed to be slipping away. *I don't know in which direction the wind is blowing,* was a line she recalled reading; it seemed appropriate now. She believed that she should try to do something, in addition to her restaurant work. She had to face the fact that the iron-bowl positions Yu and she had would, at most, satisfy their most basic material needs. The apartment fiasco had been the last straw.

Qinqin must have a different life; she was resolved. Almost everybody else in Qinqin's class had Nike shoes, and Peiqin wanted to buy a pair for him, too. In her school years, brand names did not exist, and army-green imitation rubber shoes were the norm. In Yunnan, sometimes she went barefoot, because she had mailed one pair of those she had been issued back home to her niece. Even today, she still went without cosmetics, in spite of the ever-increasing appeals of commercials on TV. At a recent class reunion, one of her former classmates arrived in a Mercedes, to the envy of most in the room. In school, he had been a nobody, copying Peiqin's homework from time to time. It was really a changed world.

And then the investigation of Yin Lige's case, unexpectedly, began to take on meaning for her. Not exactly a new meaning, nor meaningful only to her, but it was traceable as far back as her high school years. Her reading was secret at the time—secret because Chairman Mao's works alone were officially available; libraries were closed, novels and poems out of reach, and a young girl of her family background had to be careful, carrying novels in a most stealthy way, hidden under her armpit within her cotton-padded coat. Like others, Peiqin had to turn to books that had been published earlier, that were still in clandestine circulation. "Wealthy" with half a dozen books she had hidden from the Red Guards' clutches, she and several others had formed an underground network to exchange books. There was something like an "exchange rate": Balzac's *Old Goriot* would be worth Dickens's *Hard Times* plus a Chinese novel such as *The Song of Youth* or *The Story of the Red Flag*. In their network, if a member was able to get a new book through an outside contact, then the book would travel from one member to another, available to each for only one day.

She had developed a preference for certain writers. Yang, the great contemporary translator, was one of her favorites. In her opinion, hardly any modern Chinese writer was comparable to Yang for stylistic innovation, perhaps because he had a unique sensitivity to language, introducing Western expressions, and sometimes syntax too, into Chinese. In the history of modern Chinese literature, she had observed, most intellectuals who had a higher education had become translators rather than writers, for political reasons which were not difficult to understand.

When she had left high school for Yunnan, she carried some of those "poisonous" books with her. She did not talk to Yu about them. It was not that she had intended to keep something from him; rather, she was worried that her bookish passion might have made her less approachable. Besides, Yu had been too busy, doing not only his share of the labor in the field, but a lot of times hers as well.

In Yunnan she learned that Yang had written poems as well as translated novels. She found a short poem in an old anthology, which she copied into a notebook and memorized. It was not until after she came back to Shanghai that Yang's poetry collection edited by Yin appeared in bookstores. By then, Peiqin was no longer a young, sentimental girl; still, she admired those poems. It broke her heart to learn that his poetry career had been cut short even before the outbreak of the Cultural Revolution. In the collection, she also read a few poems written shortly before his death.

Now she picked up the poetry collection that Yin had edited and turned to a poem entitled "Snowman":

You have to be a snowman
To stand in the snow
Listening to the same message

Of the howling wind
With imperturbable patience,
Gazing at the scene
Without losing yourself in it
While a hungry, homeless crow
Starts to peck at your red nose,
Apparently, a carrot.

She did not think she truly understood the poem, yet she felt a sudden, almost Zen-like enlightenment, overcome by empathy for the poet. He must have been so lonely, so desolate, so chilled, standing outside alone like the snowman. Peiqin did not have to guess what "the same message of the howling wind" might have been. Or the "hungry, homeless crow." But the snowman did not lose itself in the scene: it kept its human shape, paradoxically, in snow.

She looked at the date underneath the poem. It had probably been written before he met Yin. Peiqin could understand how Yin's appearance might have made a great difference in Yang's life.

But Peiqin was drawn into the investigation of Yin Lige's case not just because of Yang, nor even because it might help her husband in his work. It was also because of a vague yearning she thought she had long since put behind her, a yearning to find something, some meaning, in her own life—like the meaning one could find in the "snowman."

Geng had suggested she become his partner when he expanded his business. She had not discussed this with Yu. It might be too early for her to let go of the iron bowl. No one could predict the future of China's economic reform. Nor was a restaurant business something in which she was genuinely interested. She had helped her husband and Chief Inspector Chen once before when they were investigating the death of a National Model Worker, but she had never thought that she would come to be so engaged in an investigation. The combined temptation of doing something for a writer she had admired, of doing something for Yu, and of doing something for herself, too, was irresistible.

Could she discover a clue Yu might have overlooked? There was no way she could investigate as he did. She still had to come to her office during the week, and the weekend was reserved for Qinqin's homework. There was only one thing she could do, Peiqin realized. Read. Yu had joked about her having lost herself God-knows-how-many times in *The Dream of the Red Chamber*. She thought she would now do a close re-reading of *Death of a Chinese Professor*.

"Peiqin, the soup will turn cold if you do not come down," someone shouted from the kitchen.

She put away the books and went downstairs.

The restaurant was full of customers. One of its new specials was rice cake with soy-sauce-braised pork steak, a popular choice. While a lot of state-run restaurants had suffered from tough competition with privately run restaurants, Four Seas had done fairly well. This was probably because of its convenient location.

Taking her seat on a bench near the kitchen entrance, she had a portion of the rice cake with pork steak in addition to a bowl of the fish-head soup. The rice cake was pleasantly soft and sticky, the steak tender, and the soup delicious, shining with the red pepper strewn over the surface. It was a pity that she could not take it back home. Once cold, the fish soup would start smelling.

Xiangxiang, a dish washer, also an ex-educated youth, came over to Peiqin. Xiangxiang had to wear rubber boots that creaked as she moved, for the sink area was always wet. As she sat beside Peiqin, she pulled one water-soaked foot out of her boot. Xiangxiang had a slight stoop from bending over the dirty dishes all year round, and her fingers were red, chapped, swollen like carrots. She worked seven days a week under a special arrangement. Her husband had been laid off. She had to support the whole family.

"We have worked our butts off, for what?" Xiangxiang complained, wiping her hands on her gray apron. "All the meat goes to the government. Nothing but the soup is left for us."

In order to compete, the restaurant had started a dinner business, instead of opening only in the mornings and afternoons as before. Business had improved, but little of the profit went to the employees, except as inexpensive perks like the fish-head soup.

"We are not doing that badly, with our location, and with our name too."

"Geng is damned smart. Now he is his own boss."

"The soup is delicious," Peiqin said, finishing her rice cake. It was true. In Yunnan, such a meal would have seemed like a banquet. She then wondered whether she was like A Que, a well-known character created by Lu Xun, a character who always succeeds in seeing the bright side, whatever the circumstances. Was it "A Que" of her to have thought that? "I have to go back to my work, Xiangxiang."

"With all the new accounting work you have, now that we work two shifts instead of one, you still have to manage all by yourself," Xiangxiang said. "It's not fair."

"Nothing is fair. Life is not fair."

Back in her own office, Peiqin took out the book and magazines again.

This time, Peqin did not read *Death of a Chinese Professor* from the beginning. Instead, she tried to focus on some pages she had already marked. This re-reading underscored something she had already vaguely noticed: the quality of the writing was not even. Parts of the book seemed to be written by a naive beginner, while other parts struck her as sophisticated. The book seemed to have been written by two different people. Especially the part about the causes of the Cultural Revolution, which was so full of analytical power. It would be hard to imagine a young, hot-blooded Red Guard possessing such historical insight. But then the next few chapters became bogged down in details about local Red Guard organizations, their conflicts of interests, their struggles for power, as well as personal grievances within them. Some of those details were both trivial and irrelevant.

The quality of a book could vary in different parts, she understood, but surely this extreme variance in *Death of a Chinese Professor* was abnormal.

She was unable to shake off a feeling that someone other than Yin must have written this book. Peiqin then laughed at herself, shaking her head at her own reflection in a small, slightly cracked mirror on the desk.

When she looked up from the book again, it was almost two o'clock. She rose and paced about in the room. It was all right for her to do so, but the manager had to walk carefully, with his head bent, in this low-ceilinged office. She called to make sure that Hua would not return that day. Then she locked the door before picking up the telephone again to call Chief Inspector Chen.

After polite routine greetings, she asked a question. "What do you think of Yin as a writer, Chief Inspector Chen?"

"I have not read her book yet. In the last few days, I've made phone calls to some people who have read it. They seem not to have a very high opinion of it. Of course, they may be biased because of her Red Guard activity."

"That I can understand. I have read the book several times.

One thing keeps puzzling me. Some parts are written so amateurishly, at least so it seems to me, almost like the diary of a high school student. But other parts are really good, like the beginning of the book, which shows historical depth."

"You have made an insightful observation," Chen said. "As to the uneven quality of her writing, one critic made a similar point, saying that Yin might have used a ghostwriter. After all, she had never written anything before."

"But that does not account for the inconsistency."

"The ghostwriter might have helped to write only part of the book."

"Perhaps you have found us the motive we are seeking. Maybe somebody demanded money from her to keep her secret—I mean either the ghostwriter or someone who had found out—" Chen paused before contradicting himself "—but no, if it she was being blackmailed, why murder her? I'm confused."

"It confuses me too."

"Still, this could be important. At least it may be a lead to a possible motive. Thank you so much, Peiqin. I have been too busy with my translation to help Yu with the case."

"You don't have to thank me. I've simply read the novel. There's not too much to do in my restaurant anyway."

"But you're doing a lot for the investigation."

That was all she could accomplish for the moment, however. She decided to go home earlier than usual.

There was something else for her to do, she remembered. Something different.

Chapter 12

Since the start of the translation project, Chief Inspector Chen had become accustomed to surprises. This morning's surprise came with a lanky workman who was supposed to install electric heaters and an air-conditioning unit in Chen's apartment. The installer was almost as surprised as the chief inspector, for Chen was positive that he had not ordered such appliances.

He remembered having read about electric heaters. Most of the new buildings in the city still had no hot water system. So an electric heater was an option, a very expensive one. He had never thought about getting one for his own apartment. After all, he could always take showers at the bureau. As for an air-conditioner, he had not even dreamed of owning one.

He guessed whose idea this must have been, and picked up the phone.

"I cannot accept anything from you, Mr. Gu. It's a matter of principle, you know."

"White Cloud says that it's too cold in your room. That's not good for your work. I have several sets left over at the Dynasty Club. So why should they go to waste? "

"No, it's too much."

"How about buying them from me?"

"I cannot afford them."

"I bought a large supply, so they came at a discount. Then there's depreciation for the three years I've had them. How about nine hundred Yuan? And you don't have to pay me right now. I'll deduct it from the payment for the translation."

"You are going out of your way for me, Mr. Gu."

"No, I am a businessman. These units are lying around, useless, in storage. And to be honest, I think a cadre of your level should have had them long ago. You're a man of integrity, and I admire you for that." Gu changed the topic abruptly. "Oh, if I could secure American investment because of the business proposal you are translating, my dream would come true."

"I don't know what to say."

"You are doing me a great favor, I mean it, Chief Inspector Chen."

But Chen remained disturbed for a long while after the phone call, staring at the translation on the desk. It was not just by the noise of the man working in the bathroom, although installing the unit in the bathroom seemed to be very complicated, with some long pipes involved. It might take quite a while for the workman to finish.

In addition to those upstarts in the private business sector, Party officials or cadres also had begun to obtain these modern devices for their apartments. It was not hard for people to notice such widespread corruption, and they pointed angry fingers at the privileged few. Chen himself had complained about this.

But some things might take place in a "gray area," Chen

reflected. An emerging Party cadre like himself had to make connections for his work, connections like Mr. Gu. And with such connections came other things. In China, in the last analysis, connections meant everything. *Guanxi.*

He checked himself from speculating further along those lines. For the moment, he had no alternative but to concentrate on the New World proposal. Sometimes, we could be most productive under pressure. He dashed through two pages before he allowed himself to take a short break.

The heater had already started working with a light whirring sound. As in the New World, where, whatever the appearance of the exterior, modern luxuries inside would be necessary. His fingers seemed to be moving deftly over the keyboard with a new rhythm. Looking out the window, he saw another apartment complex looming up not too far away. A lonesome tung tree trembled in the chilly wind. He turned back resolutely to the text on the computer screen.

The New World could turn out to be like present-day China, full of contradictions. On the outside, the socialist system under the rule of the Communist Party, but on the inside, capitalist practice in whatever disguise.

Could the combination of the two really work?

Perhaps. No one was in a position to tell, but it seemed to have been doing fine so far, in spite of the tension between the two. And in spite of a price too—the ever-increasing gap between the poor and the rich.

The rich had already started to be concerned with Shanghai's existential myth—the Paris of the Orient, the glitter and glory of the thirties—part and parcel of the superstructure to be erected on top of a socialist economic basis, the former justifying the latter, and vice versa, just like one of the Marxist principles Chen had studied in college.

For people like Gu, as well the consumers he anticipated, once the economic basis was established, a brave New World could, and perhaps should, exist. But what about the poor, who in the real world could hardly keep their pots boiling?

He was not meant to be a philosopher or economist, Chen reminded himself. He was nothing but a cop who happened to be translating a business proposal relating to the history of the city.

When the installer finally left, taking the cigarette Chen offered him and placing it behind his ear, Chen found the translation slowing down mysteriously. The new section dwelled on marketing plans in the context of globalization. He had no problem understanding the Chinese text, but he was not so sure about the exact English equivalents. Nor was it just a matter of looking up words in a dictionary, for it involved a number of new concepts, which had hardly existed in the Chinese language previously. Within the socialist state economy, for instance, "marketing" was a non-existent concept. State-run companies simply kept manufacturing in accordance with the state plan. There was no need or room for marketing. For many years, Chinese people cited a proverb: *If the wine smells really wonderful, customers will come in spite of the length of the lane.* Such an approach was not applicable to today's business world.

Perhaps that was one of the reasons why—if Gu's story was true—the first translator had failed.

Chen made himself a cup of tea. The room seemed cozy, almost intimate, with the heater purring next to the bookshelf.

White Cloud was scheduled to come in the afternoon. He looked in his notebook. She might help to find the definitions he needed in a new dictionary, but that would not be enough. As far as he knew, the latest English–Chinese dictionary had been compiled five or six years earlier, when a large number of these concepts had been far from common in China. So he'd better read some articles or books about marketing, not necessarily to get the exact meanings, but to able to convey roughly corresponding ideas in translation.

He skipped the marketing section and moved on to the part about the restaurant business in the New World. That section proved to be both pleasant and absorbing.

Around one, White Cloud arrived. She looked tired, even slightly haggard, with noticeable black circles under her almond-shaped eyes. Perhaps she had studied late the night before, as her day had been filled with her little secretary responsibilities.

She took off her jacket and draped it over the sofa. At once she noticed the change in the temperature of the room. She turned to him with a broad grin.

"Thanks for your suggestion to Gu," he said.

"You should have had these things long ago. Don't be so hard on yourself," she said. "Oh, here is a tape of my interview with some of the staff members at the university."

"You are a great secretary, White Cloud."

"Little, not great," she giggled.

He would have liked to listen to the tape at once, but her presence in the room made it difficult to focus on the investigation.

"Can I take a hot shower here?" she asked abruptly.

"Sure. But the installer was just here. I have not yet cleaned up."

"You don't have to worry about that," she said.

Kicking off her shoes, she went into the bathroom with her bag and turned back with a smile before closing the door after her. He wondered whether this was a calculated gesture, inviting intimacy.

Listening for the sound of the shower, he tried not to read too much into her status as a little secretary.

He began playing the tape. Its contents were not exactly interviews, more like a collection of various people's observations. It was little wonder, since she had neither the authority nor the training of a cop. In fact, it was surprising that the interviewees had talked to her.

The first interview was of a senior professor at the college where Yin had taught: "She was an opportunist. Why do I say so? First, she saw an opportunity by becoming a Red Guard! And all of us turned into the targets of her ruthless revolutionary criticism. When her luck at being a rebel changed, she saw her opportunity in being with Yang. He was a brilliant scholar. Like a gold mine undiscovered. Like buying valuable stocks at the bottom. Sooner or later the Cultural Revolution would end, she must have foreseen that. Only she carried the romantic drama too far—at his expense. Still, she did not really lose, did she? The book, the fame, the money, what-not!"

The next one was of a retired lecturer named Zhuang who had worked with Yang for several years and met with Yin a few times: "He was just too bookish. Even in those years, he remained so idealistic, still reading and writing, something like Doctor Zhivago, I think. As for her, she was already a plain spinster, with problems in her political dossier. That was her last chance, and of course she scrambled to take it."

The third was of a middle-aged researcher whose last name was Pang, who had read Yin's novel, but had had little personal contact with her: "As a writer, she was not so talented. If the book attracted a lot of attention, it is more because of its autobiographical nature. Now that's another shame. No big deal if the book was merely about herself. No, she was nobody without him. So the appeal really came from him. . . ."

In these interviews, White Cloud did not pose questions. As she was not a cop, it was clever of her not to try to sound like one. But in the interview with Pang, she did ask "So you don't believe she fell in love with him at the time; but didn't she, too, take a great risk by having an affair?"

"I'm not saying that she did not care for him at all—she did, in her way," Pang answered. "But I would say that, as far as she was concerned, there must have been other considerations involved."

Generally, Chen reflected, that might be true—must be true.

It was difficult to draw a clear-cut line anywhere, yet not so difficult for others to make comments.

When he heard the slow turning of the bathroom doorknob, he had been so absorbed in his thoughts that he was startled. He pressed the OFF button on his computer. He did not know how long she had been in the bathroom. There was not even a real bathtub, only a tiny space partitioned out in concrete with a shower head above, but she must have taken her time there. That was not surprising. A hot shower was still a luxury for most Shanghainese. He looked up to see her walking, barefoot, over to his desk. She was wearing his gray terry robe, which she might have noticed in the apartment at any time. The robe parted as she bent to look over his shoulder. He caught a glimpse of her breasts, her face flushed with the heat, her hair glistening with the beads of water, and he thought of several lines by Li Bai, a well-known Tang dynasty poet. They were from a poem that Yang had included in his manuscript:

The clouds eager to make

your dancing costume, the peony,
to imitate your beauty, the spring breeze
touching the rail, the petal glistening with dew. . . .

But he remembered having quoted them the first time White Cloud and he had met, when they danced together in that private karaoke room, she wearing a *dudou,* an ancient Chinese halter-like garment that had suddenly become popular, his hand touching her bare back. That might not be an appropriate scene to remind her of, so he did not recite these lines aloud now.

Li Bai, something akin to the Tang palace poet, had gotten into political trouble because of the poem. According to later critics, the imperial concubine was not pleased with the idea of being appreciated by a poet on behalf of the emperor. But the same later critics were laudatory of the poetry. The lesson seemed to be that a poet should never become involved in politics.

"What are you thinking?" she said as she stood behind him, drying her hair with a towel.

"It's not easy for people to forget what happened during the Cultural Revolution," he said. His gaze fell upon her slender ankle. No tattoo there, her red-painted toenails like fresh petals. Could he have imagined that tattoo the other day? "Nor is it easy for people not to judge from their own perspectives."

"What do you mean, Chief Inspector Chen?"

"People cannot wipe out the impression of Red Guards that they formed during the Cultural Revolution."

"Yes, I, too, was surprised that most of them seemed to be so biased against her, even some who hardly had any personal contact with her."

"Well, there is a Chinese proverb, *When three people start talking about seeing a tiger on the street, everybody else in the city believes it.*"

He added abruptly, "One of your interviewees, Mr. Zhuang, mentioned *Doctor Zhivago*. Do you have his phone number?"

"Yes. Is it important?"

"I don't know, but I think I'll look into it."

"Here it is," she said, handing him a small piece of paper.

"Now I have something else for you to do, White Cloud, but you looked a bit tired today."

"I slept late. That's nothing. The hot shower has helped."

He explained to her the problem he was having with the marketing section of the business proposal.

"Oh, I happen to have read an introductory book on marketing. A very good introduction, concise yet comprehensive. I may have given it to a friend, but I can find it in the library."

"Your major is Chinese, right?"

"The government still assigns jobs to college students, but there are no good jobs for Chinese majors," she said. "No joint venture company will hire someone capable only of reading classical poems."

"*The water flows, flowers fall, and the spring fades. / It's a changed world.*"

"Why did you recite those lines from Li Yu?" she asked.

"I am thinking of my college days, when the government assigned me to my job in the police bureau. I was interested in nothing but poetry then."

"But you have a marvelous job, Chief Inspector Chen," she said, tugging at the robe belt tentatively. "I'm going to change. I'll bring the book over today if I can get it. Don't worry."

Her departure made it possible for him to refocus on the homicide investigation. He decided to take a short cut, using his connections. Internal Security had not been helpful in providing essential information, so he would have to try to find out what they needed to know in his own way. He had a friend, Huang Shan, who was the director of the foreign liaison office of the Shanghai Writers' Association. Chen had once been considered as a candidate for the position, but had recommended his friend Huang instead. Since Yin Lige had made the trip to Hong Kong as a member of the Shanghai Writers' Association, the foreign liaison office must have kept a file on her. Her dossier should be available to Huang. Chen dialed Huang's phone number; he readily promised to help.

As Chen expected, the information he had requested arrived by special courier that afternoon.

Chen saw that Yin had recently made an application for renewal of her passport. The formalities required that an applicant first be approved by his or her work unit. Yin had chosen to go through the Writers' Association because of her membership in that group, rather than through her college. The application was based on an invitation from a small American university for a trip at the end of the coming summer.

In the past, an application of a dissident writer like Yin would have been denied at the outset. But the Party authorities must have come to the realization that the more they tried to keep dissidents at home, the more attention they attracted abroad. Once out of China, they were no longer the focus of attention, no longer even a nine days' wonder. In fact, the Party authorities had believed that Yin would not return from her earlier trip to Hong Kong. Good riddance once and for all, they must have hoped. However, she had come back to Shanghai. So there was no reason to reject her current application for a passport renewal.

Nor did there seem to be anything suspicious about her application, according to Huang. Yin had been invited as a visiting scholar for the next school year and granted a fellowship, although it was only symbolic in terms of money. So a literary agency in New York had provided a financial support affidavit. With or without the affidavit, as a well-known dissident writer, Yin would not have had a problem getting a visa from the American consul in Shanghai.

But the information surprised Chen, for Yu should have been informed of her application, whatever political considerations Internal Security or the higher authorities might have had. For the first time, Chen seriously considered the possibility that the murder might have been politically motivated. Why else would they be so cagey even after her death? But, on the other hand, if the government had intended to prevent her leaving China, wouldn't she have been denied a passport when she had applied to make the earlier trip to Hong Kong? "Murdered Before Her Trip to the United States": such a headline would be internationally sensational, would have the potential to damage the new image the government was trying hard to present to the world.

Then something else in the file caught his attention. Yin had recently had her birth certificate and diploma translated and notarized through the Writers' Association. This made no sense unless as a step toward emigration. Like so many others, she might have intended to remain in the United States. And there was something odd about the sponsorship affidavit too, although it was not exactly suspicious. For a lot of Chinese would-be emigrants, that financial affidavit served only for the visa application. The sponsoring individual had agreed beforehand with the applicant that he would not, in fact, be liable, despite signing and swearing to the document. But if an American company furnished such a financial affidavit, it might be different. Why should a literary agency have offered her financial support for a year? That was a lot of money. As far as Chen knew, *Death of a Chinese Professor* had not sold that well in the United States. The relatively small sum it had earned was out of proportion to what the literary agency had promised in the affidavit.

He made himself a pot of coffee. Whistling, he tapped lightly on the Brazilian coffee can. He hoped the cup of coffee would give him fresh ideas.

Was it possible that she had another book contract obtained by that agency? If so, they might have used her advance as the sum promised in the affidavit. There was no information, however, about Yin having written a new book.

Could it be money for Yang's poetry translation? That might also account for the presence of the manuscript in the bank safety deposit box.

But there was no information about this either. Also, he doubted that a translation of Chinese poems into English would sell so well.

Chapter 13

Yu left for home early in the afternoon. He could not do any solid thinking in the neighborhood committee office, where people were constantly coming and going. Nor did he want to return to the police bureau. He was in no mood for another political lecture from Party Secretary Li.

When he arrived home and opened the front door to the house before stepping into the courtyard, he was surprised to see Peiqin busily making coal briquettes there.

"You've come back early today."

"You, too."

There was not much coal dust left. Behind Peiqin, against the wall, stood a small mound of coal briquettes.

She had rented a briquette mold from the neighborhood coal store, an upper and lower half connected by a steel spring. The lower part was filled with coal dust, and water sprinkled over it; the upper part, which had hollow cylinders throughout, had to be pushed down hard to form each briquette. It was not yet spring, and rather windy for the time of the year. Her hands were covered with wet dust, and her wrists, chilled by the damp and the cold, were red.

In the first year of their marriage, he had occasionally made briquettes from coal dust to save money since the local coal store sold coal dust far more cheaply than ready-made briquettes. As he began to roll up his sleeves, he wondered why she had chosen that afternoon for the arduous chore.

"I'm almost finished, Yu. Don't get your hands dirty," she said, wiping the sweat from her forehead. "There is a pot of green bean soup in our room. Go in and help yourself."

A light gray smudge from the back of her hand appeared on her forehead. He chose not to mention it. But he said, "Don't do this again, Peiqin. It's not worth it. "

"It's not about the money. No ration coupons are needed to buy coal dust. And Geng's business is too good."

One problem Geng's private restaurant had was an inadequate coal supply. Most rationing restrictions had disappeared from the city of Shanghai, but there was still a shortage of coal. Peiqin had been helping Geng with his accounting work. Now, it seemed, she was helping with his coal problem.

"We will use these at home," she explained with a smile. "Then Geng can have our ration coupon."

In their room, he helped himself to a bowl of green bean soup, which was supposed to keep the body's elements in balance. Green beans were not in season; the soup must have come from her restaurant. It was already cool.

Peiqin entered their room, wiping her hands on a towel. She must have washed at the courtyard sink. There was no longer a faint smudge on her forehead. "How is it going?"

"Slow," he said, "as usual."

"Is Chief Inspector Chen still on vacation?"

"Yes, still busy with his translation."

"It must be some project to keep him away from such a case."

"Yes, it's a very lucrative commission from Mr. Gu, a Mister Big Bucks of the New World Corporation."

"*Long sleeves are wonderful for dancing.* Chief Inspector Chen has *long* connections. Because of the connections he has made in his position, those Misters Big Bucks come to him."

"That may well be true," Yu said somewhat somberly. "But he is a capable man."

"No, don't get me wrong. I'm not saying anything against your boss. At least he works for his money, instead of taking it for doing nothing."

"You should have had a rest today, Peiqin, instead of making those coal briquettes."

"It was like a good workout for me. A health club recently opened on Huaihai Road. It beats me how people *pay* to go there."

"The newly rich cannot find enough ways to waste their money."

"Well, we may be worse off than the upper crust," she said, "but we're better off than the bottom layer."

A cliché, meant to comfort, Yu thought, but it was a sort of cold comfort, like the out-of-season green bean soup. Nonetheless, it was quite true. As a cop, he did not have to worry about layoffs, and Peiqin worked in one of the few still-profitable state-run restaurants. They did not have too much to complain about as long as they did not compare themselves with those upstarts.

As he poured the green bean soup into a bowl for her, he could not help thinking of the shrimp woman again.

"Look, your hand got dirty," she said. "I told you not to bother with the coal dust."

"I did not touch anything," he said, surprised at the sight of the traces of the dust on his hand, and on his bowl too.

Strange. How had the coal dust gotten onto his hand? He had not helped Peiqin at all. Perhaps it came from the pot. He had poured the soup from the pot.

"No, I poured the soup into the pot before I started with the coal briquettes. And then I stayed in the courtyard until you came home."

"Don't worry about it," he said, changing the subject. "Have you discovered anything else in your reading?"

"A few interesting points, although I fail to see their relevance to the case. Chief Inspector Chen doesn't either. I called him this afternoon," she said. "Oh, I remember now. Old Hunter came in, carrying groceries in both hands. So I opened the door for him. My hands were wet then. That's why the dust was on the pot and how it got on your hand. I'm so sorry."

"You don't have to apologize, Peiqin, but you really do not have to make coal briquettes. Geng should be able to manage."

"It's just like making bricks in Yunnan, don't you remember?"

He did, of course. How could he forget those years in Yunnan? They'd had to make bricks with their hands, in response to Chairman Mao's urgent call "to prepare for the war." The bricks were never used, and, after years of wind and rain, they dissolved back into soil.

"If there had been no coal dust on my hand, would you have remembered Old Hunter coming back home and your opening the door for him?"

"Probably not. Opening the door was an automatic response. It took only a second. Why?"

"Nothing."

Yet it was something, Yu thought. The shrimp woman's testimony about the morning of February 7, outside the back door of the *shikumen* building seemed airtight, but the shrimp woman could have stepped away for a second, like Peiqin, without being aware of it, and without remembering it afterwards. If so, the murderer could have left through the back door unseen.

But was it possible that the murderer had been lucky enough to sneak out at that very instant?

Many things might depend upon coincidences, a phone call at an unlikely hour, a knock at the door, an unexpected glance in the dark . . . but wasn't it a little too much, too strained, for the present case? It was hard to imagine that this sequence of events had occurred unless the murderer had been lying in wait somewhere for the shrimp woman to step away from her stool. Or was there something missing in his earlier reconstruction of events after the discovery of the crime?

Yu flipped out his pocket notebook and turned to a dog-eared page. He had made a timetable of the residents' entries into Yin's room on the morning of February 7:

> 6:40 Lanlan rushed into room, and immediately started practicing Chinese CPR and shouting for help;
>
> 6:43-6:45 Junhua ran in and her husband Wenlong followed her;
>
> 6:45-6:55 Lindi, Xiuzhen, Uncle Kang, Little Zhu, and Aunt Huang arrived;
>
> 6:55-7:10 More people entered the room, including Lei, Hong Zhenshan, the shrimp woman, Mimi, Jiang Hexing;
>
> 7:10-7:30 Old Liang and members of the neighborhood committee arrived at the crime scene.

The times might not be exact, but that was basically the order in which people had entered Yin's room. Yu had checked and double-checked this with the help of Old Liang.

"What's up?" Peiqin said. "All of a sudden, you seem to be lost in thought."

He told her about the coincidence of the coal dust before pointing at the timetable in his notebook.

"What about the shrimp woman?" she asked.

"She's an important witness, because she ruled out the possibility of anyone entering or exiting through the back door. The front door could not have been the murderer's exit unless, as in those Agatha Christie novels Inspector Chen has spoken of, many people were involved in a conspiracy. So, unless the murderer remained in the building—was a resident—he must have left through the back door. The shrimp woman said that she had it in view the whole time, but what if she didn't? What if she stepped away and has forgotten about it? Or, even, what if *she* is the criminal?"

"You have a point."

"She was the closest to the *tingzijian* room. She should have heard the moment Lanlan started screaming. The back door was wide open, and she should have seen the residents rushing upstairs."

"So you mean—"

"She should have been one of the first into the room, but it took her fifteen minutes. Yes, at least fifteen minutes, according to my timetable."

The shrimp woman was familiar with the *shikumen* building, and with the habits of the other residents. Obtaining a key would not have presented a problem to her, as she had mixed with her *shikumen* neighbors for many years.

"There's no motive like poverty," Peiqin said.

"It may be true," Yu said. "The shrimp woman is desperate. She has been out of work for the last two years, and she is not even in the waiting-for-retirement program. I don't think she went up to Yin's room to murder her, but if she killed Yin in a moment of panic, she could have run back to her own room and put away whatever she had taken. That would account for her reaching Yin's room fifteen minutes late."

Yu stole a glance at his watch. He wondered whether he should hurry back to the neighborhood committee office. Then the phone rang.

Another coincidence. Chief Inspector Chen was calling about Yin's passport renewal application.

"How could Internal Security have withheld such crucial information from us?" Yu said indignantly. "Party Secretary Li must have been aware of it. It's outrageous!"

"Internal Security's acts are often very strange, understandable only according to their own logic. Party Secretary Li may be in the dark too."

"Politics aside, what relevance do you think her passport renewal application has to our case?"

"There are a number of possibilities. For example, if the murderer had knowledge of her application, he might have needed to act before her trip. But that involves a motive we have not yet discovered."

"I think you're right, Chief. There is something we do not know yet about Yin Lige."

"But who might have had knowledge of her passport application? Apparently, Old Liang and the neighborhood committee were ignorant of it."

"Apparently."

"She applied through the Shanghai Writers' Association because that office is directly attached to the city government, but I think that some people at her college may have been aware of it."

"I've talked to her department head, but he did not mention it."

"That's understandable. With someone like Yin, a passport renewal could have been classified as 'highly confidential,' and it would not be easily accessible," Chen said. "Still, some of her relatives might have heard of it. Or even Yang's relatives. She may have talked to them about her plan."

"I have discussed her possible relatives with Old Liang . He said that he had found no information about them when he did her background check. Yin had cut herself off from her own relatives years ago, let alone Yang's."

"But I think it's worth looking into," Chen said after a pause. "Yes, I think so."

Then it was Yu's turn to tell his boss about his hypothesis regarding the shrimp woman.

"That's very perceptive," Chen said.

"I'll talk to the shrimp woman."

"Yes, talk to her."

Chapter 14

Yu arrived at the neighborhood committee office quite early in the morning. It was not difficult for him to make a detailed list of Yin's and Yang's relatives, based on the information already gathered by Old Liang, even though Old Liang did not himself see any point in contacting them.

Yin's parents had both passed away. She was their only daughter. She had two aunts on her mother's side, much younger than her mother, but they had been out of contact since the early sixties. The Cultural Revolution had complicated a lot of things, including relationships among relatives. In her personal dossier, these relatives were not mentioned at all. According to several phone calls Old Liang had made, they had neither written nor spoken to her after the Cultural Revolution.

As for people close to Yang, in addition to a distant aunt in her nineties, there was only one sister, Jie, who had passed away three or four years ago. Even in the years before the Cultural Revolution, a Rightist was to be avoided like the plague. Jie had had her own family to worry about. Partially because of him, she also had been put on the "control and use" list. Jie had given birth to a daughter, Hong, in the late fifties, shortly after the commencement of the Anti-Rightist movement. When Hong was born, Yang had mailed a money order of fifty Yuan to Hong, but the money was returned to him. And that was that. Jie also got into trouble during the Cultural Revolution, and Hong went to the countryside as an educated youth, married a local peasant, had a son, and seemed to have settled down there.

When Yu had finished making the list, Old Liang, who lived only about five minutes away from the lane and spent more time in the office than at home, had still not shown up. Zhong, the security director of the neighborhood committee, was devouring a hot, oily green-onion cake. He poured a cup of wulong tea for Yu.

"Comrade Old Liang is investigating somewhere else this morning," Zhong said, taking a seat opposite Yu at the desk. "Do you need any help from us, Comrade Detective Yu?"

"Are you familiar with the background of the shrimp woman? Her surname is Peng."

"Oh, the shrimp woman! You have come to the right man," Zhong said. "She's been my next-door neighbor for years. A good, honest, timid woman, without even the nerve to kill a fly. She worked in a silk factory for more than twenty years, never having the guts to say no to her boss, never once. And then what? She was among the first laid off, and she ended up peeling shrimp in the lane early every morning."

"She has an arrangement with the food market, I've heard."

"Yes, it's part of a government effort to help those sinking beneath the poverty line. Some of the shrimp in the market do not look fresh. In order to sell them for a better price, the market has the shrimp peeled early in the morning. A lot of Shanghai wives shop there before they go to work. So the market makes a point of having the peeled shrimp on sale before seven thirty."

"So she has to start working at around six every morning?"

"She has no choice. Her family depends on what she earns from the food market," Zhong said. "Is she in any trouble?"

"No. I just have a few questions for her."

"I'll send for her."

"No, thanks. I am going to the *shikumen* house. She is probably sitting in the lane."

Sure enough, the shrimp woman was there, sitting on her bamboo stool, opposite the back door of the *shikumen* house, busy working, with a basket of frozen shrimp at her feet. She was in her late forties or early fifties, her face as thin as one of the brown sugar cakes of his childhood. She wore a pair of old-fashioned glasses smeared with broken pieces of shrimp shells.

Peng smiled nervously as Yu stopped beside her. He squatted down and lit a cigarette without speaking. It was cold; he kept one of his hands in his pants pocket.

"Comrade—Comrade Detective," she stuttered.

"You surely know why I've come to you today, don't you?"

"I don't know, Comrade Detective," she said. "Well, I suppose it's about Yin Lige. Poor woman. Old Heaven is blind, truly. She did not deserve it."

"Poor woman?" He was rather surprised by her sympathetic tone. The shrimp peeler was wrapped in an ancient imitation army overcoat, its collar raised against the cold wind, and her fingers were swollen, cracked, covered with the shrimp slime. Surely she, not Yin, was to be pitied.

"She was good-hearted. Life is not fair. She suffered such a lot during the Cultural Revolution," she explained.

"Can you tell me something more about her?" Yu asked. It was strange, he reflected: her attitude toward Yin was quite different from that of her other neighbors. "About what you call her good-heartedness. Give me one or two examples."

"A lot of people in the lane treat me like trash, complaining about the smell of the shrimp. I understand. But I have no choice. I cannot prepare them in the courtyard, or the other residents would have kicked me out of the house.

"Yin alone was really compassionate. After her piece in *Wenhui Daily*, the neighborhood committee came to her, asking whether she had some other suggestions for lane work. She put in a good word for me as well. Afterward, the neighborhood committee gave me a special permit allowing me to work in the lane."

"It sounds like she could be quite helpful to people in need."

"She was. She gave several textbooks to my daughter. And a new plastic folding chair, a recliner, to me. She gave it to me three or four years ago."

"She gave you a new plastic folding chair? Why?"

"That summer she had a visitor, her nephew, I think—"

"What?" Yu cut in. He had never heard of a nephew before. Nor had one been mentioned by Old Liang. "Hold on—her nephew? Did she describe him that way?"

"I'm not absolutely sure, but she introduced him to me. He was just a boy, maybe thirteen or fourteen years old at the time. He came from the countryside, I don't know where. He had no other relatives in the city, she explained."

"Did he stay with her here in the *tingzijian* room?"

"Yes, but not exactly. It would not be convenient to have a guest in so tiny a room. She bought the folding recliner for him to use, so he could sleep in the courtyard. It's quite common for people to sleep outside here. Some even sleep in the lane. One night, the courtyard was so full, Yin had to set up the folding chair for him in front of my door. That's when she introduced him to me, but her introduction was not that specific."

"How long did he stay here with her?"

"Maybe four or five days. Less than a week."

"Did you talk to him?"

"No, he was out during the day, I think. I saw him coming back with her one evening. She must have gone out with him. After he left, she gave the chair to me."

"Has he ever returned since?"

"No, not that I know of. Perhaps he was a poor relative from the countryside making his one visit to the city."

Yu took out his notebook. The shrimp woman wiped her hands on her apron apprehensively, which reminded him once more of the trace of coal dust on his hand the previous afternoon.

"Let me ask you another question. You said you that were busy peeling shrimp on the morning of February seventh, the morning Yin was murdered, and that you never moved a step away from here."

"That's correct. The food market pays by the weight of the finished product. I cannot even afford time to go to my chamber pot."

"You work very hard, I know. But I also know that you got to Yin's room some time between six fifty-five and seven ten. Now, with the back door open, you must have heard Lanlan shouting for help and seen others rushing upstairs. How could it have taken you somewhere between ten and fifteen minutes to reach Yin's room?"

"Fifteen minutes?" She was momentarily flabbergasted. "I don't know. I do not know what you are driving at, Comrade Detective. I heard the noise, let me think, yes, I heard the noise, and I went over."

"Don't be nervous. We don't punish innocent people," Yu said. "Did something else happen in the lane that morning?"

"No, nothing I can remember."

"Take your time. Try to recall every detail, from the moment you picked up the frozen shrimp supply from the market. It might have been trivial, perhaps an unexpected sound in the lane, or something else that distracted you."

"A sound—let me think—yes, I do remember now. There was some noise coming from the green-onion-cake booth. It's always a noisy place. Lei hawks his wares at the top of his voice, you know. But that morning the noise was louder, mixed with another voice. So I stepped out to the main lane to take a quick look."

"How long did that take?"

"I don't know. One minute. A couple of minutes, maybe. From where I stood, I could not hear clearly. It took a little time for me to make out what was happening."

"Did you walk up to the booth?"

"I took a few steps in that direction, but I never went really close to it, not with my hands covered in shrimp slime."

"Don't move, Comrade Peng," Yu said, standing abruptly. "I'll be right back."

He strode to the front lane entrance, and came back with Lei following him, his hands covered in flour. The shrimp woman, her face now a mask of anxiety, was unaware that she was crushing a shrimp to a pulp between her fingers.

"Did you have an argument or a quarrel with somebody on the

morning of February seventh, the morning Yin was murdered?" Yu asked.

"Yes, I did. Some bastard complained about a piece of hair in his onion cake, and he demanded ten Yuan as compensation. That's bullshit. He could have put his own hair into his food. Anyway, we don't claim to be a five-star restaurant!"

"Do you remember the time?"

"Quite early. Around six thirty."

So the shrimp woman's statement was true.

One fact was now established: there had been three or four minutes that morning during which somebody could have left through the back door without being seen.

Yu crossed off Lei from Old Liang's suspect list, since at least *his* time was now accounted for.

It was far from a breakthrough, though. This merely made it possible, in theory, to consider an outsider as the murderer.

Yu thanked Peng and Lei. The shrimp woman grasped Yu's hand in gratitude, forgetting about hers being wet and dirty.

Lei insisted on treating Yu to a brown bag full of his hot green-onion cakes. "Yin was a good woman. We will do whatever we can to cooperate with your investigation. As long as you are working in the lane, breakfast and lunch are on me. Free. But for her help, I would not have my business today."

Savoring a hot cake stuffed with chopped green onion and minced pork fat, Yu returned to the neighborhood committee office, where Old Liang was waiting with excitement written all over his face.

"A breakthrough, Comrade Detective Yu!"

"What?"

"Remember Cai, the cricket gambler we discussed yesterday?"

"Yes, I do. Is there new information about Cai?"

"I have been working hard on the background checkups, as I told you," Old Liang said, pouring out a small white porcelain cup of Dragon Well tea for Yu, and then another for himself. "This is extraordinary, excellent tea; all the tea leaves were picked and processed before the Yuqian festival. I keep it for special occasions, like today. It's really special."

"Oh, yes. Please tell me what you have found out," Yu said. "You surely have done a great job. *The older the ginger, the spicier.*"

On the first day of the investigation, before Yu's arrival, Cai had told Old Liang that on the morning of February 7, he was not in Treasure Garden Lane, but at his "nail" room in Yangpu District, and that his mother would support his alibi. Old Liang had tried to call the mother, but was told that public phone service there had been canceled several months earlier, as part of the government's pressure to force out those "nails." Old Liang did not let the matter drop; he himself went to the nail room. Cai's mother was not there—and, according to her neighbors, living conditions in the area were so hard that she had long since moved out to stay with her daughter. On the night of February 6 and then on the morning of February 7, no one had seen Cai at that address. As there was only one common sink with running water in the building, residents encountered one another several times a day. They had not seen him, however, for at least a week.

Old Liang had another talk with Cai, who clung to his earlier statement. Instead of contradicting him, earlier that morning Old Liang insisted on walking with him back to his nail home in Yangpu District. When the door was opened, the mail that had accumulated there for over a week stared Cai in the face. One unopened letter bore the stamped date of January 25. Cai had no explanation. Old Liang immediately took Cai into custody, and re-approached his wife and mother-in-law. They continued to swear that Cai had not been in the *shikumen* building on the morning of February 7, although they could not say where he might have been. They also proclaimed his innocence—which, of course, had no effect on the investigation. All suspects were "innocent."

"Walking him back to the nail room was really a master stroke," Yu commented.

"Cai has a motive," Old Liang said. "As an addicted gambler, he may have been desperately short of money. Cai has that history. And even more important, Cai has a key to the house. He could have sneaked into Yin's room to steal, not knowing that she would come back earlier than usual, then murdered her, and run upstairs. I don't think we can rule out the possibility that his wife and mother-in-law are attempting to cover up for him."

"What did he say after you had destroyed his alibi?"

"He denied having anything to do with the murder," Old Liang said. "Don't worry, I have ways of cracking such nuts."

"Cai is a suspect, I agree," Yu said. "But I have just a couple of questions. Somebody like Cai bets big-time, thousands or ten-thousands of Yuan on a little cricket, as you have told me. Yin seems to be too small a fish for someone with his appetite."

"No, I disagree. When you're desperate, you're desperate. As an incorrigible gambler, if he had lost several cricket fights in a row, he might have done anything for a few hundred Yuan."

"It's a possibility. But why should he have given a false alibi? It didn't help him at all."

"Well, you remember the saying, *If you had not stolen, you would not be so nervous.*"

"Yes, you have a point," Yu said. "We'll work on him."

Yu told Old Liang about his discovery, the possibility that someone could have left through the back door without being seen by the shrimp woman.

Old Liang, proud of his own breakthrough, brushed aside that possibility. "Let's say there was an opportunity to leave unseen for two or three minutes at most. So the murderer must have waited somewhere in the *shikumen* house for his chance. But where could he have waited without being seen?"

Detective Yu did not have an answer, not immediately.

黑

Chapter 15

It was Detective Yu's case, Chief Inspector Chen told himself once again.

But for the new cadre policy, with its emphasis on the candidate's educational background, it was Yu, who had more years of service in the police force, rather than Chen, who would have been appointed as leader of the special case squad. Chen did not want to give people the impression that he thought he had to be there, supervising every case. Nor should Party Secretary Li's repeated phone calls have had an effect.

With the steady progress of the New World translation, especially after he had read the introduction-to-marketing book obtained by White Cloud, however, his mind kept wandering back to the Yin case. It might have been because of his growing confidence that he would deliver the translation on time, but it was also because, ironically, it seemed that police work had somehow become the norm for him. In the midst of investigating a crime he now seemed to feel truly himself.

It occurred to Chen that he had an excuse to take a look at the progress of the investigation. He could go to Treasure Garden Lane, ostensibly for a field study of a *shikumen*-style house and lane, for the translation project.

When he approached Yu about making such a visit, the latter agreed readily even though this was, one had to admit, a fairly feeble excuse. Chen did not have to go to that particular *shikumen* building. Yu must have known this. But, close partners as they were, a lame excuse was better than none.

During this conversation, Yu also discussed with Chen the possibility that the murderer had waited somewhere in the *shikumen* building for Peng to leave before he sneaked out.

"I will keep it in mind when I look around," Chen said.

The "field study" might have served as a face-saving excuse. It was even more important to appease Old Liang, who insisted that now—with Cai in custody—the case should be concluded, though the cricket gambler still denied everything. When Yu mentioned the lack of witnesses or evidence, Old Liang took this personally. Without notifying Yu, he searched Cai's room in Treasure Garden Lane as well as his nail room in the Yangpu district, without any success. At this juncture, Chen's visit could easily be seen as a step toward rejecting Old Liang's solution. Chen did not want the old man to suffer any unnecessary loss of face. So Chen left a phone message for Old Liang, assuring the old man that he simply wanted to look around, take some pictures, and try to visualize the New World arising in similar surroundings.

When Chen arrived at Treasure Garden Lane, to show due respect, Old Liang was waiting in front of the *shikumen* house to greet him. "Welcome to our neighborhood, Comrade Chief

Inspector Chen. Your instructions will prove to be most valuable to our work."

"You don't have to say that, Comrade Old Liang. I'm on vacation, as I told you in my phone message," Chen said. "I just want to observe this neighborhood for a project of my own."

"Detective Yu is interviewing some relatives of Yin's, though I would like to say, at this stage, we really should focus—"

"You have been doing a great job. Detective Yu has told me quite a lot about you. But I'm not here to discuss the investigation with you. I know you must be very busy. You don't have to accompany me."

"Still, I'm the host here, Chief Inspector Chen. I will gladly do whatever I possibly can. If there is anything you need, please let me know."

"I have been doing some research with respect to an old architectural style. Detective Yu told me that this is a typical Shanghai lane, and a typical *shikumen* house. That's why I have chosen to come here today."

"Well, you cannot find a better guide, Chief Inspector Chen. I have done my homework," Old Liang said with a fresh air of pride. "A residence cop has to be familiar with everything in the neighborhood, even its architectural history."

Chen offered the would-be guide a Panda cigarette. He did not care much for Old Liang's company. Yu had warned him about the old man's loquacity. Still, he might provide interesting information for the translation, if not for the investigation. "Please tell me about it, Comrade Old Liang."

"Now, look at this lane. The lane, or *longtang*, in itself tells you something of the early history of Shanghai." Old Liang started speaking while they remained in front of the *shikumen* house. Perhaps the residence cop could talk more eloquently with both the house and the lane in full view.

"After the First Opium War, with the Treaty of Nanking, the city was forced to open itself to the West as a treaty port, and some areas were designated as foreign concessions. The small number of Western residents was not sufficient for the exploitation of Shanghai's potential. So a number of Chinese, who were worried about the civil wars raging outside the concessions, were permitted to move in. The British authorities took the lead in having collective dwellings built for the Chinese on designated lots. For the convenience of management, those houses were all built in the same architectural style, arranged in lines like barracks, row after row, accessible from sub-lanes leading to the main lane. French authorities soon followed suit—"

"What about the *shikumen*?" Chen, much impressed by Old Liang's narrative flow, interrupted him as Liang paused to take a long pull at his cigarette. This general introduction might go on and on, for much longer than Chen was prepared to listen. And he had already learned some of these details elsewhere.

"I am coming around to it, Chief Inspector Chen," Old Liang said, lighting another cigarette from the butt of the first one. "This is a really good brand; it's reserved for high Party cadres only, I know.

"In the early days, not too many Chinese could have afforded to move into a concession. A *shikumen* house—the typical Shanghai two-storied house with a stone door frame and a small courtyard—was originally designed for one family, usually a large, extended, and well-to-do family, with various rooms for different purposes: dwelling wings, hall, front room, dining room, corner room, back room, attic, dark room, and *tingzijian* too. As a result of the housing shortage, some of the rooms came to be leased, then subleased, with rooms undergoing further partitioning or subdivision.

"This has been an on-going progress to the present day. You may have heard of a Shanghai comedy called *Seventy-two Families in a House*. It is about such an overcrowded condition.

"Our Treasure Garden is not exactly like that. Generally, there are no more than fifteen families in a *shikumen* house."

"Yes, I have seen the comedy. So hilarious, with a mixture of so many diverse types. Life in a *shikumen* house must be quite interesting."

"Oh, you bet. Life here is colorful. There is so much interaction between residents. You practically become part of the neighborhood and the neighborhood, of you. Take this hall, for example. It was turned into a common kitchen area long ago and contains the coal stoves of more than a dozen families. It's a bit of a squeeze, but that's not necessarily too bad. When you cook here, you can learn how to prepare the dishes of various provincial cuisines from your neighbors."

"I would like that," Chen said, smiling in spite of himself.

"Take the courtyard, for another example. You may do practically anything in it, even to sleeping outside in the summer, on a rattan recliner or bamboo mat. It is so cool that you don't have to worry about an electric fan. Nor will you find it monotonous to scrub your clothes on a washboard here, where Granny Liu or Aunt Chen or Little Hou will keep you informed of the latest news of the lane. Indeed, you learn to share a lot of things with your neighbors."

"That sounds very nice," Chen said. "Here, people may have experiences unavailable in modern apartment complexes."

"People do a lot of things in the lane," Old Liang went on with unabated enthusiasm. "Men practice tai chi, brew the first pot of tea of the day, sing snatches of Beijing opera, and talk about the real weather or the political weather. As for women, washing and cooking and talking take place simultaneously. People here don't have a living room like in those fancy new apartments. So in the evening, most of them move outside, men playing chess or cards, telling stories, women chatting or knitting or mending."

Chen was familiar with similar scenes from his childhood, even though he'd lived in a different lane. Whatever differences there might be, or whatever other new information he might learn, it was the time for him to call a halt to Old Liang's speech.

"Oh, do you hear that?" Liang went on. "A cotton-candy peddler is hawking his wares. A variety of peddlers come down the lane. They offer a huge selection of goods, and services too, repairing shoes, mending coir rope bedframes or restuffing or sewing cotton quilts for the winter. It is so convenient—"

"Thank you so much, Comrade Old Liang. As the proverb says, *A talk of yours benefits me more than ten years of study*," Chen said with sincerity. "I would really like to spend some more time talking with you when I have finished my project."

Old Liang finally understood that Chen wanted to be left alone, excused himself, saluted Chen respectfully one more time, and went back to his own office.

Chen watched him walking down the lane, taking abrupt detours to avoid the laundry hanging on bamboo poles overhead. The clothing festooned on the network of poles seemed to present a scene from an Impressionist painting. Apparently, Old Liang still believed the old superstition that walking under women's underwear would bring bad luck.

Turning back, Chen tried the solid black wooden front door of the *shikumen* house. There were two brass knockers on the outside, and a solid wooden latch on the inside. After so many years of wear and tear, the door creaked when he pushed it open.

There were several people in the courtyard. They must have seen him talking with Old Liang, and they went on with their own activities, making no effort to speak to the chief inspector. As he crossed the courtyard, he saw a row of tall hall screen doors with exquisite designs of the eight immortals sailing over the ocean embossed on the panels. In an elaborate sequence, each door narrated a particular scene. The doors might be a valuable addition to the folk art museum in the New World, Chen thought.

As far as he could remember, he had never seen the hallway of a *shikumen* used for its original purpose, not even in his childhood. Without exception, a hall became common space in one way or another, since all the rooms along the wings opened into it. He smelled something like fermented tofu being fried in a wok, a favorite dish for some families in spite of its smell. It appealed to a lot of Shanghainese because of its exceptional flavor and texture. Most restaurants did not serve this dish because it was so cheap. That was a pity. There was also a faint smell, rich with a nostalgic aroma, of old hen soup with plenty of ginger and green onion.

Chen could not help wondering about the possibility of turning a *shikumen* into a restaurant. It would be unique. In a book of Chinese culinary studies he had read, it was argued that the best cooking might be done at home by a highly cultivated hostess who could spend days preparing a feast full of inspiration, to be served in an elegant ambience. Such a *shikumen* restaurant would have a pleasant family atmosphere too. The wings would be used as the dining areas, the small rooms here and there as private rooms; the intimacy of being at home, not to mention the contrast between the present and the past, would greatly enhance the proposed theme of the New World.

The courtyard, too, could be quite romantic in the evening, over a cup of wine or tea.

Some fragmented lines of an ancient poem unexpectedly came to him.

> *The moon appears like a hook.*
> *The lone parasol tree locks the clear autumn*
> *in the deep courtyard.*
> *What cannot be cut,*
> *nor raveled,*
> *is the sorrow of separation:*
> *Nothing tastes like that to the heart. . . .*

These lines were from a poem Yang had included in his translation manuscript. Some night, when all the other families in the *shikumen* were asleep, Yin, a lonely, heart-broken woman, could have stepped into this very courtyard and read it to herself.

Chen stubbed out his cigarette and walked across the hall and out the back door. He stopped to open and close the door a couple of times. Someone could have hidden behind the door, which was angled toward the staircase when it was open, but he would have been seen easily by people descending the stairs.

Outside, the shrimp woman was nowhere in sight, but a bamboo stool indicated her post in the lane, just three or four steps away. It was cold out there. It could not be easy for a woman to sit there working, morning after morning, her fingers numbed by the frozen shrimp, for the unprincely wage of two or three Yuan per hour. Her monthly income would be far less than an hour's translation earned him, he calculated.

He suddenly thought of two celebrated lines by Baijuyi, a Tang dynasty poet. *Now what merit do I have— / with my annual salary at three thousand kilos of rice?* At that time, when a lot of people could not fill their bellies, this salary was considered princely.

A recurring theme among Chinese intellectuals was a concern for the unfair distribution of wealth in society—*huibujun*. But Comrade Deng Xiaoping must also have been right when he declared that some Chinese people should be allowed to get rich first in their socialist society, that the wealth they accumulated would "trickle down" to the masses.

As for the money those upstarts like Gu were making, God alone knew where it would lead. Though China in the nineties was still socialist in name, with a time-honored emphasis on egalitarianism for the entire society, the gap between the rich and the poor was quickly—alarmingly—widening.

Chen started climbing the stairs. It was dark; finding each step was difficult. It would not be easy for a stranger to climb these stairs without stumbling. There should have been a light, even in the middle of the day. In such a building, however, with so many families, each one's share of the electricity bill would be a headache to calculate.

Some of the rooms on each floor were obviously makeshift subdivisions of space, Chen thought. There were sixteen families in the two-story building, about one hundred residents in all. Yu had his job cut out for him if each resident was a potential suspect.

Chen could not help stepping inside Yin's room, though he had not intended to examine it. Yu would have done a thorough job already.

He felt melancholy as he stood there, alone, thinking about a solitary woman whose death he should have more actively investigated. The furniture was already covered in a thin layer of dust, which somehow made the scene familiar. There was a pile of old magazines in which bookmarks had been placed. He thumbed through them; in each case, the marked page contained a poem of Yang's which had later appeared in the collection edited by Yin. A traditional Chinese painting of two canaries still hung high on the time-yellowed wall. There was nothing else left that was really personal to Yin.

Chen's interest in the room was also piqued by the term *tingzijian writer*. There were poverty-stricken writers, unable to rent better rooms, in the thirties, and then in the nineties, too. The marginal status of a *tingzijian* room, something barely inhabitable between two floors, appeared symbolic. He wondered how such a room—or the attempt to write in such a room—could have been romanticized in fiction. Not everything could have been glamorous in times past, but nostalgia made it seem so. *Things are miraculously mellowed in memories.* That was a line from a Russian poem he had read, but failed to understand, in his high-school years. A subtle transformation in comprehension had occurred with the lapse of years.

Chen started pacing around in the *tingzijian*, though there was not much room for him to do so. He wanted to concentrate.

It could not have been easy for Yin to write here; it could not have been easy to do anything, for that matter, with people going up and down the stairs, with noise coming from various directions, and with all the various smells wafting about. An unpleasant tang like that of salted beltfish sizzling in a wok was surging up from the kitchen area. He sniffed in spite of himself.

He went over to the window and rested his elbows, gingerly, on the windowsill, from which most of the paint had already peeled off.

There might be one advantage, nonetheless, for a writer in a *tingzijian* room, with its window lower than on the second floor but higher than on the first. There was an almost eye-level view of the hustle and bustle of the lane, so close yet at the same time somehow distanced.

In spite of the cold weather, several residents were out in the lane, holding bowls, talking, or exchanging a slice of fried pork for a nugget of steamed fish. Late breakfast or early lunch, Chen could not tell which. Peddlers came in and out, hawking the various goods on their shoulder poles. An old man went by, carrying a green-headed duck in his hand, stopping to feed the duck at a tiny pool in the corner, then resuming his walk, light-footed as if he were on a cloud, his mind doubtless filled by the image of sesame oil-braised duck wings. He clutched the neck of the helpless duck tightly with a look of utter satisfaction on his face. Could this be Mr. Ren, the frugal gourmet? Chief Inspector Chen then remembered having been told that Mr. Ren did not cook at home often.

Once more, Chen's glance followed the curve of the lane back to the corner where the shrimp woman was now stationed, sitting on the same bamboo stool, on the same spot, with a large bowl full of glistening fish scales at her feet. Perhaps she had another contract with the food market to make a later delivery.

As he went downstairs to the back door, something else caught his attention. It was the space—or rather something covering the space—under the staircase.

In a *shikumen* house, any usable space was precious. Since no single family could claim the space under the staircase, it became an additional common storage area for all sorts of hardly usable stuff which, in its owner's imagination, still had some potential value—like a broken bike of the Lis, a three-legged rattan chair of the Zhangs, a trunk of coal of the Huangs. But there was one difference here, Chen noticed: the space was covered by something like a curtain. It was a heavy material, possibly a once-expensive tapestry, which had been discolored by years of smoke from all the coal stoves.

The curtain seemed to be moving mysteriously. As Chen took a step toward it, out jumped two small boys. They must have been playing hide-and-seek behind the curtain. At the sight of Chief Inspector Chen, they ran away, laughing and shrieking. He lifted up the curtain; the space inside was full of the grimy discarded junk.

A middle-aged man squeezed past him to reach into a bag of coal balls that was leaning against the side of the staircase. "Sorry, lunch time," he mumbled, as he filled a ladle with coal balls.

Looking at his watch, Chen realized that he had spent nearly three hours without finding out anything of value for the investigation. He might have gained some first-hand experience for his translation, but he had no idea whether it would *really* help him to visualize the New World.

He left the *shikumen* building, cutting through one sub-lane into another, and then returned to the main lane, which was throbbing with life just as Old Liang had described it. A middle-aged woman was drying a redwood chamber pot, another trotted back from the food market with a full bamboo basket, and still another was preparing a large carp in the lane sink, splashing scales and gossip around at the same time.

Turning another corner, he saw a white-haired old man playing *go* on a board resting on a stool, the black pieces in one of his hands and the white in the other, studying the board as if he were taking part in a national tournament. Chen liked *go*, too, but he had never tried to play the game solo.

"Hi," he said, coming to a stop by the stool. "How come you are playing by yourself?"

"Have you read *The Art of War*?" the old man asked without looking up. *"Know your enemy as you know yourself,* and you will win every time."

"Yes, I have read the book. You have to figure out why your opponent has made a certain move. So you must try hard to understand your opponent."

"From my point of view, the positioning of the black piece does not make any sense, and the best I can do is to guess, to try to understand, as you put it. But that's not enough. Knowing your enemy actually means that you not only have to think as if you were reading his mind, you have to *be* him."

"I see. Thank you so much, Uncle. That is profound," Chen said sincerely. To him, it seemed as if the talk were not just about the game of *go*. "I will put your teaching into practice, not just on a *go* board."

"Young man, you don't have to take me so seriously. When you play a game, you want to win," the old man explained. "When you are absorbed in it, every piece counts, every move matters. Happy to win a corner, sad to lose a position, you are carried away with the illusion of gains or losses. Not until after the game will you come to realize it's nothing but a game. According to Buddhist scripture, everything in this mundane world is a matter of illusion."

"Exactly. You have put it very well."

Chen decided to walk back to his apartment. He could not afford to spend a whole day in the lane. The conversation about *go* had cost him another ten minutes. The translation lay unfinished on his desk at home. Still, he wanted to think a little about the case, at least on his way back, after this talk with the elderly *go* player who had been as mysteriously enlightening as the old man of the Han dynasty who had helped Zhang Liang two thousand years ago.

At the exit of the lane, he looked back toward the building where Yin had spent the last years of her life after Yang's death. Some more lines from Yang's poetry translation manuscript occurred to him.

> *Where is the beauty?*
> *Swallows alone are locked inside, for no purpose.*
> *It is nothing but a dream,*
> *in the past, or at present.*
> *Who ever wakes from the dream?*
> *There is only a never-ending cycle*
> *of old joy and new grief.*
> *Some day, and someone else,*
> *in view of the yellow tower at night,*
> *may sigh deeply for me.*

These lines were from a poem by Su Dongpo, about a courtesan who shut herself up in the tower after her lover's death. A *tingzijian* was not at all comparable to a romantic tower, but Yin, too, had shut herself up.

Chen was determined to do his level best for the investigation. He started by putting himself in the position of the government. He still couldn't figure out what it could have possibly gained from murdering Yin. While Internal Security seemed to have some concern, Chen did not consider it really surprising or suspicious for them to show interest in a dissident writer's sudden death; it could simply be their way of asserting authority. In recent years, the Party had changed its way of dealing with dissidents. Foreign investment, a vital part of China's economic reform, depended heavily on the new, improved government image. It did not make sense to assassinate someone like Yin.

After all, she was not someone fighting for democracy and freedom under a red banner in Tiananmen Square.

Then he tried to think about Yin from the perspective of her neighbors. Yin was not rich; they all must have been aware of this. Someone might have been desperate for money, like Cai, but even then there must have been better targets: Mr. Ren, for instance, who was alone, and went out in the mornings too. Besides, no one would have kept much cash at home in this neighborhood.

As for the possibility of someone stealing Yin's checkbook so he could withdraw her money from the bank, it was way too risky. Banks in the city did not open until after nine o'clock, and, by that time, Yin would surely have discovered that her checkbook was gone and notified the authorities. So it didn't seem like it could have been a planned robbery gone wrong because of Yin's unexpected return.

There seemed to be no reason to suspect an insider, a neighbor, whether he or she had intended to kill Yin or not.

But why would an outsider sneak in to kill her?

Chen caught himself shaking his head in resignation. The theoretical possibilities seemed to be unlimited. He could go on conjuring up one motive after another, but they remained nothing but theories; he did not have any facts to support them.

On the corner of Shandong Road, Chen came in sight of the New China Bookstore. To his surprise, the portion of the store devoted to books had been reduced, and now one large section was devoted to tawdry art and craft products, while another portion, under an impressive array of red paper lanterns, was selling Japanese noodles. He had not been to the bookstore for several months, and it had changed almost beyond recognition. It was like seeing an old acquaintance after he'd had plastic surgery: recognizable, yet different.

He decided not to go inside, for he wanted to focus on the case. He merely took a look at a bunch of new magazines and newspapers near the entrance: *One Week in Shanghai, Shanghai Culture, Bund Pictorial, One Week's Life*. All of them featured big color photos of stars. He did not read any of these new trendy magazines, and only recognized one picture, that of a Hong Kong actress, on one cover.

Things had been changing very fast in the city.

Chen then tried to tackle the case from another perspective. Motive aside, what would an outside murderer have done after committing the crime?

Surely he would have tried to escape immediately.

In his attempt to get away, there was a possibility of his being seen by someone in the building. But that would not be too much of a risk. In a *shikumen* building, people might have relatives or friends staying over or visiting early, and a stranger's presence would not have caused instant alarm. No one would have taken drastic action to stop him from leaving. In the worst-case scenario, if Yin's body was immediately discovered, one of the neighbors might be able to produce a rough sketch of the suspect for the police bureau later, but such a sketch alone would not be much help to a homicide investigation.

To stay in her room with the dead body, with the growing possibility of a knock at the door, would have presented a much greater risk. The longer the murderer stayed in the room, the more people would go upstairs and down, passing by the closed *tingzijian* door, and the more suspicious they would grow if Yin did not emerge.

According to Yu's hypothesis, the murderer could have waited in hiding, either in the *tingzijian* room or somewhere else, until an opportune moment to leave the *shikumen* building.

In terms of hiding places, Chen did not think it totally impossible for someone to hide briefly amidst the broken furniture pieces and other junk stored here and there in various nooks and crannies in the building; he might have hidden behind the open back door, for instance, or behind the tapestry under the staircase.

So either when the shrimp woman stepped away from her position, or when all the neighbors rushed upstairs, the murderer could have escaped in the confusion if he had been waiting in hiding.

But hiding and waiting involved another risk. If he were found lurking, he would instantly be seen as a suspect and grabbed, or at least questioned.

Why would the murderer have taken that risk? And why kill Yin? For what?

Those were questions to which he did not have answers.

In the afternoon Chen threw himself into his translation work. He had told White Cloud that he would spend the day in the Shanghai Library. Whether she believed him or not, she neither called nor came to his door.

He had told himself that he had probably done all he could in the criminal investigation. Cops may spend days, or weeks, on a case without getting anywhere. And he could not afford, despite his determination to do his best, to spend any more time on it.

Toward the evening, he got a phone call from Overseas Chinese Lu. As always, Lu started by referring to a loan Chen had made to him in the early days of his restaurant, Moscow Suburb, and then Lu repeated his usual dinner invitation.

"Now I have several Russian waitresses dressed in white, tightly laced corsets and garters, as if they were walking out of those posters of old Shanghai. Absolutely sensational. Customers have come pouring in. Particularly young customers. They say the atmosphere is full of *xiaozi*."

"*Xiaozi*—petty bourgeoisie?"

"Oh, yes, it is a fashionable new term. *Xiaozi*—petty bourgeoisie, a sort of trendy, highly cultivated, status-conscious consumer. It is particularly hot among those white-collar workers employed by foreign joint ventures. 'If you are not a *xiaozi*, you are nothing.'"

"Well, the language surely changes," Chen said, "and it changes us too."

"Oh, by the way," Overseas Chinese Lu said at the end of the conversation, "I called your mother yesterday. She had some stomach problem. Not serious. Nothing to worry about, I trust."

"Thanks. I'll give her a ring. I talked to her two days ago; she didn't mention anything to me."

"She talks about a lot of things to me, you know, about your ginseng, about your work, and about you, too."

"I know, my dear old pal. Thank you so much."

Putting down the receiver, Chen thought that if he were going to take White Cloud out to dinner one of these evenings, it would not be to Moscow Suburb, even if Overseas Chinese Lu insisted, as always, on treating.

His buddy and his mother had in common an overanxiety about what they both called "the most urgent matter" in his personal life, what Confucius regarded as the most important duty of a filial son. *The worst unfilial thing is not to provide offspring for the family.* Overseas Chinese Lu had somehow become his mother's loyal and enthusiastic consultant on that particular aspect of

Chen's life. Any girl seen in Chen's company, however unlikely, would immediately give rise to fantasy, no matter how unsubstantiated, on both their parts.

For one second, Chen almost envied Overseas Chinese Lu—a successful businessman, and a good family man too. Lu managed to keep up with the newest fads, but at the same time he remained conservative, traditional in his concern about his friend.

Perhaps Lu had adapted better to the times, combining the old in his personal life and the new in business.

Chen cracked his fingers, and moved back to his desk. Back to work, which alone did not disappoint him. In fact, his work often gave him a place to hide.

A new idea occurred to him. Even if he could not uncover the murder motive, he could speculate as to why the murderer chose to hide and wait, in accordance with Detective Yu's hypothesis. A possibility at once suggested itself. The murderer might have been afraid—not of being seen, but of being *recognized* by the neighbors in the *shikumen* building. That opened up a number of new possibilities. The murderer could be someone who had once lived in the house, someone who had stayed there, someone who had been there before, even though not as a resident, someone who had met other residents in the *shikumen* building—or even in Yin's company. When Yin's body was discovered, he might be found easily because his identity was known. That's why he had to hide himself at such great risk.

Soon, however, Chen's excitement began to fade. He realized that this way just another possibility, like all the other possibilities in his mind. There was no evidence to back them up.

Chapter 16

Then the investigation took a surprising turn. Wan Qianshen turned himself in to the police for the murder of Yin Lige.

This happened on February 14, a week after Lanlan had discovered Yin's body in the *tingzijian* room and two days after Old Liang had taken Cai into custody. According to his own statement, Wan had murdered Yin not for the sake of money, but out of a long-held, class-conscious grudge against her.

Initially, Old Liang was nonplussed, but then he readily embraced the surprising turn of events which, after all, fit his original inside-murderer theory. Wan had been on his list of suspects from the very beginning. Yu, too, should have been pleased with the breakthrough, but he was not. In fact, as he sat in the company of Old Liang and Wan in an interrogation office of the district police station, he was confounded.

"Yin Lige deserved it," Wan said in a low controlled voice. "She had slandered the Party and our socialist country. Indeed, her death was long overdue."

"None of your political lectures," Old Liang said.

"Tell us how you did it," Yu asked, taking out a cigarette but not lighting it. "Give us all the details."

"I did not sleep well the night before. That is, the night of February sixth. So I got up later than usual on the seventh, but I still wanted to go to the Bund. As I went downstairs, Yin came up. By accident, I brushed against her on the stairs. I did not mean anything by this; the stairs were narrow. She snapped, 'Still a Mao Zedong Thought Propaganda Worker Team Member?' That was *way* too much. She had the damned nerve to insult the working class to my face. In a moment of uncontrollable rage, I turned back, followed her into her room, and smothered her with the pillow before she could shout or struggle."

"Then what did you do?"

"I realized that I had killed her in a moment of blind anger. I had not intended this. So I pulled out the drawers and tossed the contents around, so that people might suspect a different motive."

"Now, the first time I talked to you," Yu said, "you told me you had been out on the Bund practicing tai chi. Why this sudden confession?"

"What would have happened to me if I had told you the truth? I knew. Besides, it was not premeditated. If she had not provoked me that morning, I would not have lost control. Why should I suffer for this?" Old Wan said. "But now that you have taken Cai into custody, the situation's different. I had to do some serious thinking. Cai is a criminal, perhaps, but he should not be punished for something he did not do."

"So you are no longer worried about what will happen to you?"

"I did what I did, and, as a man, I take responsibility."

"Now, what did you do after you killed Yin?"

"I went back to my room. I saw no one on the stairs, but it was touch-and-go; the moment I stepped back into my room, I heard somebody coming up, and then shouting for help. I waited in my room for a couple of hours. I did not leave it until nine, the hour I usually come back from the Bund."

In view of all their theorizing and the work they had put in, this sudden confession seemed to Yu like an anticlimax, but Wan's statement seemed to make sense. Some of the details fit.

"One question for you: you said you pulled out the drawers and tossed the contents around, right?"

"Yes, I did."

"Do you remember what was inside the drawers?"

"No, I do not remember. It all happened so fast, like in a movie, I did not have time to think."

"Surely you can remember something," Yu said slowly, patiently, "if not every item."

"Well, there was some cash, I now remember, some ten-Yuan and five-Yuan bills."

"Did you take the money?"

"No, of course not. What kind of man do you think I am?"

"Well, we will find out. We will talk to you again."

Yu signaled for Wan to be taken out of the interrogation room.

"Wan might have a motive," Yu said to Old Liang when they were alone. "But what prompted his confession? Cai has not even been charged; he's only in custody. What is the relationship between these two, Cai and Wan?"

"Come on, Detective Yu. They are neither relatives nor friends. Wan might do anything *but* cover up for Cai. Wan had a fight with Cai not too long ago."

"Oh? What was that about?"

"Neither Lindi nor Xiuzhen makes much money, and they are a family of six, including the son's live-in girlfriend. If Cai did not help financially . . . in fact, that's one of the reasons Xiuzhen married him, so the family could eke out a living. Wan urged Cai to give his family more support, and Cai retorted that it was none of Wan's business."

"Well, neighborhood squabbles are not surprising."

"There's another thing, Detective Yu."

"What?"

"Both you and I have questioned him about his alibi, and asked him to name someone who could support his statement. But he never did."

"That's true."

"So Wan is the murderer. It's obvious. There's no need for us to continue to investigate."

"But there are still some things for us to do before we can conclude the investigation."

"For example?"

"Wan touched a lot of things in Yin's room, according to his own account. So he must have left his fingerprints there. The initial report about the fingerprints is not conclusive, as there were so many blurred or indistinct prints on every surface, but I don't think Wan's fingerprints were listed. We should double-check the fingerprint report. "

"Yes, we can do that."

"Also, Wan mentioned some cash, five- and ten-Yuan bills, in a drawer, but we only found some coins. That's suspicious."

"Well, Wan may not have remembered so clearly."

"At the moment, we have only what Wan himself says. If that's true—I mean, about his getting up and moving about after six on that morning—some of his neighbors might have seen him, though they did not pay him any special attention at the time."

"We may check that too, but I don't think you have to worry. In addition to his words, we do have some hard evidence," Old Liang said in a suddenly boastful voice. "In Wan's loft, I found a train ticket to Shenzhen for next week."

"Have you already searched his room?"

"Yes, as soon as he made his confession. This is the ticket. I came across it in a notebook in his desk drawer. I had not really expected to find the murder weapon, but the ticket speaks volumes."

"So—" Yu had intended to ask if Old Liang had obtained a search warrant from the police bureau, but the question might have sounded pedantic. In the years of class struggle, Old Liang could have searched any home in the neighborhood without bothering about a search warrant. "Let me take a look at the ticket."

"It means that Wan planned a trip to Shenzhen," Old Liang said as he turned the ticket over. "I have double-checked with the neighborhood committee. Wan does not have friends or relatives there. He is a retired worker, and he has no business there. The answer is self-evident. From there, he could try to sneak over to Hong Kong. A lot of people have done that. Wan knew that if he did not make his getaway, it was only a matter of time before we got to him."

It sounded logical, except that the ticket was for a soft sleeper, a detail Old Liang had overlooked, Yu thought, as he studied the piece of paper that he held. Why should Wan have paid the extra money for a soft sleeper if he were going to Shenzhen for the purpose suspected by Old Liang?

"What did he tell you about the ticket?"

"That's more or less what he said."

"Can I keep the ticket?"

"Sure." Old Liang looked up at him in surprise. "When you think about it, there's something else suspicious about him. As a residence cop, I should have noticed it earlier. About half a year ago, Wan started going out early in the morning—allegedly for tai chi exercise on the Bund. Yin also went out for tai chi in the morning. But there's one marked difference. She practiced not only in the park, but in the lane too, especially on rainy days. Wan has never practiced here. That's not like a tai chi devotee. No, I don't think he told us the truth."

"Well, Wan may not be such a wholehearted exerciser. He only turned to tai chi, he told me, because the state-run company he had worked for can no longer cover its retirees' medical insurance."

"That old die-hard still lives in the days of the Mao Zedong Thought Team, and he grumbles all the time. That's why he committed the murder. Tai chi or whatever is just an excuse. He followed her around, to become familiar with her routine. Then he acted."

"Did he have to follow her around for months in order to kill her at home early that morning?"

"Is it so impossible?" Old Liang said, becoming impatient with these questions from Detective Yu.

"Let me make a phone call to Dr. Xia first, Old Liang, to ask about the fingerprints."

"Whatever you want, Comrade Detective Yu."

Afterward, alone in the office, Detective Yu admitted to himself that it was not absolutely impossible.

Wan's entire life—or most of it—had been the product of a totally different society. In the sixties and seventies, Chinese workers had been praised to the skies as the masters of society, the makers of history. People like Wan committed themselves unreservedly to Mao's revolution, believing in their contribution to the greatest social system in human history, which, in turn, promised them a lot too, including retirement benefits: a generous pension, full medical coverage, and the political honor of being retired masters basking in the warm sunlight of communist China. Now these retired workers found themselves, helplessly, at the bottom of the heap. The praise for them as the "leading class" was irrelevant. They had a hard time making the ends meet. What was worse, state-run companies, going downhill, could keep few of their earlier promises.

And things must have been even more unbearable for Wan, who had once been such a prestigious Mao Zedong Thought Propaganda Worker Team Member.

Yu phoned Dr. Xia, asking him to recheck the fingerprints, focusing only on Wan's.

He made a second phone call to the Shanghai railway station. He thought he remembered that there were regulations regarding sleeping-car tickets. The information he received confirmed his suspicion. According to the railway station, tickets to Shenzhen were very hot, especially sleeping-car tickets. New entrepreneurs flocked to the special economic zone to seek their fortunes. Normally, tickets were sold out on the first day of the fourteen-day advance purchase period. The date on Wan's ticket was February 18, which meant Wan could not possibly have obtained it after

February 7 unless he had paid a ticket scalper a much higher price
for it.

Yu wanted to discuss this with Old Liang, but Liang did not
return to the neighborhood committee office for lunch.

Shortly afterward, Party Secretary Li called. The Party boss
sounded very pleased with the latest development, for it meant the
conclusion of Yin's case as a simple homicide, with no suspicion
falling on the government.

"Great job, Comrade Detective Yu," Li repeated over the phone.

"This conclusion is too dramatic, too sudden, Party Secretary Li."

"I don't find it surprising," Li said. "You kept the pressure on,
and Wan cracked. *With enough fire burning under the pot, the pig's
head will be cooked to your satisfaction.* You need not doubt that Wan
killed Yin."

"But we put pressure on Cai, not on Wan."

"Wan stepped forward," Li said slowly, "because he couldn't
endure the thought of an innocent man being punished in his stead."

"There are holes in Wan's statement, Party Secretary Li. We cannot depend on a so-called confession like this," Yu said. "At least,
I need to get some questions answered first."

"We cannot afford to wait too much longer, Comrade Detective
Yu. A press conference will be held early next week, Monday or
Tuesday, no later than that. It's time to end all the irresponsible
speculation surrounding Yin's death."

Chapter 17

Chen finished the first draft of his translation of the New World proposal into English. He was amazed at his own speed, though the job was still far from complete: he would have to spend more time polishing and revising before it would be presentable.

It proved to be a good day for the murder investigation, too. Though it came as a surprise that Wan had turned himself in, it looked like a plausible solution as well as an acceptable one.

Yu was still so full of misgivings that Chen did not even try to share with him some half-formed ideas of his own. After all, a lot of things in the process of writing, or leading to publication, seemingly inexplicable to others, could turn out to be significant, if only to the writer himself.

In the late eighties, when Chen, a published poet with some renown in literary circles, had suddenly started translating mysteries, no one knew why. But it was because of a Beijing roast duck—at least partially because of it, he recalled. That duck turned out to cost more than he had in his pocket at the end of a wonderful dinner, in the company of a friend who liked his poetry so much that she snatched the bill with her slender fingers. It was a humiliating lesson about money—which, as he happened to discover through that friend, came much quicker from mystery translations than from poetry. But a few years later, when another friend of his published an interview about him in *Wenhui Daily*, she claimed that he did the translations to "enlarge the horizon of his professional expertise."

So those mysterious abbreviations in the margins of Yang's manuscript could have referred to anything; "ch" might stand for a chicken, for all Chen knew. The uneven quality of Yin's writing noticed by Peiqin could be just another of the mysteries of a creative mind. Chen had not written novels, but he guessed that a novelist might not be able to keep up the same intensity of creativity in a long work as in a short poem. He could never explain how he was capable of producing a horribly poor poem after penning a fairly decent one.

So all these hypotheses, including his own theory regarding the murderer's hiding for fear of recognition, were nothing but hypotheses, which did not weigh much, and were eventually irrelevant, if Wan had committed the murder as he had confessed. His motive might not make sense to someone else; it was enough if it had made sense to him.

The bottom line was, as Chen had realized from the beginning, there are things a man can do, and things a man cannot do. That was also applicable to being a cop, in the present case.

He considered giving himself a break that evening, in the company of White Cloud. It might be an opportunity to find out more about Gu, and about the New World project.

He suggested a dinner at a karaoke club, a different one than the Dynasty, as a gesture of his sincerity—he had told her that he liked her singing. White Cloud would not decline such an invitation, he hoped.

She did not, but she suggested that they go to a high-class bar, the Golden Time Rolling Backward.

"It's on Henshan Road. An up-and-coming place."

"That will be great," he said.

Perhaps she did not like to be reminded of her K-girl status. He liked the name of the bar, which suggested a nostalgic atmosphere in common with the New World.

They took a taxi to the Golden Time Rolling Backward, which turned out to be an elegant bar that had opened in a grand Victorian mansion; he supposed it had still been a private residence in the thirties. A number of celebrities had lived in European-style mansions in the area then.

They chose a table next to the tall french window looking out to a well-kept garden just visible in the gathering dusk. The bar, according to White Cloud, was known for its classic elegance. She failed to recall the name of the original owner of the house. "She was a celebrated courtesan who became the concubine of a triad tycoon. He bought this mansion for her," was all White Cloud could remember.

Inside, it was fairly dark; the candlelight barely illuminated the somber background. After a minute or two, he managed to make out a black, old-fashioned telephone, a gramophone with a trumpet-shaped speaker on a corner table, an Underwood typewriter in a corner, and an antique grand piano with ivory keys, all of which contributed to the period effect, as well as the dark-colored oak paneling, the antique pictures and posters on the walls, and the carnations in a cut-glass vase on the mantelpiece.

"Perhaps we should come in the early afternoon, in warmer weather, when the light is better," he commented. "Then you would be able to take in all the period details. The illusion would be even more vivid and convincing."

Still, the whole scene was ingeniously designed. It was as if the life of the city had continued, uninterrupted, from the thirties. The years under Mao's communist rule seemed to have been wiped out by the pink napkin in the hand of a young waitress, who wore a scarlet *qi* dress with high slits through which one could see flashes of her white thighs.

The only difference from an old movie scene was that the customers here this evening were Chinese. Then a middle-aged foreign couple arrived, looked around, and moved to a table in the corner. The woman had on a Chinese-style cotton padded jacket with embroidered buttons. They were the only Western couple there. No one seemed to pay them any special attention.

Studying the bilingual menu in the candlelight, Chen ordered coffee, and White Cloud, black tea. In addition, she had a bowl of popcorn. It was still too early for dinner. There were several excellent Chinese restaurants in the area. He was not in a hurry to decide whether to dine here. He was not experienced at dining in a Western-style restaurant. White Cloud was so fashion-conscious, he was not confident of making the right choice.

To his surprise, the black tea came in a tall glass with a Lipton tea bag. The popcorn tasted too sweet and was as tough as rubber. The coffee was fine, but not hot enough. He had no objection to the tea bag, except that it did not appear as authentic as tea served in the Chinese way. Then he tried to mock himself out of such an antiquated idiosyncrasy. This was a modern Western bar, not a traditional Chinese teahouse. Still, he missed the feeling of the tender tea leaf on his tongue. He took another sip of the lukewarm coffee.

"Americans eat popcorn when they are enjoying themselves," she said, filling her mouth with a handful.

"They eat it while at the movies, I've heard," he said.

What surprised him was not the poor quality of the food they were served, but that people were content in spite of it. It seemed as if the atmosphere more than compensated for anything else. For the first time, he had a feeling that the New World project would work in Shanghai. Whether or not the customers here were exactly the middle-class ones in Gu's mind, Chinese people wanted to find new ways of enjoying life—"value-adding ways," the phrase he had read in the introduction to marketing.

As for the added value, he wondered who was going to define it. It would have to depend on one's taste. For instance, the passion for "three-inch golden lotus feet," which had endured for hundreds of years in China, was a matter of fashion. In some men's imaginations, the deformed, white-cloth-bound feet were transformed into lotus blossoms blooming in the black night. If people chose to look for value, they would find it in one way or another. Chen scribbled a few lines on the paper napkin, lines probably for a poem.

"What are you thinking about?"

"I'm just making some notes. If I don't write my ideas down, I may totally forget them by tomorrow."

"Tell me about your work in the police bureau, Chief Inspector Chen." She lifted the tea bag by its paper tag, then let it sink to the bottom of the glass.

"Detective Yu has been handling a special case that was recently assigned to my squad. I'm on vacation, but we have a daily discussion about developments."

"I do not mean just this week," she said.

"What do you mean?"

"How could somebody like you have turned out to be a cop? A fine scholar, a good translator, and a first-class poet, and you seem to be doing a great job in the police bureau too."

"You are flattering me, White Cloud. I'm just a cop. You cannot always choose to do what you would like, can you?"

He had not meant this as an allusion to her work in the K club. He regretted having spoken so. He had been asked this question too many times, and his answer came out almost automatically.

She fell momentarily silent.

He tried to maneuver the talk in the direction he had intended it to take. "It's the same with Mr. Gu, perhaps. He probably didn't expect as a child to grow up to be a millionaire businessman."

To his disappointment, she did not know much about Gu. It was all business between Gu and her. As an employer, Gu was not too bad, according to her. He did not take advantage of the girls working for him. Nor was he tight-fisted, at least not with her. As for his connections with the triad world, that was nothing uncommon, she declared. A businessman needed protection.

"Gu has to burn incense, that is, to burn his money to the triad gods, and he is good at what he does. Now he has established connections almost everywhere, in both the white way and the black way." She added, with her sly smile, "Connections with powerful people like you—"

It was not unpleasant to hear her referring to him as "powerful," but he cut her short. "Don't count me in. But have you met any of those really powerful people with him?"

"On a couple of occasions, including several important figures in the city government. One from Beijing as well. I recognized them from their pictures in the newspapers. Do you want to know their names? I can find out."

"Don't bother, White Cloud."

A lambent melody began to waft through the bar. Looking round, he failed to find a karaoke TV set. Then it hit him: karaoke had not existed in the thirties.

"Sorry, there is no karaoke today."

"Well, I do not enjoy singing that much, Chief Inspector Chen."

This was not what he had expected. Perhaps she felt the same way he did, preferring not to talk about his job outside the bureau.

The waitress came by again. He ordered a glass of white wine, and she chose a double scotch on the rocks.

Another melody followed. It was an old one, but it belied the period effect—the singer was an American pop star giving a contemporary rendition. For White Cloud, however, it seemed to be even more enjoyable. She was rapt, her face cradled in her hands.

Something soft touched his foot under the table. She had kicked off her shoes, her bare feet were beating out the rhythm, and they were brushing his in her trance. Perhaps.

Sitting so close together at the table, Chen was not unaware of the age difference between them. And of all the other differences, too. They practically belonged to different generations.

To someone like him, whose elementary school years had been in the sixties, a bar or a café carried with it associations with bourgeois decadence, decried in all the official textbooks. He might be something of an exception because of his English studies. Still, if he visited a café, it was first of all for a cup of good coffee, and occasionally, if time allowed, to spend a couple of hours reading a book over the coffee.

White Cloud, however, had studied no such textbooks. Perhaps a place like Golden Time Rolling Backward symbolized a cultivated taste a notch above that of the common folk who drank tea with leaves in their cups, a sense of being part of the social elite. Whether she genuinely enjoyed the taste of the Lipton teabag tea or not did not matter that much.

An elderly couple rose from their table. The music was good for dancing. They started doing slow steps in a space in front of the grand piano, a hardwood area large enough for ten or fifteen people. Chen caught White Cloud looking at him expectantly. He was going to reach out to her when she touched his hand, tentatively. Dance could be an excuse, he had read, to hold someone it was otherwise impossible or impropriate to hold.

But why not? It was fun being a Mr. Big Bucks for the evening, with a young pretty girl—a little secretary—stroking his hand across the table. He did not have to be Chief Inspector Chen, a "politically correct" Party cadre every minute of the day. He, too, was doing well. He had a powerful position, and a generous advance payment from a business project.

However, it was not destined to be an evening of Golden Time Rolling Backward for Chief Inspector Chen.

His cell phone rang. It was Zhuang, the senior lecturer White Cloud had interviewed. Chen had left several messages for him, and now Zhuang was finally calling back.

"I'm glad you called me," Chen said. "I have just one question for you. In your conversation with White Cloud about Yang, you mentioned Doctor Zhivago. Now, was Yang reading the novel, or writing a novel like it, or writing poetry like Doctor Zhivago?"

"Did I say that?"

"Yes, you did. The exact words were, 'still reading, and writing, something like Doctor Zhivago.' You don't have to worry, Comrade Zhuang. The case has nothing whatsoever to do with you, but your information may help our work."

There was a short silence from the other end of the telephone.

A young man approached their table, holding out his hand to White Cloud in a gesture of invitation. She flashed Chen an apologetic smile. Chen nodded in encouragement as he heard Zhuang continuing in a more subdued voice. "Now that both Yang and Yin are dead, I don't think that anybody can get into trouble."

"No. Nobody. So please go ahead and tell me."

Another short silence ensued.

He took a sip of wine. Not too far away, White Cloud started moving gracefully with the young man in front of the piano. A perfectly matched couple, both of them young, energetic, dancing with a rhythm perhaps slightly too wild for this upscale bar.

Zhuang spoke. "I met Yang in the early sixties, during the so-called Socialism Education Movement, you know, shortly before the Cultural Revolution. The school authorities assigned Yang and me to the same study group. We were both single then, and both listed as special targets for brainwashing, so we were put into a temporary isolation dorm room for 'intensive education' at night. Yang said that he did not sleep well, but one night I discovered that he was writing—in a notebook, under the quilt. In English. I asked him what it was about. He said that it was a story of an intellectual, something like Doctor Zhivago."

"Did you take a look at what he was writing?"

"I did not understand English. Nor did I really want to read a single word of it."

"Why, Comrade Zhuang?"

"Yang said it was a story of an intellectual, and he was an intellectual himself. That's it. If the school authorities ever looked into the matter, I could claim that it was his diary—at least so I thought. It was no crime to keep a diary. But if I read it, and it was a book, I would have turned into a counterrevolutionary by withholding the information from the authorities."

"Yes, I see: you did not want to get him—and yourself too—into trouble. Did Yang tell you anything else about it?"

"It was really naive of him to tell me that he was writing a story. Fortunately, I had no idea then who or what Doctor Zhivago was—perhaps a doctor Yang knew personally. Zhivago surely sounded like a Chinese name. The Chinese translation did not appear—let me think—until the mid-eighties. It had been banned, as you know, as an attack on the great Soviet Revolution. In those years, a Nobel-Prize-winning book *had* to be counterrevolutionary."

"I know. I happen to know someone who went to jail because of a copy of *Doctor Zhivago*. You were lucky that you remained in the dark," Chen said. "Did you ever talk to Yang about it again?"

"No. Pretty soon the Cultural Revolution broke out. All of us were like broken clay Buddhist idols drifting down the river—already too disintegrated to care about anybody else. I was thrown into jail for the so-called crime of listening to the Voice of America. When I got out, he was already away at that cadre school. And there he died."

"Do you have any knowledge about his continuing writing during the Cultural Revolution?"

"No, but I doubt it. It's hard to imagine somebody like him writing in English in those years."

"Well, Yang was actually allowed to keep English books because of one particular word—fart, I think it was—in Chairman Mao's poetry translation."

"Oh, yes, I have heard that."

"Do you think anybody else may have known about this manuscript?"

"No, I don't think so. It would have been suicidal for him to tell anybody," Zhuang said. "Except Yin, of course."

When he finished with Zhuang, Chen scribbled something else on another napkin. He had also come to a different decision about dinner. There was no point moving to another restaurant. He could use some time to himself, just thinking. White Cloud dancing, away from the table most of the time, was all to the good.

The abbreviations on the poetry translation manuscript started to make sense. If it were a novel Yang had been writing, as Zhuang had supposed, "ch" could refer to chapters. Yang might have tried to use poems in his novel, to insert them at various places in the text, in a way similar to *Doctor Zhivago*. And Peiqin's suggestion of plagiarism would fit in, too. The portions of Yin's novel that seemed to be too well-written—

But where was this novel manuscript? Chen could not be sure that such a manuscript had ever really existed.

Often, Chen put down some thoughts in his notebook, on a piece of paper, or even on a napkin like this evening, but afterward, for one reason or another, he failed to develop these ideas, and what he put down remained in fragments.

So, too, could Yang have written down some ideas on a sleepless night, in the days of the Socialism Education Movement when he was with Zhuang in that dorm room. But those notes might never have been developed into a novel. Still, Chen added a few more words to the napkin and put it into his pocket before he looked up.

White Cloud seemed to be thoroughly enjoying herself in Golden Time Rolling Backward, like a fish in water. Although the new culture of nostalgia did not appeal that much to him, he found it quite pleasant to spend an evening in such a trendy place, in the company of a pretty girl. She was popular here; her face became flushed as she danced with one young man after another. They kept coming over to the table, like flies drawn to spilled syrup.

Chen refrained from dancing with her. With a touch of quizzical self-scrutiny, he diagnosed something akin to jealousy. Naturally a young girl preferred companions of her own age; a temporary boss meant nothing but business to her.

He thought of several lines by Yan Jidao, an eleventh-century poet.

> I was so happy drinking with you,
> heedless of my flushed cheeks, dancing
> with the moon sinking
> in the willow trees, singing
> until I was too tired
> to wave the fan that unfolds
> a peach blossom.

The narrator of the poem was a young girl like White Cloud, and then he thought of another line by an American poet, already paraphrased in his mind: *I do not think she will sing to me.*

He had the waitress bring the dinner menu as White Cloud returned to their table. He did not have much experience choosing non-Chinese cuisine, but a medium-done steak was something he could not order in a Chinese restaurant. She had Red House baked clams as an appetizer, and French roast duck for her entree. He tried to encourage her to choose the more expensive items, caviar and champagne. People at other tables appeared to be doing so. He felt he was obliged.

To his surprise, she chose a bottle of Dynasty, a fairly inexpensive domestic wine from Tianjin. "Dynasty is good enough. No point choosing the imported XO whiskey or champagne," she said, pushing aside the wine list.

The steak was tender. The waitress insisted that it was genuine American beef. He did not know whether this made any difference, except in price. The clams appeared exquisitely done, golden in the candlelight, with the clam meat picked out, mixed with cheese and spices, and put back onto the shells. It was easy for her to pick up the mixture on her fork.

"So delicious," she exclaimed, putting a second helping on her fork, and offering it across the table to him to taste.

For Chen, it was still not going to be an evening of Golden Time Rolling Backward. His cell phone started ringing again. This time it was Yu, reporting the latest development in the investigation. Chen smiled apologetically to White Cloud.

"I have just received a new report from Dr. Xia. None of the fingerprints in the room matches Wan's. That throws his statement further into question. At the very least, we may assume that the drawer-searching part is a fabrication."

"Yes, that's an important point."

"I tried to discuss it with Party Secretary Li again, but he said that Wan might not have remembered everything while he was committing the murder in a moment of rage; afterward, since everybody talked about the emptied drawers, Wan spoke of them too."

"No, Party Secretary Li cannot brush it aside like that."

"Absolutely not," Detective Yu said in a voice of mounting frustration. "But when I pressed the point, Li lost his temper, shouting 'It's a case of high political significance. Someone has already confessed, but you still want to go on investigating forever. For what, Comrade Detective Yu?'"

"Li understands nothing but politics." Normally, it was Chen who had to deal with Party Secretary Li about "politically significant cases," and he understood how frustrating it must have been for Yu.

"If political considerations override everything else, what is the point of being a cop?" Yu asked. "Where are you, chief? I think I hear music in the background."

"I'm with a business associate on the translation project." That was true, Chen thought, to some extent. He felt upset, not with the question, but because of it. "Don't worry. Go on speaking, Detective Yu."

White Cloud poured more wine into his glass, in silence.

"And then, after the talk with Party Secretary Li, guess who I met just in front of the bureau? Li Dong."

"Ah, Li Dong." Li, a former member of the special case squad, had quit the police force to run a private fruit store. "How is he?"

"Li Dong has developed that single store into a business chain that supplies fruit for the Shanghai airport and the Shanghai railway station. He's used the connections he made in the police force. And he talks like another man. 'Nowadays, one month's profit from the airport alone is more than the bureau pays in a year. You are still working here, Comrade Detective Yu, but for what?'"

"That little rascal. Now that he has gotten a little money, he speaks like a rich man. How could he have changed like that? It's only a year since he quit the police force."

But that was not the answer Yu sought, Chen knew. What had

Detective Yu been working so hard for? The official answer was that people worked for the sacred cause of communism. Party newspapers might still occasionally say this, but everybody knew it was a joke.

Chief Inspector Chen worked hard too, yet at least he could say that he worked for his position, for the benefits of his position: the apartment, the bureau car, the various bonuses—including this well-paid project from Mr. Gu. That, too, came from his position; there was no question about it.

In terms of social Darwinism, what was happening was not too surprising. In any social system, the strong stay in power, whether they be the CEOs of capitalism, or the Party cadres of communism. Actually, he had first read this argument in *Martin Eden*, an American novel translated by Yang.

"The steak is getting cold," White Cloud whispered as she cut off a small piece with his knife to feed to him.

He stopped her with a wave of his hand.

He could also say that he worked for a night like this, with a little secretary at his service.

"Where are you, Yu?"

"At home."

"Let me call you back in five minutes."

The cell phone bill for this month was going to be staggering. The police bureau would pay it, but Chen did not want the accountant to raise her eyebrows at him again. Nor did he want to say more in front of White Cloud.

The antique phone in the corner still worked, he had noticed. It was a pay phone for the bar. Most of the status-conscious customers here, with their cell phones, would never consider using the pay phone.

Chen picked it up and dialed Yu's number.

"I have been doing some thinking about the case," Chen resumed. The sound quality of the phone was affected by the wear and tear of time, but it was reasonably clear. "In a *shikumen* house like that, with so much broken stuff and furniture stored here and there, it would not have been impossible for someone to hide until he had a chance to sneak out, especially if the shrimp woman was temporarily absent. But a question occurred to me: why should the murderer have wanted to hide if he was an outsider?"

"That's a good question," Yu said.

"One possibility is that he was not so much afraid of being *seen* as of being *recognized*. With that in mind, I called the Shanghai Archives Bureau. I asked them to check all Yin's relatives, with special focus on information about a possible nephew of hers. But the information they provided is the same you had obtained."

"She could have referred to someone who was a boy as a 'nephew.' He did not have to be her real nephew."

"Yes, that's possible. But would she have let someone totally unrelated stay with her, and for a week?" Chen asked. "And then there is Peiqin's point. Now that I have read a few chapters of the novel, I agree with Peiqin: Yin may well have plagiarized somebody else's work."

"Peiqin reads too much. I believe she applies Yang's high standard to the work of others," Yu said. "But I just do not see how this can possibly be related to our investigation."

"I have a feeling that there may be something in it. Coincidentally, I had a phone call earlier this evening, from a former colleague of Yang's. According to him, Yang had been writing a novel before his death. There may be a connection," Chen said slowly, feeling something eluding him in the hidden recesses of his mind as he spoke.

White Cloud had finished yet another dance and returned to their table, Chen noticed. The music had stopped.

"Had Yang written a novel?"

"We don't know for sure. He might not have finished it," Chen said, "but he could have left part of one behind. So far, we have not found a novel manuscript of his, not even a few pages. We have only that manuscript of poems translated into English."

"That's true."

"And finally, I cannot figure out why Internal Security should have withheld the information about her passport application. Was their reason related to her writing or to her trip to United States? If so, which? And why keep us in the dark?"

"We may continue to work on all these possible leads but do we have time, Chief Inspector Chen? Party Secretary Li will hold a press conference early next week. How can we be sure that we will make find the right answers in just a few days?"

"Let me stall him. It's your case, but it's also our special squad's case," Chen said. "It will be difficult, however, to hold him off for long, if we come up with nothing but some inconsistencies in Wan's statement. For Li, Wan is ideal, but the culprit does not *have* to be Wan. Anybody will serve as a murderer, so long as we give him a quick solution."

"Yes, we have to make progress. Once the real criminal is apprehended, we won't have to worry about Wan *or* about Party Secretary Li."

Finally, Chen put down the antique receiver and went back to the table.

"Sorry, White Cloud," he said, "we simply cannot have a nice quiet evening."

"An important man like you cannot expect a quiet evening, but it is nice. I appreciate your taking me out tonight."

"The pleasure is all mine. Those interruptions aside, I've enjoyed the evening—and your company." He said, turning toward the approaching waitress, "Another double scotch for the lady."

He did not know whether scotch was a proper choice after dinner, but it was what she had ordered earlier, and on the wine list it appeared to be expensive.

It was late. Some people began to leave, but others were arriving. A couple of new waitresses appeared, perhaps a later shift. Here, the night was still young.

In those myths of the thirties, Shanghai was called a nightless city—a place of red neon and white wine, of intoxicating money and glittering gold.

When he suggested to White Cloud that he take her back home in a taxi, she looked at him before responding in a low, husky voice. Perhaps she had drunk too much wine. "It's too far from here. The taxi fare will be very expensive. Can't we go back to your apartment? I'll have to come over tomorrow morning anyway. I can sleep on the sofa."

"Don't worry about the taxi money, White Cloud," he said hastily. "The police bureau will reimburse me."

It was out of the question for her to stay overnight at his place. In these new apartment complexes, the arms of the neighborhood committee might not reach as far, but people still watched. Stories traveled up and down in the elevators, if not on the staircases. Chief Inspector Chen could not afford to have such stories circulating about himself.

Nor did he consider himself a Liu Xiahui, a legendary Confucian figure who kept himself under restraint with a naked girl sitting on his lap. Chen doubted he was capable of imitating Liu Xiahui with a pretty young girl, a little secretary, asleep on the sofa in his room.

It was a long drive. She did not speak much. He wondered whether she was slightly disappointed or even displeased with his rejection of her offer. At one point, she leaned against him in the back seat, as if she was slightly drunk, then she straightened up again.

She had the taxi pull up at the street corner. "The road ahead is under repair. I can walk from here to my home. It's only two or three minutes away."

"Let me walk you home. It's late," he said before turning to the taxi driver. "Wait here for me."

Even at this late hour, there were still several young men loitering around the corner with lit cigarettes shimmering between their fingers like fireflies. One whistled shrilly as they passed by in the chilly night. They walked into a long, dark alley. Originally it must have been a passageway between two blocks of houses, but people had built illegal makeshift one-story huts or shelters along both sides. The city government did nothing, because those people had to live somewhere. So the passage was squeezed into a much narrower lane, not even wide enough for two people to walk abreast. He followed her in silence, stepping carefully between the coal stoves and piles of winter cabbages stored outside. This was too sharp a contrast to the Golden Time Rolling Backward.

It was no wonder that White Cloud studied at Fudan University while working hard at the Dynasty Club. She had to get a life that was different from her parents', by whatever means possible.

It was easy to say that poverty was no excuse for what people chose to do with their lives. It was not easy, however, for a young girl to follow the Party's principles of a simple life and hard work. In fact, few Party members, as far as he knew, still adhered to those principles.

He parted with her before a ramshackle one-story shelter and started back toward the taxi. A minute later, he turned to see her still standing by the door. The hut appeared stunted, its roof looming merely inches above her hair. In the dark night, he was surprised to make out a small pot of flowers blossoming on top of the roof tiles, placed there as a decoration.

As the taxi started winding out of the slum area, he had a weird feeling, as if the city had suddenly turned into two disparate halves. The first city was made up of old *shikumen* houses, narrow lanes, and slum alleys like the one he was leaving, in which people still had a hard time making ends meet. The second city was composed of trendy places like the bars on Henshan Road, the new high-end apartment complex in Hongqiao, and the would-be New World.

When Gu had first approached him about his ambitious business project, Chen had almost considered the New World and its like as myths, but he was wrong. A myth would not survive if it was not rooted in present realities.

There was also an untold part of that myth, of course: the suffering of the people shut out of it; that was the part familiar to Chief Inspector Chen from his elementary-school textbooks. At that time, all the glitter and glory were represented as decadent, evil, sustained at the cost of the working class. The emphasis was then on what was in back of the glamour, an emphasis that had justified the Communist Revolution.

It had been true to some extent. What had changed was the emphasis. Now it was on the facade, the glitter and glory, an emphasis that justified the reversal of the Communist Revolution, although the Party authorities would have never acknowledged this.

Chen was momentarily confused. History in textbooks was like colored balls in a juggler's hands.

If truth could not be found in textbooks, then where else could one look?

But what could he do? He was just a cop. He had once beleaguered himself with those questions. He had long since given that up.

Even as a cop, Chief Inspector Chen wondered, when he started thinking about his conversation with Zhuang earlier in the evening, whether he had done a decent job.

黑

Chapter 18

Yu awoke early on Saturday morning. He decided not to get up immediately. This was a decision reached from necessity. In his family's small room, if one got out of bed, the others had to follow.

Qinqin had stayed up late last night studying. Nowadays, middle-school students worked like crazy, and Peiqin pushed him like crazy too, insisting that Qinqin had to enter a first-class college at all costs. "He must never end up like us."

She might not have meant anything by it, but this statement did not sound pleasant to Yu, especially as he was unable to do anything to assist Qinqin. Peiqin was the one responsible for helping with their son's homework; it had already proven too much for Yu.

Qinqin was still sound asleep on the fold-out sofa, his feet hanging over the edge. He had grown into a lean, tall boy. The sofa bed was no longer long enough for him.

Normally, Peiqin would have been up and about by this time, but it was a weekend. She had stayed up late with Qinqin, going over math problems with him. In the morning light, her face looked pale, tired.

Lying awake, Detective Yu could not help becoming increasingly upset by the latest developments in the Yin investigation. He was aware of the pressure being brought to bear on the bureau, pressure that was especially maddening to Party Secretary Li. The news of Yin's tragic death had caused wild speculation not only in China, but overseas as well. The case had been reported in several foreign newspapers, which added fuel to the fire back in Shanghai. In addition, Yin's novel had now been reprinted by underground publishers, and it was selling like hotcakes in private bookstores. Fei Weijin, the Propaganda Minister of Shanghai, was so concerned that he had visited the Shanghai Police Bureau in person to declare that the longer the case remained unsolved, the greater would be the damage to the new image of China.

As a result, Party Secretary Li was anxious for the immediate conviction of Wan for murder in spite of Yu's arguments. All Yu's efforts to persuade Li that they had to look further were like eggs thrown against a concrete wall.

Yu tried to recall how Chen had worked his way through the jungle of bureau politics, though he was not too pleased with Chen either. Last night, he was sure he had heard a girl's whisper and some music in the background of their phone conversation. What Chen had been up to was none of his business. Perhaps the chief inspector could afford to enjoy himself, with his position, with his "lucrative project," with his promising career, and with a free "little secretary" too. Still, Yu felt uncomfortable at the thought.

At the same time, he was amazed by Chen's suggestions. He had no idea how, in the midst of working on a rush translation, Chen had managed to come up with those theories. Still, they were no more than hypotheses, with nothing substantial to support them. Yu himself had made tentative forays in these directions without result.

Peiqin stirred beside him—still dreaming, perhaps.

Suddenly he felt sorry for himself, but more so for Peiqin and Qinqin. All these years, they had been together, squeezed into this tiny *shikumen* room, in this shabby lane. Working on one homicide case after another, he was more often than not away even on weekends, and he earned so little. Why was he doing it?

Perhaps it was time for him to rethink his future career, as Peiqin had suggested.

When Yu had first entered the police force, his objective was a clear-cut one: to do better than his father, Old Hunter, who, though a capable policeman, never rose higher than sergeant in rank. It was from him that Yu had inherited the job in the Shanghai Police Bureau. In terms of rank, Yu had already achieved his objective. As a detective, he was one notch higher, but he did not feel nearly as good as Old Hunter used to feel—in the years of the proletarian dictatorship. In those years, people were not that different from one another, each had the same paycheck, the same housing, and believed in the same Party doctrine of "hard work and a simple life." A cop was just one of the people, and he might take extra pride in being the tool of the proletarian dictatorship.

But to be a policeman nowadays was not that rewarding. In an increasingly materialistic society, a cop was nobody. Take Chief Inspector Chen, for example. Though a much more successful cop, Chen still had to take a vacation to earn some extra money for himself.

And then there were stories about corrupt cops, true stories, as Yu knew. What was the point being a cop at all?

As he got out of bed, he announced a decision, which was a surprise even to himself.

"Let's go out to Old Half Place for breakfast."

"Why?" Qinqin asked, rubbing his eyes.

"Our family deserves to enjoy a good weekend."

"It's a great idea. I've heard of the restaurant," Peiqin agreed sleepily, looking startled, for it was not like Yu to take the family out for breakfast in the midst of an investigation.

"So early, for breakfast?" Qinqin said, getting up reluctantly from the creaking sofa.

"Old Half Place is well-known for noodles from the first pot of the morning," Yu said. "I've read about it in a restaurant guide." He did not want to explain how he had actually learned about the restaurant.

In half an hour, the three of them arrived at Old Half Place, which was located on Fuzhou Road. Sure enough, many customers were already sitting there waiting, most of them elderly people who held bamboo chopsticks in their hands before the noodles even appeared on the tables.

Above the front counter, the variety of noodles listed on the blackboard menu was impressive. Yu hardly had time to choose. People standing behind them were growing impatient. They must be regular customers, familiar with their favorite noodles, capable of telling the round-faced cashier their choices without having to consult the menu.

Yu ordered noodles with pickled green cabbage and winter bamboo shoots, plus a small dish of xiao pork—a must at this restaurant, according to Mr. Ren. Peiqin had noodles with fried rice paddy eels and shrimp, and xiao pork too. Qinqin chose noodles with a smoked carp head, in addition to a Coca-Cola.

The service was far less impressive. The oil-and-soup-smeared round tables were large enough for ten or twelve people, so the Yu's could not have a table for themselves. The first floor of the restaurant was large, but there were only two middle-aged waitresses who bustled around, carrying plates and bowls overlapped along their outstretched arms. They were unable to clean up the tables in a timely way, especially since other customers were still eating. That might be one of the reasons the restaurant was able to keep prices low.

Two other noodle-eaters shared their table. One looked as thin as a bamboo stick. The other appeared as round as a winter melon. They seemed to know each other well.

"Eat and drink while you can. Life is short." The thin one raised his teacup, took a sip, and buried a piece of chicken deep under his noodles.

"This bowl of plain noodles has the same delicious soup," the round one said, smacking his lips. "Besides, I need to keep to my diet."

"Come on." The thin one sounded sarcastic. "It's a miracle that you look so prosperous and can come here every day—on your waiting-for-retirement pay."

Plain noodles must be the cheapest in the restaurant, but for someone in the waiting-for-retirement program, with a monthly paycheck of around 200 Yuan, a bowl of plain noodles for 3 Yuan might be all he could afford.

From a bamboo container, Peiqin picked out chopsticks which were still wet, dried them with her handkerchief, and gave a pair to each member of the family. Qinqin took the old-fashioned black pepper bottle and studied it like a math problem. As they waited for their orders, Yu noticed some less patient customers going to the kitchen counter and bringing back their orders with their own hands.

Finally, their noodles arrived. Following Mr. Ren's advice, Yu immersed slices of xiao pork in the soup, waited for a minute or two until the warmed pork grew nearly transparent, and then let it melt on his tongue. The noodles' texture was indescribable, resilient but not too hard, seasoned by the tasty soup.

To impress Qinqin, Yu tried to analyze the special ingredients of the noodle soup, but he ended up remembering only that some tiny nameless fish were boiled in a cloth bag in its preparation. Qinqin appeared to be quite interested.

Yu was pondering whether to order a portion of xiao pork for his son when an old man took a seat at a table next to them. The newcomer wore a long purple down-padded jacket and a cotton-padded hat with two long earflaps, which nearly masked his face. He kept rubbing his hands which seemed to be stiff from the cold morning air outside. He also ordered a bowl of plain noodles, over which he breathed a long sigh with an air of utter satisfaction.

"Look," Qinqin whispered to Yu. "He took pork out of his pocket."

It was true. The old man actually produced plastic-wrapped slices of pork from his jacket pocket, put them into the soup, and waited for the celebrated soaking effect.

"Is that pork really so special?" Qinqin asked in amusement.

Yu did not know how to answer. For regular customers here, he supposed, it could be a ritual to place a piece of xiao pork on top of the noodles. But he did not know what kind of pork the old fellow had brought with him. Perhaps it was ham, processed in a very special way.

But there was another mystery: xiao pork was prepared only at

Old Half Place. What the old man brought must have been home-cooked pork. If so, why had he bothered?

Then, when he took off his hat and turned toward them, Yu recognized the old customer to be none other than Mr. Ren.

"Ah, Mr. Ren!"

"Comrade Detective Yu, I'm so glad to see you here in Old Half Place!" Mr. Ren said with a genial smile. "You have taken my advice, haven't you?"

"Yes, I have brought my wife and son as well. Peiqin and Qinqin."

"Great. A wonderful family dining out together. That's the spirit," Mr. Ren said with an energetic gesture. "Please go ahead and enjoy your noodles or they will get cold."

Turning back, Yu whispered in Peiqin's ear, "He is someone I met at Yin's building."

"I should have known better," she whispered back. "Imagine you having the leisure to take us out for breakfast in the midst of your investigation."

"No, our breakfast has nothing to do with the case."

But that was not exactly true. Yu might have intended, subconsciously, to check the accuracy of Mr. Ren's statement.

"He told me a lot about Old Half Place when I interviewed him. Does that count as something related to the case?"

"He's one of the suspects on your list, I remember," she said with a smile of subtle sarcasm. "And are you satisfied now?"

"Well, he's not on my list any longer, but I'm satisfied with breakfast."

That was true. The breakfast, at a total of sixteen Yuan for the three of them, was inexpensive yet delightful. It was also good for the whole family to go out occasionally, like this.

Wiping his mouth with the back of his hand, Mr. Ren turned around to their table. His noodles were finished. "You may be surprised that I took some pork out of my pocket. That's a trick only an old gourmet knows how to play." He grinned at Qinqin.

"Yes, please tell me why you did that," Qinqin said.

"After lunchtime, the restaurant sells xiao pork by the kilo. Fifty Yuan for one kilo. It sounds expensive, but it is not really. If you slice the pork at home, one kilo will make about seventy-five or eighty portions. How much do you pay for a side dish here? Two Yuan. So I buy half a kilo, put it in the refrigerator—you must have a refrigerator at home—and take out a few slices before I come here."

"You surely don't have to be so hard on yourself, Mr. Ren, with all—" Yu did not say *all your compensation money.*

"You don't have to worry about me, Detective Yu. An old gourmet will do anything but let his stomach down. I'm too old to care for what's called—oh, conspicuous consumption. The xiao pork I bring with me tastes the same in my mouth. Old Half Place is a good place. I hope I'll see you here again."

"We will certainly come back," Yu said. "When the investigation is over, you will have to tell me more about your gourmet tricks."

"Come to my restaurant some day, Mr. Ren," Peiqin said. "Ours is not well-known—it is called Four Seas—but we have some quite good specialties, and they are inexpensive too."

"Four Seas? I think I've heard of it. I will be there. You may count on that. Thank you, Peiqin."

They rose from their tables, ready to leave.

Near the entrance, Qinqin stopped to look over the counter into a window, behind which two white-clad, white-capped chefs were slicing the chunks of xiao pork deftly on huge stumps. There were rows of chickens, dripping oil, hung on the shining steel hooks overhead.

"It's like in Zhaungzi," Qinqin said.

"Really!" Yu said vaguely, without catching the reference. Perhaps Peiqin had.

Then he saw Mr. Ren, who had walked out ahead of them, walking back toward the restaurant.

"Did you forget something, Mr. Ren?"

"No—that is, I forgot to *tell* you something."

"What's that?"

"Maybe it is nothing, but I'd better tell you about it, I think," Mr. Ren said. "On the morning of February seventh, when I went out of the *shikumen* building, I saw somebody leaving in front of me."

"Who?"

"Wan."

"Really! Do you remember the time?"

"Well, as I have told you, it was around five forty-five."

"Are you sure it was Wan, and that it was that morning?"

"I'm pretty sure. We may not be close as neighbors, but we have lived in the same building for many years."

"Did you talk to him?"

"No, I did not. As a rule, I do not talk much to my neighbors—after so many years of being a black capitalist."

"Neither did my father. He was a black capitalist too, when he was alive," Peiqin interjected. "He was in the import–export line of business."

"Yes, it's understandable only to those who have lived through the years of humiliation. I used to be so black, politically black, and Wan used to be so politically red," Ren said, his lips hardening into a bitter smile. "Of course it's possible that Wan, too, came back that morning—earlier than usual—to commit the murder, but isn't that too far-fetched?"

"You are absolutely right, Mr. Ren. That is a very important point. In his statement, Wan did not mention going out earlier that morning."

"Now there's another thing. I've heard people talking about a train ticket found in Wan's room as the piece of evidence that pinned the crime on him, but I happen to know something else about it."

"What is it, Mr. Ren?"

"Another coincidence," Mr. Ren said. "As a frugal gourmet, I eat around, not just at Old Half Place. Another of my favorite restaurants is close to the Shanghai railway station. Western Hill is known for its mini soup buns. The soup inside the bun is so juicy and delicious.

"One morning half a year ago, I happened to see Wan standing in a long line in front of the railway ticket window. I did not pay too much attention then. He might have been buying a train ticket for a relative, if not for himself.

"Then one morning several weeks ago, I saw Wan standing in a long line there again."

"That's strange," Yu said. "Wan seems to have lived by himself. I have not heard anything about his making frequent trips out of Shanghai."

"It's none of my business. But that morning, Western Hill was so packed with customers that I had to wait for more than an hour and half before a bamboo steamer of mini soup buns appeared on my table. On my way out, I caught sight of Wan again. This time, he was not standing in line; he was selling tickets to some provincials in the railway station square. So Wan earned a little money by selling tickets to those unable to stand for hours in line."

"That's the very information I need. Instead of going out for tai chi practice, Wan goes out early every morning to buy and sell train tickets. Now I see."

"I have never talked to anybody about this. Wan is a man who cannot afford to lose face. It's terribly humiliating for an ex-Mao Zedong Thought Propaganda Worker Team Member to end up being a train ticket scalper. So he told the neighbors he practiced tai chi in the morning.

"A Propaganda Member could be as relentless as a Red Guard during those years, but I have no personal grudge against them. No one should be wronged, Wan or anybody else, just to conclude a murder investigation."

"Thank you so much, Mr. Ren. This is a real breakthrough."

Yu was now convinced that Wan was not the murderer. But this did not mean that he could throw out Wan's confession. He would have to have another discussion with Party Secretary Li.

It had turned out to be a more interesting breakfast than Detective Yu had expected.

Chapter 19

Chief Inspector Chen's morning was again punctuated by phone calls.

The first was from Detective Yu. Yu recounted for Chen the "breakfast discovery" he'd made earlier at Old Half Place.

"The case against Wan has too many holes," Yu said. "I cannot conclude my investigation yet."

"You don't have to." Chen added, "We don't have to."

"But Party Secretary Li is in a great hurry to do so."

"Don't worry, I'll call him."

"What will you say?"

"Well, isn't Comrade Wan himself a political symbol? A Mao Zedong Thought Propaganda Member during the Cultural Revolution, and a murderer in the nineties? Party Secretary Li will not like it."

"So you are piercing his shield with his own lance, so to speak."

"Exactly," Chen said, catching the note of excitement in Yu's voice. This was a card he knew how to play. "Hoisting him with his own petard. I'll discuss this with Party Secretary Li."

Chen brewed himself a pot of tea. Before he finished the first cup, as he was chewing a tender green tea leaf and preparing his speech to Party Secretary Li, the phone rang again.

The caller was a nurse at Renji Hospital. His mother needed to be hospitalized for a test in connection with her stomach trouble. According to the nurse, the doctor was very concerned.

This news came at an untimely juncture. Apart from the new development in the investigation, he was also putting on a final spurt to complete the translation. He had made a promise to Gu. Time mattered for the New World, he knew. For a moment he wished he had not accepted the project which interfered with his responsibilities as a cop, and now as a son.

Still, there was also some benefit to working on the translation. The hospital demanded a deposit before a patient would be admitted. The advance would come in handy now, as it was more than enough to cover the deposit.

Of course, he could have made a couple of phone calls to his "connections." His mother might have been admitted then without the deposit. He chose not to do so; now at least he had a choice.

This was another aspect of China's economic reform that he did not like. What about those who could not pay the deposit and had no connections? There should be a touch of humanity in the management of a hospital.

Everyone looked for the money in the nineties. *Xiang Qian Kan, Look to the future,* the revolutionary political slogan, was cruelly parodied, as *qian* could mean money as well as the future. In the market economy, hospitals made no exception. Doctors and nurses were human too. Their own incomes depended upon the hospital's profit.

While he was still talking with the nurse on the phone, White Cloud came into the room.

"My mother has to be admitted to a hospital for a test as an inpatient," he said as he put down the receiver.

"Hospitals make a point of doing tests now. The test may not even be necessary, but the hospital will collect a large fee for it. They like to make money," White Cloud said. "Don't worry too much, Chief Inspector Chen."

"That may be true. Thank you," he replied.

He, too, wondered why this test required that his mother be hospitalized. She had been complaining about her stomach trouble for years. No one had said it was so serious.

"Let me go to the hospital for you this morning to deliver the admission money, to make any necessary arrangements, and to keep your mother company. It's really up to me—as your little secretary. Call me any time if you have questions. You have my cell phone number."

What would his mother think? He had never told her anything about having a little secretary who worked for him at home. At this moment, however, he could not afford to hesitate.

"Fine. Tell her that I will come over in the afternoon or in the evening. Thank you so much, White Cloud."

"Don't mention it," she said as she put a brown paper bag into the refrigerator. "Oh, here is roast beef with steamed buns. Last night you did not even have time to finish the steak. You like beef, I guess. For lunch, put them in the microwave."

Again, he was lucky to have her help.

Then it was Party Secretary Li's turn to call.

"Detective Yu said that you wanted to talk to me about something. What's it about, Comrade Chief Inspector Chen?"

"Oh, yes. Detective Yu discussed the latest development in the investigation with me. So I would like to talk to you."

"Go ahead."

"Since our last talk, I have been giving a lot of thought to the case. As you have said, we should be aware of the political repercussions of the case. Just as you explained, the higher authorities have every reason to want us to solve the case without any political complications. So in my understanding, it is necessary for us to depoliticize the case."

Chen went on after a meaningful pause. "Now if we conclude in a hurry—with Wan as the murderer—this might be against the interests of the Party—"

"What do you mean, Chief Inspector Chen?"

"I mean, if Wan proves to be the real murderer beyond any reasonable doubt, we will punish him. No question about it. But there are still holes in his confession, as Detective Yu pointed out, so why not wait for a couple of more days?"

"I'm still confused. Please explain."

"Once the press conference is held, people will come to know who and what Wan is. He is an ex-Mao Zedong Thought Propaganda Worker Team Member, who was once very politically red, but now what? Unfortunately, Wan is not alone. Many retired workers are having a hard time. Wan may well be seen as an example of an old worker going downhill, going to ruin. If Wan was capable of committing a murder in his desperation, then so could a lot of other people in a similar position. Wan might be seen as highly symbolic."

"You have a good point, Comrade Chief Inspector Chen," Li

said after a long pause, "but the city government is putting a lot of pressure on the police bureau."

"That's what we have to take into consideration," Chen said equivocally. "If some of the details were seized upon by a reporter, and published, and twisted—think about it—'the antagonism between an ex-Mao Zedong Thought Propaganda Worker Team Member and a dissident writer who denounced the Cultural Revolution.' Such political associations could be disastrous."

"Then we have to apply strict information control."

"I doubt if it will work. Following your suggestion, I went to the *shikumen* house last week. There're so many people there, all mixed together, that news and rumors spread as if they had wings. And reporters could go there too. Today, some of the newspapers are no longer what they used to be—they're not so loyal to the Party authorities any more. To increase their newspaper's circulation, they need sensational news."

Li said, after a slight hesitation, "If Detective Yu wants to take a couple of more days for his investigation, I think it should be okay. But it is important for people to know that the government is not involved in Yin's death. And for them to learn this as soon as possible."

"I have one question, Party Secretary Li."

"Yes, Chief Inspector Chen."

"It's about Internal Security. There's something that puzzles me. It's not their case. No one has told us about any involvement on their part. Yet they had searched Yin's room even before Detective Yu first reached the building. And then they withheld information about Yin's application for her passport renewal. Why, Party Secretary Li?"

"Well, Yin was a dissident writer. It is understandable that

Internal Security would be interested in the case. They are not responsible to us, as we know."

"But if it was such a politically sensitive case, they should have shared information with us."

"If they had found something of substance, I believe they would have informed you," Li said. "Have you discovered anything that might interest Internal Security?"

"No," Chen said. Of course, he would have denied it even if he had found something. "That's why I asked you the question."

"The ministry in Beijing has called us, too. Minister Huang has a high opinion of you, you know. Since you have given a lot of thought to the case, what about your taking it over?"

"No, Party Secretary Li. My mother is in the hospital. I've just gotten a phone call about it."

"I'm very sorry to hear that. Is there anything the bureau can do for you? You are still on your vacation. If necessary, you can take a few more days. Or we can send someone to the hospital to help. Have you any particular request?"

"No, not at the moment. But thank you very much. And I will assist Detective Yu in whatever way I possibly can. I give you my word, Party Secretary Li."

For a while after this conversation, Chen found it hard to concentrate on the translation, but he finally managed. Not too long afterward, however, White Cloud called. Everything at the hospital had been taken care of, and his mother was not in any real danger. The doctor explained that they wanted to admit her to the hospital for the test because of her age. That seemed reassuring. So Chen went on revising the translation.

Before lunch time, he dialed Yu's home number, but it was Peiqin who answered the phone. It was just as well; he had questions for her too. After their last talk, he had obtained a copy of *Death of a Chinese Professor*, and tried to read as much as possible in the little time available. Peiqin had been right: the novel was uneven, with striking contrasts in style and content, so much so that it was difficult not to notice them.

"I think you are right," he said. "Yin may have plagiarized. Her source was probably not newspapers or bestsellers. Some parts of the novel are of high literary quality."

Peiqin said, "Some parts are far better written than others. But I cannot see the connection between her novel and the murder."

"Neither can I. If somebody—either the writer of the work she copied, or a reader—had discovered this, he could have contacted her or the media. In a similar case, I remember, the plaintiff sued for monetary compensation. But nothing could have been gained from killing her," Chen said. "Have you discovered anything else, Peiqin?"

"Nothing new," she said, "except for one small point. As Yu must have told you, I have read a number of translations—I was a bookworm in my high school years. In a close reading, books translated into Chinese often read quite differently from those originally written in Chinese. Linguistically, I mean."

"That's a very interesting point. Can you try to be a bit more specific, Peiqin?"

"There are certain ways of putting a phrase or a sentence in one language that are changed in another. Sometimes even a word can be different. For instance, Chinese writers seldom if ever use the pronoun 'it,' and experienced translators like Yang are aware of this. But not so with third- or fourth-rate translators. Exotic expressions keep popping up in their texts. Perhaps there is nothing wrong with the meaning, but Chinese sentences should not read that way."

"You are right. Some paragraphs do not read smoothly; that's my impression too. But I have not done as close a reading as you."

"There's another example. Ten years ago, the word 'privacy' hardly existed in Chinese. If used at all, it was with a negative connotation—indecent or evil, incapable of being open and aboveboard. But in *Death of a Chinese Professor,* Yin used the word in a positive sense, like some fashionable young people use it today."

"Your English is really good, Peiqin!" he said. "Even today, some people would still use the word cautiously, because of its lingering negative connotation."

"No, don't laugh at me, Chief Inspector Chen. I have to help Qinqin with his English homework, and he asked me how to translate 'privacy' into Chinese just a couple of weeks ago."

"You are perceptive, Peiqin. I have done translations, but I have paid little attention to such linguistic complexities."

"Oh, forgive me. This is really like an apprentice giving a lesson to Master Ban. I know you have done a lot of translations. But some paragraphs in the *Death of a Chinese Professor* read like a literal translation."

"So you are suggesting that Yin might have plagiarized an English text and translated it herself?"

"It's possible, isn't it?"

It was possible. A number of books about the Cultural Revolution had been written in English. As a college English teacher, Yin could have read some of them. But, then, *Death of a Chinese Professor* had subsequently been translated into English too. Yin would surely have considered the possibility of discovery.

Perhaps Peiqin was like him, too focused on what she could do to help in the investigation. The only help she could provide was through her reading; as a result, she was susceptible to exaggerating some possibilities. Still, she did all this for her husband, who had been left to deal with a difficult case all by himself.

Then Chen spoke on the spur of the moment. "Yu told me about your family breakfast at Old Half Place this morning. That's great. He deserves a break."

"Yes, he does. He's been under a lot of pressure of late. Due to a lot of things."

"I understand. Detective Yu and I are in the same boat. I depend on him, and of course I will do whatever I can for him. He is a great cop. I consider myself fortunate to be his partner."

"Thank you. It's kind of you to say so, Chief Inspector Chen."

Afterward, he regretted having made such patronizing statements, which might have sounded like the empty compliments Party Secretary Li usually paid. It was perhaps little wonder that he was in line to become Party Secretary Chen. What had he really meant, he wondered. And what would Peiqin think?

He brewed himself another pot of coffee before he resumed reading his own translation.

He put the roast beef and steamed buns into the microwave. It was a clever combination. The roast beef was prepared in a Western way, for in traditional Chinese cuisine there was only soy-sauce-stewed beef. The mixing of the opposites, like yin and yang—he stopped himself with the first bite. The digital timer on the microwave read 3:00 in green lights and there was a sharp beep. There was some strange correspondence between this sound and his new thought.

Was it possible that those parts Yin had plagiarized came from an unpublished manuscript, and the original author was in no position to complain?

He had not really considered this possibility because he was aware that Yin had been a nobody until the publication of *Death of a Chinese Professor*. No one would have given her a manuscript to read—except Yang. But the missing English manuscript that Zhuang had mentioned might have been Yang's version of a Chinese *Doctor Zhivago*.

Of course, Yin would never have told anyone if Yang had left the manuscript to her, for it would have brought her no end of trouble. If the Party authorities had gotten wind of it, they would have demanded the manuscript. They would never have left anything potentially damaging to the glorious image of socialist China in such hands. Especially a manuscript written in English, meant for the market abroad. It might also have exposed her to unpleasantness if word got out about the money she might receive in the event of its publication. That, he could understand from personal experience. So far he had hardly talked to anybody about his current translation project—except to Yu. But even to Yu he had not mentioned the exact amount he was being paid. What would others have thought?

Yang could not have sued—or murdered—Yin, of course.

But who else could have known about the existence of such a manuscript? Yin had long since cut off all ties with her relatives. As for her friends and colleagues, Yin must have been too much of a dissident to ever trust anyone with something like that.

What about someone on Yang's side? He had started the book prior to the Cultural Revolution. In the early sixties, perhaps. Though he would not have talked to people about it, it was possible that one of his relatives might have visited him and stumbled upon his writing, the way Zhuang had discovered it in the dorm.

The other possibility, of course, was Internal Security. They might have somehow learned of the existence of the manuscript, and decided to take matters into their own hands. It was possible—especially if Yin had started contacting people abroad. That would fit with their decision to withhold information about her passport renewal application. That was also why they would have searched her room before Yu's arrival: Yu was not supposed to look in that direction. Even Party Secretary Li's emphasis that it was *not* a political case fit this hypothesis.

He suddenly realized that he had almost finished the roast beef and steamed buns without having tasted them. The beef, warmed in the microwave, still juicy and tender, put between the two sides of a bun, like a Chinese sandwich, was really not bad.

White Cloud was good—not just because of this culinary invention that combined oriental and occidental cuisine.

Before he discussed these ideas with Yu, however, Chen decided to take some action on his own.

First he got in touch with Comrade Ding, an officer in charge of tapping the phones of people designated for "inside control." Chen could have done so earlier, but with Party Secretary Li and Internal Security prowling in the background, he did not want to cause any alarm. Also, Ding was one of his connections it would be better not to use too frequently.

Ding turned out to be more cooperative than he had expected. In about forty-five minutes, Ding called back. Yin's telephone line in the college had been tapped for some time. According to the records, there had been nothing unusual in her conversations over the last few months, but that did not prove anything. Yin would not have made any important phone calls from the office she shared with her colleagues. As for the public phone booth in Treasure Garden Lane, she almost never used it. She could have been either so lonely, or so cautious, that she made no phone calls or else made them away from the lane. Chen was more inclined toward the latter idea. There was no controlling pay phones.

Ding promised that he would check all the records with respect to Yin for the last several years. It would take time. Chen understood.

Then he made another call to the Shanghai Archives Bureau, asking for a detailed list of Yang's relatives.

Chapter 20

There was not a lot that Detective Yu could possibly do. Party Secretary Li had agreed that Yu might continue his investigation a little longer, but Li also emphasized that the investigation could not drag on forever.

However unreliable his confession might be, Wan had come forward of his own free will. There was always a possibility that Wan had committed the murder on the spur of the moment. Whether or not he had a specific deadline, Yu would have no more than a few more days. He doubted this additional time would make any real difference. If nothing happened soon, the case would conclude with Wan being charged with murder.

Yu did not know which way to turn now.

He discussed the investigation with Peiqin over breakfast. It was a much simpler one, with rice reboiled in water plus fermented tofu and a thousand-year egg. Peiqin, too, was disappointed; after having put in hours reading and doing research, all her efforts seemed to have come to nothing.

"According to the proverb, *Miraculous discoveries are often made without effort*," she said, slicing a tender thousand-year egg immersed in soy sauce. "But it takes time and luck."

"That's true with police work," he said. "An investigation can take weeks or months. It does not conclude when a Party boss sets a deadline."

"Isn't there anything new at all?"

"Well, I had a free meal with Lei. He insisted on it—because of Yin. Really, this is something new for me, being treated by a businessman, just like Chief Inspector Chen," he said. "Yin did not get along with most of her neighbors, but she could be helpful to some."

"It's hard to judge people. She might have lived too much in the past—together with Yang—to get along with her neighbors," she said, "or to move out of the shadow of the Cultural Revolution."

"What a life! I, too, have read a few pages of her novel. She said her life started with Yang in the cadre school, but how long were they really together? As lovers, less than a year. Now she may have died because of him."

"Still, she got fame and money because of him," Peiqin said. "And the book, too, of course."

Perhaps this was meant to comfort him, but Yu did not see how. "You may be a bit too hard on her," he said. "After all, it was her book; she earned her royalties."

"I have nothing against her. But it's a fact that the novel sold so well because of him, because of her relationship with him." She added, "What about his poetry collection, the one she edited, then?"

"Poetry earns no money, as Chief Inspector Chen always says."

"But Yang's collection sold out." She added, "It was a large printing. In those years, a lot of people read poetry. I bought a copy too."

Afterward, at the neighborhood committee office, Yu mentioned Peiqin's point in a phone conversation with Chief Inspector Chen.

"Things have changed a lot," Chen said. "Several years ago, the publisher would have paid just a one-time fee of about fifteen Yuan per thousand characters, or ten lines of poetry. So all in all, she would not have received much money."

"That's what I guessed."

"But if her contract provided that she would earn royalties based on sales, it might be another story. Have you talked to the editor about it?"

"No. Why?"

"Well, he may tell you the amount she received," Chen said thoughtfully. "I don't know. Maybe you should give him a call."

A large sum could have been a motive for murder, but it seemed to Yu that since Chen was a passionate writer and Peiqin a passionate reader, they might be overemphasizing the literary aspects of the investigation. Still, Yu made a phone call to Wei, the editor of *Death of a Chinese Professor* at Shanghai Literature Publishing House.

"About Yin again?" Wei was not very patient on the phone.

"Sorry, we have to ask you some more questions," Yu said.

He could understand Wei's impatience. Wei had gotten into trouble because of *Death of a Chinese Professor*. If anything politically incorrect was published, not only the author, but the editor too, was held responsible. Should the author be well-known, he would sometimes get away with little punishment, while the editor became the one to shoulder the "black pot." Wei had been criticized for having not foreseen the political repercussions of *Death of a Chinese Professor.*

"I have told you everything I know about Yin, Comrade Detective Yu. What a trouble-maker—even after her death."

"Well, last time, we talked about Yin's novel, *Death of a Chinese Professor*. But Yang also had a book published by your house. A poetry collection."

"That's right, but I am not the poetry editor. Jia Zijian edited the poetry collection. It came out sometime before the novel."

"Has Jia talked to you about it?"

"We did not discuss it. A poetry book, you know, does not find too many readers, or make much money. Yin was involved with the book, of course. She was some character: she would not have let a single drop of fertilizer fall into anyone else's field."

"Can I talk to Jia?"

"He's not in the office this morning. Call back in the afternoon."

This did not appear to lead anywhere. Wei, too, was sure that the poetry collection had not earned much money. For a while after their conversation, however, Yu could not shake off an uneasy feeling, as if he had missed something.

Old Liang did not appear in the office in the morning. It was a silent protest, perhaps. For him, the case was finished when Wan confessed and any further investigational effort was an attack on Liang's judgment.

Because Yu had been turning the conversation with Wei over in his mind, he called Peiqin.

"Wei only guesses," Peiqin said, not ready to acknowledge that the sum involved would be so small. "You need to talk to the poetry editor."

"I don't know why Wei reacted so negatively against a dead woman," he said.

"It beats me too. Why would he have a grudge against her?" Peiqin added abruptly, "He said she would not spare even a drop of fertilizer for anyone else. Who could he have meant?"

"Somebody else who wanted to edit the collection?"

"But no one could have competed with her. She alone had possession of many of Yang's original poems."

The proverb Wei had quoted was commonly used to describe a greedy person, or a person in a given business transaction who was overreaching. "I'll call you later." It was Detective Yu's turn to be abrupt. He put down the phone and then immediately picked it up again to dial the editor.

"Comrade Wei, excuse me for one more question," he said. "In our earlier talk, you used a proverb—not letting a single drop of fertilizer fall on another's field. What did you mean?"

"That's something Jia said—in connection with a relative of Yang's, I remember." Wei hardly tried to conceal the impatience in his voice. "So what?"

"Thank you so much, Comrade Wei. This may be very important for our work. I really appreciate your help."

"Well, I don't know much about it. You'd better talk to Jia. He will be back soon." Wei added, "Oh, one more thing. About a year ago, somebody called to inquire about the publication date of the poetry collection's second edition. The call was transferred to me, and I did not have any information for him. He might have been a reader interested in the poetry, but I somehow got the feeling that he called for some other reason."

Yu decided to visit the publishing house.

The Shanghai Literature Publishing House was located on Shaoxing Road. It had been a large private residence in the thirties. There was a new bookstore café on the first floor. Detective Yu called Jia and waited for him there.

Jia, a man in his late forties, walked into the café in big strides. As Yu broached his topic, Jia eyed him in surprise.

"The second edition has not come out, has it?"

"What do you mean?" Yu said, reminded of the conversation with Wei.

"Then why do you ask, Comrade Detective Yu?"

Yu's puzzlement was mirrored on Jia's face. He apparently knew nothing about the murder investigation.

"I don't know anything about the first edition or the second edition, Comrade Jia. Can you tell me what you know, from the beginning?"

"Well, it was several years ago," Jia said slowly. "Yin asked me to arrange a meeting here at the publishing house to explain her contract for Yang's poetry collection to Yang's grandnephew."

"Yang's grandnephew?"

"Yes, a boy named Bao, from Jiangxi Province."

"Hold on here—a boy, from Jiangxi Province—" Yu interrupted Jia. It fit the description given by the shrimp woman. The time was right, too. It made sense for Yin to have referred to him as her nephew. In view of the difference in their ages, it would have been too much to call him her grandnephew. "Yes, please go on, Comrade Jia."

"His mother is an ex-educated youth, who married a local farmer and settled in Jiangxi. Bao must have come here to claim the money as the legitimate heir to Yang. After all, Yin had not been married to Yang."

"That's true. How did the meeting go?"

"It was not a pleasant one. He did not understand why she got such a large share of the money—too large a portion, to his way of thinking."

"I do not really understand. Can you tell me a little more?"

"When we publish the work of a dead author, we sometimes engage a special editor. Such an editor would collect the author's various publications, compare different versions, annotate some of the text, and write an introduction if necessary. As special editor for Yang's poetry, Yin did a lot of work, searching out poems from old magazines, and retrieving quite a few from his notebooks or scrap paper. It was no exaggeration to say that the collection would not have been published without her hard work. For such a job, we normally pay about fifty percent of the going rate."

"Fifty percent of what you normally pay an author?"

"Yes. That is, of course, when the author is no longer around and no one else makes claim to the royalties. At that time, it was fifteen Yuan for ten lines, I remember, regardless of the print run. If there's anything not conventional in our agreement with Yin, it was the additional twenty percent she claimed as a copying fee. We agreed, since it was still less than what we would have paid Yang. The sudden appearance of the grandnephew rattled us. There's no precedent for a relative like him claiming anything, especially so long after publication. Yin maintained that what she earned was rightfully hers. In a way, she was right. So she refused to pay Bao.

"I talked to my boss. Not that much money was involved. We did not want to cause a scandal. So we paid Bao an amount equivalent to the remaining thirty percent."

"In other words, you ended up paying the normal rate—100%—for the book."

"That's correct."

"Did Bao accept the arrangement?"

"He did, but in a grudging way."

"So he protested?"

"He did not know anything about the publishing business, but he didn't trust her. Obviously, he didn't think it was fair. That's why she wanted us to explain, I think. She was a very shrewd woman. There was nothing he could do. In those years, people did not sue each other over things like that."

"Do you think he hated her?"

"That's difficult for me to say. Nobody was happy. She even asked us to draft an agreement that he had to sign, specifying that he would never bother her again, before he received the money."

"So she ended up not paying a single penny to him?"

"Not a single penny came from her pocket."

"Did he come back to you?"

"No. He's not in Shanghai. There will be no more money, he understands, until the book runs into a second edition. If it ever does."

"Will it?"

"Well, we did a large printing for the first edition, which sold out. We thought about doing a second. Then her novel was published. Her name appeared on the government inside control list. We decided not to print a second edition."

"I'm confused, Comrade Jia. The poetry volume is not her book, is it?"

"But her name's also on the cover—as a special editor. Whether we remove her name or not, when people read the poems, they may think of the novel. My boss said it was not worth it."

"Do you have any other information about him—I mean the youth, Bao?"

"No, nothing," Jia said as he stood up. "Oh, he stayed with her for a few days, I remember. He had no relatives left in the city. She told me about it. But after the meeting, he must have gone back to Jiangxi immediately."

"I see. Thank you so much, Comrade Jia. Your information may be extremely important to our work."

It was like a missing piece of a puzzle that unexpectedly popped up at the last minute, Detective Yu thought, as he stepped out of the publishing house.

Outside, it was a sunny, yet cold, day. A middle-aged, scantily clad idiot was searching in a trashcan not too far away, singing a doggerel verse:

When red is black,
Old time comes back.
Oh, Oh, Oh, Oh,
You've got to pack
A Big Mac, a Big Mac!

Behind Detective Yu, from the café, came a line from a Revolutionary Modern Model Beijing Opera, "Chairman Mao's teaching thaws the ice in the dead of winter." A contrast in cacophony.

Yu had to find Bao, now perhaps a young man, he decided. From a pay phone at the end of Shaoxing Road, he called Chief Inspector Chen about the new lead.

"I have contacted the Shanghai Archives Bureau again," Chen said. "They have faxed me a list that contains some basic information about Hong and her son, Bao, and several pictures. I'll fax it to you. It may help."

It would be difficult for Yu to find these people in just a few days. He started by contacting Hong's middle school. According to the dean, there had been a class reunion the previous year. Hong had not attended, but one of her former classmates still had her address. With the address he obtained from her, Yu dialed the number of the Jiangxi Police Bureau.

Their reply came in the late afternoon. Hong was there, still in the village where she had already spent more than twenty years. A poor lower-middle-class peasant's wife, she had become just such a peasant herself. Chairman Mao's theory of the transformation of educated youths still applied. Hong did not want to come back to Shanghai, not because of her continuous belief in Mao, but because of her successful transformation. A poor lower-middle-class peasant would be a laughingstock in Shanghai today.

Bao was not there. He had left the village again for Shanghai about a year ago. In the nineties, millions of farmers found it impossible to stay on in their backward villages as they watched TV and saw how the fashionable, free-spending middle class lived in the coastal cities. In spite of the government's efforts to balance the development of the city and the countryside, an alarming divide between rich and poor, urban and rural, coastal and inland had appeared—these were the differences that the economic reforms Deng had launched a decade ago had helped create.

Like so many others, Bao had left home to seek his fortune. The first few months, he occasionally wrote home, and once even mailed fifty Yuan to his mother but the correspondence became less frequent, and then stopped. According to someone from the same village, Bao had not been doing too well in the city. The latest information Hong had was that about six months ago, Bao had shared a room with some other people from Jiangxi. Then he had moved out without leaving a new address.

So the problem was how to find Bao in a city where millions of people kept pouring in from every province. With new construction going up everywhere, provincials provided an ever-growing mobile labor force. Naturally, they did not bother to register their residences; they stayed wherever they found cheap housing.

Yu went over to the old address, where Bao had lived until six months ago; only one of Bao's former roommates remained. He did not know where Bao was. They did not keep in touch.

A notice was sent out to the neighborhood committees, particularly to those areas where provincials were known to gather together.

In normal circumstances, three to five days would be considered a reasonable period before any feedback started coming in, but Yu did not think he could wait that long.

Chapter 21

Chen had several days left of his vacation, but he went to the office because he had turned in the translation of the New World business proposal. It had not taken as long as he had expected. Of course, he anticipated that he would have to make minor changes when Gu's American partner faxed back corrections and suggestions. But according to Gu, the initial response from across the Pacific Ocean was positive. Chen himself was now quite satisfied with the English proposal, which presented a comprehensive, convincing argument for the potential success of the project.

It would be nice to have a secretary working for him here in the office too, he thought, but he knew he'd better wait patiently, until he moved up one more notch in the bureau hierarchy before making this request.

There was a noise outside the window. He looked out. Not too far away, another matchbox-like apartment complex, supposedly postmodern, seemed to look back at him with a dull stare. Each building in the area seemed to be identical, each lost in the other's reflection.

After all, the New World might be a good addition to the city, a fresh alternative to the commercially designed metropolitan landscape, even though the New World itself had been conceived out of commercial considerations.

What convinced him of its plausibility was not the study of the city's architectural history, as elaborately presented in the business proposal, but his realization that there was now a rising middle class eager to claim a culture of its own. China was no longer a society of utopian egalitarianism as it once had been under Chairman Mao.

From the various documents littering the desk, he managed to dig out the latest bulletin of the city housing committee. Turning to the last section of the bulletin, he started checking through a list of rooms that had been turned back in to the city authorities.

Housing assignment was a very complicated issue. Because of the severe housing shortage, some of the new apartment assignees had to hand over their former rooms in exchange. Most of them were single, all-purpose rooms rather than apartments. Invariably, they were smaller, or shabbier, than the newly assigned housing. But they would in turn be reassigned by the city housing committee. Those on the top of their respective working unit waiting list, like Detective Yu, might not be interested in such second-hand rooms with neither bathrooms nor separate kitchens.

Chen wanted to see if there was a room listed in the area designated for the construction of the New World. To his pleasant surprise, he found one—actually, one and half rooms, converted out of an original *shikumen* front wing, facing the courtyard. The former resident had even partitioned the wing into two areas, though the small back room thus created could contain only a single bed.

And there was an extra bonus. Rooms in *shikumen* houses built in the thirties never had an indoor flush toilet; the chamber pot was a necessary nuisance. Here the previous resident had installed a kind of electric chamber pot. It was not as good as a toilet, but it would spare its owner the trouble of getting up early every morning to perform the routine of chamber pot emptying and washing.

He placed a phone call to the city housing committee. The associate director of the committee gave Chen a positive answer regarding the availability of that particular room.

"We will hold it for *you*, Comrade Chief Inspector Chen."

Such an old-fashioned room might not appear to Yu to be a satisfactory substitute for the new apartment in Tianling New Village that he had lost. But this *shikumen* room had potential that Chen alone knew about: it was on the street where the New World was going to be built. The value of properties there would increase tremendously when construction started. And as Gu was the potential buyer, Chen was sure he would be able to put in a word or two on behalf of Yu. According to the newest policy, compensation to the resident would be negotiable depending upon the value of the property—and, even better, the original resident could claim a new apartment of similar size in the same area when the project was completed.

Then Chen started to think about buying a room in that area, too. Perhaps he could buy a modest room for his mother, who refused to move in with him. At least it would be better than the attic she had lived in for thirty years. With the payment from the translation, he reflected, it was not unimaginable.

He wondered if there might be a conflict of interest. There was no hurry for him to make up his mind though. He would decide later.

At this moment, he had to think of a way to talk Yu into it—without saying a single word to him about the New World.

A hint might be enough.

He lit a cigarette as he started visualizing a future visit to Yu in his new quarters, taking part in a game of *go* in a quaint courtyard, drinking a cup of Dragon Well tea. Perhaps there would be some neighbors in the background, merely as part of the traditional scenery. The picture was a pleasant contrast to his own apartment building, where people met, if at all, briefly, quickly, impersonally, on the stairs or in the narrow hallway. People were simply classified as Room 12, Room 35, Room 26.

He wondered whether he had been influenced by the business proposal for the New World. It was possible. People could be influenced by a book, a movie, a song, a proverb, not to mention a proposal interrelated with the cultural history of the city. He was no exception.

It was then that, like an apparition, Party Secretary Li dropped by his office.

"Great! You are already back at work, Chief Inspector Chen."

"I just stopped by to take a look at the paperwork that has piled up. There may be some urgent documents or letters that need my attention."

"The Propaganda Minister of the city government has talked to us again. We have decided to hold the press conference this Friday. It's time the Yin case was concluded. We cannot wait forever, you know." Li added, "It's really *his* decision."

The last sentence might have been added for face's sake. Chen had opposed the termination of the investigation, but the contrary decision might be a little more acceptable if, supposedly, it had been made by somebody outside the bureau.

Chen knew he was not in a position to argue. Yu had informed Li of the new lead, about Bao, but Li had brushed this aside. There were no witnesses and no direct evidence to connect Bao with the murder.

"With all the notices that have been sent out, some information about Bao should reach us soon, Party Secretary Li," Chen said, making a feeble attempt to stall.

"If you could find Bao and prove him to be the murderer before Friday, it would be satisfactory. We have also spoken to Internal Security, and they have no objection to that conclusion. But they want us to keep them informed if you find out anything," Li said amiably before leaving the office. "It's all in the interests of the Party authorities."

As Party Secretary Li's footsteps faded along the corridor, Chen picked up the phone, and decided that he was justified in dialing the number. In a Confucian classic, Chen recalled, there was a long paragraph on the term "expedience." It seemed relevant now.

"Hello, Gu."

"Hi, Chief Inspector Chen. I was just thinking of giving you a call. My partner has already showed the English proposal to an American investment banker."

"But the text has not been finalized yet."

"Well, it was too good an opportunity to miss. Mr. Holt decided to go ahead. We may have to make some minor changes later, of course. You have really done me a great favor."

"You are flattering me again. But I have to ask a you a favor, Gu."

"Anything, Chief Inspector Chen."

"If your are not too busy at the moment, how about meeting for lunch at Xinya? We'll talk there."

"Xinya, that's great."

They were seated in a private room in the state-run restaurant on Nanjing Road. Like other large restaurants in the city, Xinya had been resplendently redecorated. Its facade shone in the sunlight, and its rear connected with a new American hotel, the Amada.

"You made an excellent choice," Gu said. "Xinya used to be my grandpa's favorite place."

In his childhood, Chen's parents, too, used to take him there more often than to any other restaurant.

"Beef in oyster sauce. Fried milk. Garlic fried fish in a bamboo basket. Gulao pork. These were the dishes we ordered almost every time," Gu said. "My grandfather had a superstitious belief in them."

A waiter in a bright yellow uniform took their order down on a small pad, after suggesting many exotic, expensive possibilities.

Gu selected those specials his grandfather had always chosen. Chen asked for slices of winter bamboo shoots fried with dried winter mushroom, which had also been one of his parents' favorites.

"I am sorry, we do not have bamboo shoots."

"How can that be?"

"Bamboo does not grow in Guangzhou. Xinya is known for its genuine Guangdong-style cuisine. All our vegetables are from there. We get them delivered by overnight air freight."

"That's ridiculous," Chen said, shaking his head as the waiter stepped out of the room. "What about buying bamboo shoots in the local market?"

"Well, that's what a state-run restaurant is like," Gu said. "It's not their own business. Profit or no profit, the people here get the same pay. They don't care. Soon, you will come to dine in the restaurants of the New World. All of them will be privately run, and you may have whatever you like."

"Really, I am not such a fastidious gourmet," Chen said. "I wanted you to meet me here because I need to discuss something with you."

That was true. Chief Inspector Chen did not want to talk too much on the bureau phone, with people like Party Secretary Li dropping in without knocking; Li, for one, still did not have the word "privacy" in his vocabulary.

"Yes, please go on."

"Detective Yu, my long-time partner, has been looking for a young man named Bao," Chen said, producing a picture from his briefcase. "That's his picture, taken about a year ago in Jiangxi Province. Like other provincials, Bao has not registered his residence in the city. Detective Yu is having a hard time tracking him down. I do not think Bao is connected with the Blue or other triads, but those organizations may know more about the provincials than we do. The police do not have direct control over them."

"Let me ask around. There is one thing I do know about those provincials: if they are from Jiangxi, they will stay together in a certain new area, like Wenzhou village, where the police have not established control yet, but where the Blues have their contacts."

"Exactly. It's an important case for my partner. If you can find out something before this Friday, I would be very grateful."

"I will do my best, Chief Inspector Chen."

"I owe you a big one, Gu," Chen said. "Let me know as soon as possible. I really appreciate this."

"What is a friend for? You, too, are helping your friend."

The arrival of their order prevented them from saying more, but Chen thought he had covered what was necessary.

The lunch was not so satisfactory. The Gulao pork looked like sweet and sour pork done in a hurry at home. The beef in oyster sauce did not taste as delicious as he remembered it. The fried milk was a joke.

And Gu paid the check once again. The waiter took Gu's gold credit card—an unmistakable sign of his wealth—ignoring the cash in Chen's hand.

Later that afternoon, Chen arrived at the Renji Hospital with a small bamboo basket of fruit. At the front desk, he was told that his mother had been transferred to another room. Panic-stricken, he rushed upstairs, where he found that she had been moved to a better room, a semi-private which also had more advanced equipment. His mother was pleased to see him; she reclined in the adjustable bed, looking more relaxed than he had seen her in weeks.

"I'm really fine," she said. "They've been running one test after another. You don't have to come every day. And don't bring me anything more, I already have so many gifts."

It was true. There were so many things on top of the nightstand that it was almost like a display at an expensive food store: smoked salmon, roast beef, white bird nest, American ginseng, pearl powder, black tree ears, and even a bottle of Russian vodka.

Chen thought he could guess from whom this array came.

"No, they're not from Overseas Chinese Lu alone," his mother said, shaking her head, as if in disapproval of something invisible in the air. "Some are from a certain Mr. Gu. I had never met him before he came to see me here. He must be a new buddy of yours, I guess. He insisted on calling me aunt, like Lu does. He also summoned the head of the hospital to my room, and right in front of me, he pushed a bulging red envelope into his hand."

"He's incorrigible, that Mr. Gu."

But he was not completely surprised. White Cloud would have kept her real boss informed of everything concerning Chen, but Gu should have mentioned his visit over lunch.

"Since then the doctors and nurses have been extraordinarily nice to me. They moved me here. This is a much better room, normally for high cadres, they said," she told him and shook her head. "You must be somebody nowadays, son."

"No, not me, but Mr. Gu. I've been doing some translation for him."

"Really!" She appeared to be in better spirits and there was amusement in her voice as she said "Perhaps I'm too old to understand things in today's world, but since when have you had a secretary working for you at home?"

"She's no secretary." He had foreseen that his mother would mention this. In her eyes, he must have strayed far enough from his father's path. Now the news that he had a "little secretary" would only confirm her opinion. "She is just a temporary assistant for the translation project."

"She is young, clever," his mother said. "And she makes a very good home-made chicken soup."

"Yes, she is very capable." He doubted that the soup had been made in White Cloud's home. She bought the soup from a restaurant with Gu's money, probably. But he decided not to correct his mother.

"And she's a university student. She likes your work, she has told me."

He realized that his mother was already launched in a different direction. It should not have surprised him. "Yes, she's a Fudan University student," he said. He was not about to disclose that he had first met White Cloud when she was working as a K girl in a private room of the Dynasty Club.

Fortunately, his mother was still too weak to push this topic any further. He decided to leave well enough alone. If she wanted to cherish hopes, in spite of everything, especially in her present frail health, why not let her?

He did not like Confucianism, despite his late father's influence. Like many other people of his generation, Chen believed that Confucian ideology had caused rather than solved problems in the course of the history of Chinese civilization. Still, the chief inspector considered it only human nature to be a filial son. That was the least a man should do—to provide for his parents in their old age, and, whenever possible, to make them happy.

He shuddered to think of those who refused to pay the deposit for their parents at the hospital. And for those who were unable to do so. It was not their fault, of course. Chen was able to do so, in the last analysis, because of his Party cadre position.

Someday, he might be able to make his mother happy in that particular aspect, but his first priority must be to do a good job as a chief inspector of police. In the Confucian ethical system, responsibility to one's country was more important than to one's family.

As for White Cloud, she was just a temporary assistant, as he had told his mother. He did not know whether the future would ever throw her into his path again. There was no predicting with

Mr. Gu, of course. Two lines came to mind: *Waving my hand lightly, I'm leaving, / leaving, carrying not a cloud with me.*

He thought he had forgotten this poem by Xu Zhimo, and he wondered whether it had come back to him now because of her name. Or was it because of something else?

Chapter 22

The ringing of the telephone woke Yu.

Chen told him, "Bao's address is 361 Jungong Road. Second floor. It's in the Yangpu District."

Yu said, "How did you get this information?"

"Through one of my connections," Chen replied vaguely.

The boss did not sound too willing to go into detail. Yu understood.

"I'm on my way," Chen continued. "Not a word to Old Liang or anybody else. Meet me there."

This was a surprise to Yu. So far, Chen had made a point of staying in the background. When Yu reached that section of Jungong Road, the chief inspector was already waiting for him, smoking a cigarette.

In the pre-1949 era, this area had been a slum. It had been upgraded in the early fifties, when some workers' housing was built there to show the superiority of the socialist system. Nothing further had been done, as the city was overwhelmed by one political movement after another. The area was now considered a depressed neighborhood that had a markedly different living standard from other parts of the city. It had acquired a nickname—"the forgotten corner."

In recent years, it had also become one of the streets where provincials gathered because of the cheap rentals that they could obtain there by means of illegal subleases. Five or six people usually squeezed into a single room when they first arrived in the city. When they bettered their finances, they moved out into other areas.

"According to my information, Bao lives by himself in a small room here," Chen said. "He moved in about two months ago. He does a not have a regular job; he survives by working part-time for an interior construction company."

"If he has a room for himself, he is better off than others," Yu commented.

Bao's building, 361 Jungong Road, was one of the old two-story workers' houses from the fifties. It boasted neither the sophisticated style of a *shikumen* house nor the modern facilities of the new apartment buildings. The house consisted of units, rather than apartments; each unit was inhabited by several families; each family had one room and shared the common kitchen area. Bao's room had originally been a balcony accessed from the kitchen area of the unit. Beneath it was a small restaurant on the first floor of the building. It, too, looked like it had been converted from a residential room.

Chen and Yu went up the stairs. Their knock on the door was answered by a tall, lean young man of sixteen or seventeen. Bao looked like an undeveloped green bean sprout. His small eyes dilated with fear at the sight of Detective Yu in uniform. His room was one of the barest Yu had ever seen. There was hardly any furniture. A hardboard had been placed on two bamboo benches as a bed, and beneath it stood a disorderly pile of cardboard boxes. A broken chair and something like a student desk completed the furnishings, which appeared to be castoffs Bao had found and brought back.

"Let's crack this nut here before we take him to the bureau," Chen whispered.

This was not like Chen, who normally made a point of following procedure. But they were pressed for time, Yu knew. If they took Bao to the bureau, Party Secretary Li and others might join their interrogation. In one way or another, they might slow things down.

It was Thursday. They had to get the truth from Bao before the press conference on Friday.

"You'd better spill the beans," Chen told Bao. "If you come clean about what you did on the morning of February seventh, Detective Yu may be able to work out some sort of a deal for you."

"We know everything, young man," Yu said, "and if you are cooperative, we will recommend leniency."

Detective Yu did not know if he could guarantee this, but he had to back up Chen.

There was nothing for them to sit on, except for the broken chair. Bao squatted against the wall, like a wilting bean sprout.

"I don't know what you're talking about, officers," he said, without looking at either of them.

"You question him, Detective Yu," Chen said. "I will search the room."

Again, Chen was departing from his usual standard of behavior this morning, Yu observed. They did not even have a search warrant.

"Go ahead, Chief," Yu said, playing along. "Where were you on the morning of February seventh, Bao? We know what you did, so there's no point denying it."

Perhaps Bao was too young. He did not know that the police had to have a search warrant before they could go through his room. Still he evaded Yu's questions, mechanically proclaiming his innocence of any wrongdoing.

Chen, searching under the bed, pulled out a couple of cardboard boxes. Inside a shoebox he found a bunch of paper, rubber-banded together.

"This is the manuscript you took from Yin's place on the morning of February seventh," Chen said in a composed voice, as if this discovery was a foregone conclusion. "This is the manuscript of the novel that Yang wrote in English."

Yu manage to conceal his surprise as he said, "The game is over. Better come clean right now."

Bao looked like a green bean sprout that had been boiled and shrunken.

"I have the evidence now; you took this from Yin's room," Chen said. "There is no use denying it. This is your last chance to cooperate."

"Use your brains, Bao," said Yu.

"I did not mean it—" Bao started, all in a fluster. "I really did not mean to do it."

"Hold on," Chen said, taking out a mini tape recorder from his pocket.

"Yes, we can tape him here," Yu said.

"It's your case, Detective Yu. You question him. I'll take a look at the manuscript over a bowl of noodles in the small restaurant downstairs."

"Come on, Chief. You should question him too. Surely you can read here."

"I have not had breakfast yet. I'll be back as soon as I've had a bite."

So Bao began to confess. His head buried between his hands, squatting in a posture Detective Yu had seen in a movie about the farmers in the northwest region, with the tape recorder on the floor in front of him and Yu, seated on the hardboard bed gazing down on him, Bao spoke.

It had all started with Bao's first trip to Shanghai three and a half years earlier, on the occasion of his grandmother's death. The dying Jie had asked to see her grandson for the first and also the last time. Theirs was one of the numerous tragic stories from the Cultural Revolution. Hong, who had been a teenager then, had tried to join the Red Guard, but had been rejected because of her family background. Hong felt she had no choice but to prove her revolutionary fervor by cutting all her family ties. She denounced her parents as well as Yang, the Rightist uncle she had never seen. Hong was among the first group that went to Jiangxi Province in the movement of educated youths going to the countryside. She went one step further by marrying a local farmer, a decisive break with her former self.

At the end of the Cultural Revolution, Hong must have come to regret those "revolutionary decisions" of hers, but there was little she could do. Her father had passed away, and her mother would never forgive her. After the first two years of her marriage, she had practically nothing to talk about to her husband. All her hopes rested with her son Bao. She made him read books, and she told him stories. Most of the stories were about the wonderful city in which she had grown up. And there were a few about Yang too.

With the passage of time, Yang no longer appeared so black or counterrevolutionary to her; now he was a glamourous intellectual.

When her mother's dying request reached her, it took Hong several days to borrow enough money for a train ticket for Bao. The old woman still had not forgiven *her*. Bao alone boarded the train. By the time he reached Shanghai, Jie had passed away. Her room had already been reclaimed by the government. What she had left behind had been divided among her neighbors. One claimed that Jie had given her all her furniture, and another took Jie's old clothes. They were not worth much, but to Bao this was a huge disappointment. Hong had sent him forth with the expectation that he would receive an inheritance.

When Jie had lain dying, she had been alone. Now that she was dead, her grandson arrived out of nowhere to claim his due. No one wanted to put themselves out on his behalf. Bao did not even have a place to stay in the city. From the neighborhood committee, however, Bao learned one thing: among those who had attended the funeral service for Jie was Yin Lige. She had taken away with her an old photo album, as well as several old letters that no one else wanted.

One of the committee members suggested that Bao approach Yin for help. Hong had also mentioned Yin's name. She had heard that some of Yang's earlier translations had already been reprinted. Or maybe it was his poetry. There might be money awaiting him or at least Yin might have some information about it.

That's why Bao first went to Yin's room in Treasure Garden Lane.

Yin was all hospitality when he introduced himself. After all, Bao was closely related to Yang. She urged him to stay on for a few days. The location of the lane was convenient, and she suggested that he go sightseeing while she was busy with her teaching. She took him out when she had time. She even treated him to a meal at the Xinya Restaurant on Nanjing Road. Everything went well, until the moment he made known why he had come to Shanghai.

Her attitude changed completely. She had not earned any money from Yang's earlier translations, but Yang's poetry collection was another matter. She showed him the statement the publisher had sent to her. It did not specify how much was due to her as special editor, so she arranged a meeting for them with the editor. She insisted on the condition that, in return for a small payment from the publisher, Bao promise that he would never bother her again.

But Bao did not think it was fair. He believed that these city people, especially Yin, had taken advantage of a country bumpkin like him.

He went back to his village with less than a thousand Yuan. It was not such a small a sum to the villagers, but Bao was no longer the same young man, content to work there like his father and forefathers, toiling in the rice paddy, his legs covered in mud. The trip to Shanghai had opened his eyes to a new world. The fact that his grandmother had lived in the city all her life, and his mother for seventeen years, and, more than anything else, the legend of his granduncle, made it impossible for Bao to stay on in the poor, backward village.

He told his mother he was going to become a success in the city of Shanghai.

He was not alone. Several young men from the village had already left for big cities.

Shanghai, however, did not turn out to be the city of Bao's dreams. He had neither capital nor any skills with which to compete. Low-paying, hard-working temporary jobs on construction sites were all he could find. Yet he saw with his own eyes how the rich wallowed in money and luxuries, while his wages for a month were not even enough for one karaoke night. Still, if he had been willing to work hard like other provincials, it would not have been impossible for him to survive. But that was not enough for Bao.

With his Shanghai background, he considered himself different. He could not forget his great expectations, his hopes that there would be a lot of money awaiting him as the grandnephew of Yang.

He started reading about Yang and discovered the novel, *Death of a Chinese Professor*. Like others, he believed that its success was derived from Yin's relationship with Yang. So Bao felt that his claims as Yang's legal heir should not have been forgotten.

And if one poetry collection had been left to Yin, he thought there might have been other manuscripts, perhaps translations or novels. His mother had once mentioned that Yang had been writing a story before the Cultural Revolution. Then he learned that, but for the notoriety of *Death of a Chinese Professor*, Yang's poetry collection would have gone into a second or even a third printing, from which he would have gotten some money.

Bao did not simply lose himself in such speculations. While working at menial jobs, he tried hard to make a fortune in the ways that occurred to him. He started gambling on mah-jongg. This did not work out. He did not lose much, but those long, sleepless nights at the mah-jongg table cost him several odd jobs. Then he threw himself into the stock market with borrowed money. While he made a couple of hundred Yuan at first, he soon began to pile up losses as the money seemed to sink into a quagmire, and his creditors began hounding him, knocking at the door at all hours of the night.

In desperation, he thought of approaching Yin again. She had a lot of money—at least, it seemed so to him.

He thought she should have helped him.

Yin would have been nobody without Yang. The book, the money, the fame . . . all of it had come to her because of her relationship with him. And what was that relationship? They had not even been married. She did not even have a marriage certificate.

He, Bao, was Yang's only legal heir.

Bao hesitated to approach her because of the agreement he had signed. And the effort would most likely be useless, he supposed. When he learned about her visit to Hong Kong, however, he had an idea. At the time, those who came back from their visits to foreign destinations, including Hong Kong, were entitled to a certain quota for imported goods, such as a Japanese TV or an American stereo system. If they did not want to use the quota for themselves, they could sell it on the black market for a fairly large amount of money. Bao did not think Yin would have the space for this kind of equipment in the *tingzijian* room, or the guts to sell the quota for a profit on the black market. So what he was going to ask of her was to let him have the quota, something that would probably be of no value to her.

He phoned her but before he could begin to explain his proposal, she flew into a rage, threatening to call the police if he came to the lane again. Instead, he paid a visit to her at the school where she taught, calculating that a college teacher like her would not choose to make a public scene about something in her private life. He got through the college gate by claiming to be a former student of hers. And he found her in her office, alone.

"If you are not using the quota, you don't lose anything by giving it to me," he explained in a voice he thought full of reason. "As Yang's only grandnephew, I am asking you to please help me."

"Well," she said after giving him a long look. "I've been trying to save some money to buy a color TV for myself, but the quota is only valid for six months. Give me a call in two months. If I still do not have enough money by that time, then you can have the quota."

It was not an outright refusal, and she was already standing up. "You have to leave now. I have a class in ten minutes. Let me walk you to the door."

Before she marched him to the end of the corridor, however, two young female students came over to her with notebooks in their hands.

"You know the way out from here, " she said to him.

He did, but he heard something that made him pause and hide behind a concrete pillar.

"Professor Yin. You must remember me," one of the girls said in a sweet voice. "You taught me two years ago. You said I was your favorite student. And I will need your help when you get to the United States. I will need a letter of recommendation."

From what he overheard, he concluded that in two months Yin would be far away in the United States. So her promise was worthless.

The more he thought about it, the more upset he became. In his mind, even her opportunity to go abroad was derived from her relationship with Yang. He had to take action, he decided, before it was too late.

He remembered that she had left the keys dangling from the keyhole of her desk when she had literally pushed him out of her office, and that she had not locked the door because one of her colleagues happened to be coming in at that moment. So he sneaked back to her office. Her colleague was not there, and the office door was not locked either. No one had seen him enter the room, but his search of her desk drawer was not successful.

The only money he could find was some coins in a small plastic box. But then he realized that on the key ring were the keys to the back door of the *shikumen* and to her room. And he remembered something. During his previous stay with her, Yin had had him duplicate these keys for his own use. Perhaps because he had an accent, or because of his countrified appearance, the locksmith produced two duplicates for each, and charged him for them. Bao did not tell Yin for fear of losing face and he paid for the extra set out of his own pocket. Later on, he only gave back one set. He kept the keys together with the key ring decorated with the image of the dancer from the ballet *Red Woman Soldier*, as a souvenir. When he returned to Shanghai, he brought the keys with him.

He started to make plans, but he was cautious. He remembered her habit of getting up early in the morning for tai chi. Normally, she left the *shikumen* building at around five fifteen, and she did not come back until after eight. In that period, he could get into her room, take whatever there was, and leave either through the back or the front door. The earlier, the better, of course, as most residents would not get up before six. As long as he was not actually seen leaving Yin's room, he would not be in danger. The only possible risk was that one of her neighbors might recognize him. But since his previous visit, he had grown up, and that risk was slight. Even if he were to be identified as the thief, the police

would probably not exert much effort to track down a mere bur-
glar, nor would it be easy to trace him in Shanghai.

To make sure of his plan, he did some surveillance work. After
having observed the lane secretly for a week, he decided to act. He
sneaked in through the back door shortly after Yin left on the
morning of February 7. He did not really consider that he was
doing anything wrong, for he believed that it was only fair that he
receive a share of Yang's legacy.

But it took him much longer than he had anticipated to find
anything valuable to steal. There was less cash than he had
expected and no checkbook, much less a credit card. Then he
found the English manuscript in a cardboard box under the bed.
He could not read it, but he could tell what it must be.

When he heard footsteps mounting the stairs, he paid no attention. There were so many people in the building. Some of the
women went to the food market quite early in the morning.
But when he heard the sound of the key being inserted in the lock,
he was thrown into a panic. He rushed to hide behind the
door, hoping he might somehow sneak out unseen. Her face registered horror upon the sight of the ransacked room, in which
most of the drawers had been emptied out, and the shoeboxes
shoved into the middle of the floor. As she turned in his direction,
he jumped out, snatched up the pillow from the bed, and covered
her face while pushing her body hard up against the wall. He was
trying to stop her from shouting, but he used too much force.
When he finally let go of the pillow, she collapsed to the floor like
a sack.

It was impossible for him to stay with her corpse in that tiny
room.

He knew that he could not take the slightest risk of being seen or recognized by a neighbor, now that this had happened. It was a murder case now. He picked up the manuscript and the few valuables he had found, opened the door to her room, and stepped out onto the stairs. He could not leave the building through the front door. At any second, people might come from the rooms in the wings on either side.

As he went downstairs toward the back door, he saw the woman peeling shrimp outside. He could not retreat, so he had no choice but to hide in the space under the staircase. He did not have a plan; he was just bumping about like a headless fly. After the longest two or three minutes of his life, he heard some commotion in the lane. He peered out and saw that the shrimp woman was no longer there.

He dashed out.

Bao's narration lasted nearly two hours. Yu almost used up the tape. A few minutes before Bao finished, Chen returned carrying his briefcase and the manuscript under his arm.

A large part of Bao's tale confirmed Yu's earlier hypothesis, though some details surprised him.

"He did it," Yu said, nodding to Chen.

Chen put the manuscript on the bed, in front of Bao. "Did you know that Yin had this English manuscript?"

"No, I had no clue," Bao said. "But I had wondered about it. My mother thought she might have it. My mother had never met her uncle Yang, you know."

"Shall we take him to the bureau now?" Yu asked.

"Yes. I called Little Zhou from the restaurant downstairs. He said he'd be here at one o'clock in a bureau car. He may be waiting downstairs now."

They walked Bao down. Sure enough, Little Zhou was waiting for them in a Mercedes.

"Chief Inspector Chen, we will always have the best bureau car for you."

Chen seemed to be lost in thought as he tapped his fingers on his bulging briefcase, which rested on the seat beside him.

"I have one question, Chief Inspector Chen," Yu said. "Yang's novel manuscript should have been kept in the bank safe, together with his translation of Chinese poetry into English. Why did she leave it in her room?"

"She was too clever for her own good. Do you think the safety deposit box would be safe enough for someone like her?" Chen said. "She might have purposely rented a bank box so people would assume her valuables were there and would not suspect that she kept anything important in her room."

Chapter 23

The investigation of Yin Lige's case had been successfully concluded, Chen could assure himself, and the translation of the New World business proposal was finished. But the phone in his apartment started ringing early in the morning, like an alarm clock set at the wrong hour. It was Gu.

As Chen listened to him, a line came to mind. *What will come, eventually comes.*

That line had been inscribed beneath a traditional Chinese painting of a wild white goose carrying an orange sun on its wings, an exquisite painting he had seen years ago, in Beijing, in the company of a friend. It had hung on the wall of her room in Muxudi.

The line would often come back to him unexpectedly. This morning, what brought it back was a request for a multi-level garage, or, to be exact, for additional land close to the New World upon which such a garage could be constructed. Gu had a number of good reasons for this request, which he had made to the city government, and now he was telling Chen about it.

"So many people will come to the New World, not only in taxis, but in their own cars. For most of these customers, private cars will be a matter of course. The middle class is no longer interested in shopping along Nanjing Road. Why? There is no parking and no garage space. That's at least one big reason. GM has already signed a multi-year agreement with the Shanghai government for a gigantic automobile joint venture. In addition to Volkswagens, you will soon see as many Buicks in Shanghai as in New York. The New World will be a landmark for this century, and for the next one. We have to be foresighted in our business planning or the neighboring area will be terribly jammed with traffic."

"That may be true," Chen said.

"This concerns the image of our city, especially from perspective of the city traffic control office. I believe it's important to take preventive measures." Gu added, "You were the director of that office, I remember."

"Acting director. I was only the acting director for a short while."

"Oh, what's the name of that secretary of yours? Meiling or something. She simply adores you. 'The temple is too small for a god like Chief Inspector Chen,'" was what she said, the night she was with you at the Dynasty Club. The traffic control office will surely do whatever you say."

So Gu was asking him to put in a word on his behalf to the city traffic control office.

"You cannot rely on Meiling's words, Mr. Gu," Chen said. "Why didn't you put this request in your earlier proposal to the city government?"

"It's such a big project that some details may have been overlooked."

But Gu had not overlooked this necessity, Chen was sure. Gu

must have had in mind Chen's former position when he'd offered him the well-paid translation project, and sent him White Cloud as a little secretary, as well as the air-conditioner that now stood against the bookshelf, the heater in the bathroom, the presents on his mother's nightstand in the hospital—and the tip about Bao's address, too.

There's no free lunch. He should have known better.

After having translated the New World business proposal, however, he believed that the request was a reasonable one. In fact, he found himself attracted to the vision of the New World, and not only because he had been paid so generously for the translation of the proposal; he had come to believe that the project would enhance the cultural image of the city. For a fast-developing city like Shanghai, cultural preservation could be of great significance, even though the New World was designed to meet only the demand for an exterior retro look.

And for a grand project like this, a multi-story garage would be necessary. It would be a disaster for Huaihai Road, as well as the neighboring areas, to be jammed with cars of New World shoppers parked everywhere at random. So the traffic control office might make a suggestion to the city government.

For Gu, the grant of land in the heart of the city, in the name of cultural preservation, would save him a huge amount of money, and perhaps even the project itself. Businessmen applied to the city government for the use of land and the government charged them in accordance to the specified land usage. For a high-end commercial use like the New World, Gu would have had to pay a very large sum. But, as he had confided to Chen, Gu had applied instead for a cultural preservation project. Of course he had not included a multi-level garage in that proposal, for it would have aroused suspicion. But as an add-on, backed up by the traffic control office, he might get quick approval. What Gu had paid for the translation was nothing, like a feather plucked from a Beijing duck, compared with what he hoped to gain.

From another perspective, however, the grant of Gu's request would mean a loss of revenue to the traffic control office. A large modern garage would put a lot of cars out of sight, but it would also put a lot of patrol officers out of work and eliminate the fines they might otherwise collect. So it might not be that easy for him to back Gu's request, he understood, and Gu understood this too.

"Well, when it is convenient, put in a word for the New World," Gu said very smoothly.

Chen could always claim that he was still waiting for that convenient moment, but he would probably not do so. The bottom line was that he was obliged to help Gu with respect to the garage request. "I'll make a couple of phone calls," he said vaguely at the end of the phone conversation. "And I will call you back, Gu."

Chen decided that first he had better go to the hospital. He had to pay the medical bill there. His mother would be released that evening. She had been worried about the expense. There was no point letting her know how much it cost; in any case, the money from the translation would surely cover it. This gave him an extra sense of self-justification, he reflected, as he arrived at the hospital accounting office. In the age of the market economy, the hospital made no exceptions, so neither need he, as long as he made money in a way that was acceptable to the system.

To his surprise, he learned that his mother's factory had already paid the hospital bill. "It's been taken care of, Comrade Chief Inspector Chen," the hospital cashier said with a broad grin.

"Comrade Zhou Dexing, the factory director, wants you to give him a call when you have time. This is his number."

Chen dialed the number from a pay phone in the lobby.

It was no great surprise to him to hear a warm speech from Comrade Zhou Dexing: "Our factory is having a difficult time, Comrade Chief Inspector Chen. The national economy is in a transitional period, and a state-run factory meets with one problem after another. For an old worker like your mother, however, we will take responsibility for her medical expense. She has worked all her life with utter dedication to the factory. We know what a good comrade she is."

"Thank you so much, Comrade Zhou."

What a good comrade her son is; somebody must have tipped him off about that, thought Chen. Whatever his motivation, what Comrade Zhou had said and done was politically correct, even an appropriate subject for an editorial in the *People's Daily.*

"For our work in the future, we will continue to enjoy her support, I hope, and yours too, Comrade Chief Inspector. I have heard so much about your important work for the city."

These official courtesies were a polite veneer. But Chen was not worried. *There are things a man can do, and things a man cannot do.* This Confucian dictum could also mean that no matter what others might ask him to do, he would make his decision in accordance with his principles.

A new sort of social relationship, cobweb-like, seemed to have developed, connecting people closely together along the threads of their interests. The existence of each thread depended on the others. Like it or not, Chief Inspector Chen was bound up in this network of connections.

"You really flatter me, Comrade Zhou," Chen said. "We all work for socialist China. Of course we will help each other."

That was not the Confucian ideal of a society, not the one envisioned by his father, a Neo-Confucian intellectual of the old generation. Ironically, Chen reflected, it was not totally irrelevant to Confucianism either. *Yiqi*, or the *oughtness* of the situation, a Confucian principle that emphasized moral obligation, had somehow evolved into oughtness of one's own interest.

But Chen reminded himself that he had no time for such philosophical speculation.

He walked into his mother's room. She was still asleep. Although the test results had excluded the particular possibility that had worried him, she had been growing visibly weaker in the last few years. He decided to stay with her for a while. Since the onset of the translation project, almost simultaneously with the murder of Yin Lige, this was the first day that he could spend some peaceful time with his mother without worrying about this clue or that lead, or about definitions and phrasing.

She stirred in her sleep, but she did not wake. It might be as well. Once awake, she would probably lead their talk to her number one question: Now that you are established in life, what about your family?

In traditional Chinese culture, both "establishment" and "family" were at the top of a man's list of priorities, though the latter appeared more urgent to his mother. Whatever he might offer about his career and Party standing, his personal life was still a blank page to her.

Again, he thought of the line under the painting of the goose in Beijing, although in a different context: *What will come, eventually comes.* Perhaps it was not time yet.

He started peeling an apple for his mother. That was something White Cloud had done in his place, he remembered. Afterward, he put the peeled apple in a plastic bag on the nightstand. He looked into the drawer of the nightstand. He might as well start putting things together for her. Perhaps he would have to leave before she woke up.

To his surprise, he found a small photograph of White Cloud in a book of Buddhist scripture his mother had brought with her. In her uniform as a college student, White Cloud looked spirited and young as she stood in the impressive gateway of Fudan University. He understood why his mother had kept the picture. For his mother, as Overseas Chinese Lu had once put it, *Anything that came into her bamboo basket must be counted a vegetable now.*

White Cloud was a nice girl, to be sure. She had helped a lot: with the translation, with his mother in the hospital, and with the investigation. For all this, he could not but be grateful to her. He did not want to denigrate her because at their first meeting she had been a K girl with whom he had danced, his hand on her bare back, nor for being a "little secretary," with all the possible connotations of that term. Chen considered himself above that sort of snobbishness.

What his mother had obviously thought about her in connection with him, however, had never entered his mind. This was not so much because of the difference in their ages, or in their backgrounds, it was just that it seemed to him that they lived in two different worlds. But for the business of the New World, their paths would never have crossed. The translation was now finished, and he was pleased that she could go back to her life, whatever it might be like. There was nothing for him to be sentimental about. She was paid for her work as a little secretary. "Paid handsomely," as she had put it; the way he was paid, although at a different rate and for a different reason.

But then, was he really so sure about himself?

Was the filial son sitting with his mother the same man as the Mr. Big Bucks drinking with his little secretary in the Golden Time Rolling Backward?

"Are you Chief Inspector Chen?" A young nurse poked her head into the room. "Someone is waiting downstairs for you."

Chen took the steps in long strides. To his surprise, he found Party Secretary Li waiting in the lobby, carrying a large bouquet of flowers, in sharp contrast to the familiar image of the serious senior Party cadre in his high-buttoned Mao jacket. A bureau Mercedes was parked in the driveway.

"They told me your mother is still sleeping," Li said, "so I think I'll just say a few words to you here. I have a city government meeting this morning."

"Thank you, Party Secretary Li. You are so busy; you shouldn't have taken the trouble to come here."

"No, I should have come earlier. She is such a nice old lady. I have talked to her a couple of times, you know," Li said. "I also want to thank you on behalf of the Shanghai Police Bureau for your excellent work."

"Detective Yu did the work. I only helped a little."

"You don't have to be modest, Chief Inspector Chen. This was an excellent job. No political complications. Simply wonderful.

"That's what we are going to say at the press conference. The motive for the crime was some money dispute between Yin and a relative. Nothing to do with politics."

"Yes, nothing to do with politics," Chen repeated mechanically.

"In fact, we have already had some positive reaction. A *Wenhui* reporter said that Yin should not have been so mean to Yang's grandnephew. And a *Liberation* reporter said that she was really a shrewd woman, too calculating for her own good—"

"You have not held the press conference yet, have you?"

"Well, these reporters must have heard about our conclusions one way or another. Their stories may not be so helpful to her posthumous reputation, but I don't think we have to worry about that."

"Who can control stories, the stories after one's life? / The whole village is jumping at the romantic tale of General Cai—except that this story is not so romantic."

"You are being poetic again, Comrade Chief Inspector Chen," Li said. "By the way, we don't have to mention Yang's novel manuscript. We should not. Internal Security has made a point of this. It's in the best interest of the Party not to say anything about it."

That was the real reason for Party Secretary Li's visit, Chen realized. Li would be in charge of the press conference, and he had to make sure of what would—and would not—be said by the cops in charge of the case.

After Li left, Chen noticed fallen petals from the bouquet on the ground. As with White Cloud, he did not want to judge Yin. In spite of Bao's statement made in his self-defense, or the reporters' comments made from their journalistic perspectives, Chen chose to see Yin as a woman who had had complexities forced upon her.

It was true that Yin had a monetary interest in the publication of Yang's poetry collection. To be fair to her, however, she had put in a lot of work as editor. A labor of love, done in memory of him. Yet she could have earned more by giving private lessons, like many English teachers in the nineties. In the last analysis, she, too, had had to survive in an increasingly materialistic society.

It was also true that Yin had kept Yang's novel manuscript a secret and that she had no intention of sharing it with Bao, whose position was that he should have inherited it according to law.

But what *was* the legality of this situation?

A piece of paper called a marriage certificate had been denied to the lovers in those years of the Cultural Revolution.

What would have happened to the manuscript had she handed it over to Bao? He had no idea of its contents or value. He would have tried to make money by selling it to an interested publisher, but he could never have succeeded. He would have ended up by having the manuscript confiscated by Internal Security. So Yin was justified in keeping the manuscript a secret from Bao, and from everybody else. She must have waited for her opportunity, Chen reasoned; then, on her visit to Hong Kong, gotten in touch with a literary agency, reached an agreement, and prepared to take it with her when she went to the United States as a visiting scholar.

That also explained her rental of a safety deposit box at this time. She must have thought of it as a sort of camouflage. She had had to be careful. Internal Security might have heard rumors arising from her trip to Hong Kong.

As for her use of the American publisher's advance—from Yang's novel—as her means of financial support in the affidavit, Chen did not see anything improper in this either. In the event the novel was published in the United States, she would surely be overwhelmed by political troubles here. So she had had no choice but to go to the United States for the publication of the novel. For her, that must have been more important than anything else.

And Chen was also more than willing to overlook her "plagiarism." If she had been unable to publish Yang's book, she would have made at least part of his writing available to readers. And she must have regarded herself as one with Yang, as in that celebrated poem, "You and I," quoted in *Death of a Chinese Professor*. There was no point distinguishing between the two of them when they had already turned into one.

Of course, a lot more could have been involved, a lot more than Chen might ever come to know, or than he might ever want to know. What he chose to think was, perhaps, just one version of the story, seen from one perspective. Perhaps, as in the proverb, *When the water is too clear, there will be no fish;* as long as things were not too muddy, it was not up to him to investigate.

For the moment, he would choose to believe that it was a tragic love story, one that lightened up the darkest moments in the lives of Yin and Yang. After Yang's death, Yin had tried hard to continue living in the story, through her writing and through his writing too, but in the end she did not succeed.

Chen produced a photocopy out of his pocket. It was a poem which, for some reason, was not included in Yang's poetry collection. The poem was titled "Hamlet in China":

A rustle of the synapses rushes me
to the stage, to a sea of faces
drowning in the dark, and clutching
for a straw of meaning, in my stepping
into the light. A role, like
all others, is to be played in
[in]difference, mad or not
mad. A camel, a weasel, and a whale,
to construct and to deconstruct,
when reality is the ever-changing
signifier. What is the meaning? A dictionary

entry that defines me with a sword
killing a rat or a rat-like noise.
O father, whatever it is, tell me.

In his novel, Yang had tried to emulate Pasternak's narrative structure with twelve poems grouped together at the end of the novel, lines supposedly written by the protagonist, in sequential reflections on his life, crushed in the those years of socialist revolution under Chairman Mao. Chen wondered when Yang had written "Hamlet in China." Judging from its order in the sequence, it might have been composed during the Cultural Revolution. If so, the stage in question could have referred to the "stage of revolutionary mass criticism," upon which Yang had stood as a black target, with his "crimes" written on a blackboard hung around his neck. Yang had rendered it in such a universal way, however, that a reader unfamiliar with Yang's real experience might have come up with a totally different interpretation. It needed such an impersonal distance—which reminded Chen of another great poet—to represent Hamlet in the waste land.

Even today, Chen felt connected to that poem. After all, a role is to be played, whatever meanings or interpretations may be imposed on it, like the role of Chief Inspector Chen.

Surprisingly, the novel manuscript did not have a title. Chen thought he might as well call it *Doctor Zhivago in China*. Eventually, he would find a way to have the manuscript published. He made a pledge to himself. He did not really consider it a conflict with his political allegiance as a Party cadre. Like Boris Pasternak, Yang had passionately loved his country. The novel was not an attack on China. Rather, it represented an honest, patriotic intellectual's unwavering pursuit of his ideals in an age when everything in his country had been turned upside-down. It was a novel written with unrivaled passion and masterful technique. China should be proud of such an excellent literary work produced in the darkest moment of its history, Chen concluded.

But there was no need to act in a reckless hurry, nor to take any unnecessary risk. The manuscript had been finished years earlier, and it still retained its power. First-class literature does not suffer with the lapse of time. It should not matter too much if the manuscript were to lie unpublished for a few years more.

Internal Security was still on the alert. They had inquired about how the chief inspector and his partner had come to find the manuscript, and he had simply said that it had taken Detective Yu's hard work to trace Bao and obtain his confession, and that they had at once marched Bao over to the police bureau with the manuscript. The press conference was scheduled for the next day. They could not afford to delay any longer.

He had not mentioned that he had had the manuscript in his hands for about two hours, and been busy copying every page of it at a street-corner copy shop, before he returned with it to Bao's room. His story was plausible, but Internal Security had never really gotten along with him, and he had to be very careful.

Besides, the way things were changing in China, in five or ten years, publication of Yang's novel might not be totally unimaginable—

"Chief Inspector Chen." The young nurse approached him again in the lobby.

"Oh yes, how is she?"

"She is doing all right, still asleep." she said. "But when she is out of the hospital, you have to pay more attention to her choice of food."

"I will," he said.

"Her cholesterol level is still too high. The expensive delicacies on the nightstand may not be good for her."

"I understand," he said. "Some of my friends are incorrigible."

"She must be proud of a successful son like you with all those important buddies."

"Well, you'd really need to ask her that."

As he walked toward his mother's room, he was surprised at the sight of White Cloud making a call at the pay phone. Her back was toward him, but she was wearing the same white, large-collared wool sweater as on the first day she had reported to his apartment. She must have come to visit his mother again.

She had a cell phone, he remembered, but it was not surprising that she should use a pay phone, considering what her cell phone bill at the end of the month might amount to. He, too, had used the pay phone in the lobby.

Was it possible that Gu had given her a cell phone only for her assignment? And now that the job was finished, he had taken it back? In any case, it was none of his business.

She seemed to be engrossed in a long conversation. He was about to step away when he heard his title mentioned. He snapped to attention, and took a few steps to the side until he was out of sight behind a white pillar.

"Oh, that chief inspector. . . . What a prig . . . impossible . . . so self-important."

There was no justifying his decision to go on eavesdropping. But he remained fixed by the pillar, hardly able to convince himself that he was lurking there for the purpose of finding out more about Gu.

"Those Big Bucks at least know what to do with a woman. . . .

Not so goddamned bookish, so busy keeping his official neck untouched. He will never take a risk for something he wants."

From the position in which he stood, he could not quite make out every word she spoke. He could tell himself that she was probably talking about somebody else, but he knew it was not so.

"He loves only himself. . . ."

Was she so aggravated by his "political correctness" or "Confucian morals?"

Perhaps he was too bookish to figure this out. Perhaps she was so modern or postmodern that in her company, he was hopelessly old-fashioned. Hence the inevitable conflict. Perhaps he did not understand her at all.

In a Zen episode he had read long ago, a good lesson came with a blow. *When you are knocked out of your usual self, things may be seen from a totally different perspective.*

Or perhaps it was nothing but business. In business, every gesture was possible, for a possible reason. Hers would have been made for his approval, and more importantly, for Gu's approval. It was not every day that she could have landed such a job. Now that their business was finished, she was making her objective comments.

Yet these objective comments hurt.

I am a cloud in the sky, casting a reflection, / by chance, in the heart of your wave. Don't be too amazed, / or too thrilled, / in an instant I'll be gone without a trace.

Those were lines from another poem by Xu Zhimo, also with a central image of a cloud. The poem would read far more naturally in her voice. She was not meant for him. Still, he should be grateful to her, whether their relationship had been all-business or not. In those hectic days, her help really had made a difference. He wished the best for her now that everything was over.

He decided not to go back to his mother's room. White Cloud would be there too. It was time for him to return to the routine bureau work which he had become accustomed to, the way a snail becomes used to its shell.

No more little secretary, nothing. He was truly like the blank page he had thought of in his mother's company a short while earlier.

Afterward, on the way to the Shanghai Police Bureau, he dropped in at a travel agency, where he booked his mother a trip to Suzhou and Hangzhou with a tour group. She had not had a vacation for years—not since the early sixties, when she had taken him to Suzhou on a one-day trip. He had been a Young Pioneer, in his pre-school days, and his mother, wearing a red silk *cheongsam*, had been very young as they stood together in the Xuanmiao Temple. A trip might help her to recover, he thought. A pity that he would not be able to accompany her. There was no possibility of his taking another vacation, not after he received a phone call from the Central Party Discipline Committee in Beijing urging him to be prepared for larger responsibilities. He decided not to discuss that with his mother.

"What a good son you are," the travel agent said.

Perhaps it was not too bad being Chief Inspector Chen.

And he also decided that instead of waiting for a distant future opportunity, he would start trying to do something now about the manuscript Yang had left. Chief Inspector Chen was prepared to take a risk for something he really wanted.

Chapter 24

Yu was pleased with the conclusion of Yin Lige's case. He was sitting in the courtyard while Peiqin was preparing a special dinner in the common kitchen area "in celebration of the successful conclusion of the case," she told him.

Qinqin was overwhelmed by the need to study for an important test next week. "Extremely important," Peiqin had declared. So the only table in the room was reserved for Qinqin until dinner time.

Incoming phone calls would not help Qinqin to concentrate. Nor did Yu want to smoke like a chimney with Qinqin studying hard in the same room. As a result, Yu had to remain in the courtyard, although it was chilly for this time of the year. Seated on a bamboo stool, with a pot of hot tea, a cordless phone, and a notepad resting on a slightly shaky chair in front of him, he looked almost like a lane peddler. He was going to write the report concluding the Yin case. It was his case, after all.

It was true that Chief Inspector Chen, while on vacation, had played a crucial part in the breakthrough but Yu believed that he had performed well as officer in sole charge. Police work could sometimes be like a blind cat jumping on a dead rat, dependent on a lot of luck. Still, the cat had to be there, capable of jumping energetically at the right moment. Whatever others might think, Chen and he had moved beyond the stage of splitting hairs over who should get the credit for each contribution to the solution of a case.

It was also true that Peiqin had helped a great deal. Chief Inspector Chen had praised her perception when she had shared her insight into the textual problems of *Death of a Chinese Professor*, which proved to be a crucial lead.

Even Old Liang had contributed in his way, pushing and pressing his theories, by the *ironic causalities of misplaced yin and yang*, a phrase Yu had recently learned from Chen.

As Party Secretary Li had declared, "The homicide case would have remained unsolved but for Detective Yu's hard work." What the Party boss did not admit was that but for Yu's hard work, the case would have been "solved" by the arrest and conviction for murder of an innocent man. Li would not say a single word about this at the press conference, of course, and he had taken pains to arrange for Yu to take a break at home while the conference was being held. As Chief Inspector Chen was still on vacation, it made sense for the senior Party cadre to talk about the significance of their work to the media. Yu readily agreed.

It was still a moment of triumph for him, Yu thought; a moment of redemption as well, in spite of his pathetically low pay, of his bottom-level rank, and of the fiasco that had taken his promised new apartment from him. What's more, it was a moment that might reinspire him to hang on to his position as a policeman.

The telephone calls kept coming as he sat in the courtyard. He had no more time to think about himself. There was still plenty to do to wrap up the murder investigation.

Whatever defense Bao might drum up, it was all over for him. Not only the city government, but the central government too, had expressed concern over the tragic death of Comrade Yin Lige. The murderer had to be punished. That was a foregone conclusion.

It remained for Yu to notify Hong, the poor mother who still had all her hopes vested in Bao. It would not be a pleasant job, and he was not in any hurry to do it.

The remaining loose end to the investigation was the manuscript Bao had stolen, even though it was Yang's rather than Yin's. It had at once been seized by Internal Security. To his puzzlement, Chief Inspector Chen had made no protest. Later he would have to discuss this with Chen, Yu decided.

Then, in accordance with the terms of Yin's will, whatever was left of Yin and Yang's money would go toward a scholarship for college students writing in English. It would not amount to a great deal, and it was not police business, but Yu had volunteered to help with this arrangement. To his surprise, Party Secretary Li had not objected.

The neighborhood committee was so pleased with the special commendation from the city government that they honored Yu by asking him to make a speech at the entrance to Treasure Garden Lane.

Lei, the food stall proprietor, telephoned to express his thanks to Yu for his investigative work. "I thank you from the bottom of my heart, Comrade Detective Yu. Finally, Yin may rest in peace. She must be in heaven, I know, looking down at this lane and at my business at the lane entrance, with a smile.

"And you know what? My lunch business is growing. So I am going to give it a formal name: 'Yin & Yang.' That will be my way of commemorating that remarkable woman, and it may also bring in more business. A magazine has already contacted me for the story of how she helped me at the lowest ebb of my fortunes. She's the *guiren*—important person—in my fate."

"We can never understand the workings of fate," Yu said, "but the restaurant's new name is catchy and should even attract customers who know nothing about the story behind it."

"Exactly. Yin & Yang. And it goes without saying, Detective Yu, whenever you come to the lane, lunch is on me—on the Yin & Yang Restaurant."

It had been much tougher, on the other hand, to deal with the two men who were in custody, Cai and Wan.

Cai should have been released days earlier, the day Wan turned himself in. Old Liang had objected, insisting that there was still something suspicious about Cai, for he had never provided an alibi for the night of February 6 or for the morning of February 7.

Finally, Yu had to put his foot down. "If Cai was detained as a suspect, he must be released now that the case is closed. I'm in charge, and that's my decision."

Grumbling, Old Liang realized that he had no choice but to let Cai out.

But for Wan, the situation seemed far more complicated. To begin with, no one could understand why Wan had come forward. He did not utter a single word when he was informed of Bao's arrest. He sat with his chin on his chest, like a statue, offering no explanation as to why he had confessed to a crime he had not committed.

According to one neighborhood committee member, Wan must

be assumed to be more or less demented—Alzheimer's disease or something like it must have been behind his confession. Another suggested that Wan had sought the limelight he had long missed. According to a third, Wan must have imagined himself to be the last soldier of the Cultural Revolution. And, finally, according to neighborhood hearsay, Wan was secretly in love, and he confessed in order to impress his undisclosed lover. Or a combination of various factors might have motivated him. For, as Chen had pointed out, Wan was like a fish out of water in present-day China, a factor that must have influenced his thought processes.

Old Liang was furious with Wan. The residence cop insisted that *some* charge should be pressed against him. "He should be sent to prison for at least three or four years. Wan deserves it. Deliberate false testimony! This ex-Mao Zedong Thought Propaganda Worker Team Member is crazy. He must believe he can do whatever he likes and get away with it, like in the days of the Cultural Revolution. He's simply lost in his spring-and-autumn dream! Our society is a legal society now."

It was Party Secretary Li, however, who decided against prosecuting Wan. "Enough is enough. We have had so many stories about the Cultural Revolution. There is no point bringing Wan into troubled water, too. People have to move on. Let the old man alone."

Politically, it was not a good idea to harp on the disastrous aftermath of the Cultural Revolution, or even to remind people of it. This was the very card Chen had played, though Li did not say this in so many words. Anyway, Wan's case was not to be interpreted politically, so Yu did not have to say anything. Outraged as Old Liang might be, Party Secretary Li had the last word regarding Wan's fate.

Still, the unsolved mystery of Wan's confession kept intruding itself into Yu's thoughts.

Stubbing out his cigarette, Yu got up and carried his phone into the kitchen area.

Peiqin was busy cooking, moving about in a maze of pots and pans. There was hardly enough space for the two of them.

She was genuinely pleased with the outcome of the investigation and with the part she had played. "So everything is finished," she said, turning to him with a bright smile, her hands still stuffing tofu with ground pork.

"There is still a lot to do to wrap it all up."

"Imagine I—imagine both of us—having done something for Yang," she said. "Yin was his only comfort in his last days. Now her murderer has been caught. In heaven, if there is a heaven, Yang must be pleased."

"Yes, the conclusion. . ." Yu found it hard to complete his sentence—*that his grandnephew killed the woman he loved.*

"Can you take out his poetry collection for me? It is in the second drawer of the chest."

"Of course. But why?"

"I think I have just gained a new understanding of Yang's poetry while I was busy cooking," she said. "Sorry, my hands are not clean. But when you bring the book here, I have something to tell you that is related to the case."

Yu came back with the poetry book in his hand.

"Please find the poem titled 'A Cat of the Cultural Revolution,'" she said. "Can you read it to me?"

He started reading in a low voice, still totally mystified. At times, Peiqin could be too wrapped up in books, just like Chief

Inspector Chen. Fortunately, she did not have too many idols like Yang. And there was no one else in the kitchen area just then.

My fantasy came true / with the Cultural Revolution / of being a cat, jumping / through the attic window, stalking / on the dark roof, staring / down into the rooms now peopled / with the strangers wearing / the armbands of "Red Guards." / They had told me "Go away, / bastard, you hear!" I heard, / only too glad to come / to the roof, where I found, / for the first time, that starlight / could shine so long in solitude, / and that Mother had changed / beside the Red Guards, her neck / bent by a blackboard like / a zoological label. I couldn't tell / the words written on it, but I knew / she's in no position to stop / my leaping into the dark night.

Morning brought me down / brandishing a slate, Mother sprang back / at the sight, as if the slate too / were designed for her swollen neck. / I couldn't help shouting / in a voice I had learned overnight, / "Go, and fetch a bowl of rice / for me, you hear!" Away she / scampered. A mouse scuttled / in the debris of a night's "cultural revolution." And / I decided, not being human enough / to be a Red Guard, to be / felinely ferocious. Back / from a visit to the dentist / one day, I caught her squealing, "No, / your teeth are sharp." "Alas, / she was born under the star of the mouse," a blind / fortune-teller said, sighing / by her deathbed. "It was / predestined, according / to the Chinese horoscope." / I ran out wild. There were / nine lives to lose, and I jumped / into the jungle.

I see a paw-print / on this white paper.

"Yes, it's about the Cultural Revolution," Yu said, after reading the long poem aloud.

"Now that I have learned more about his life," Peiqin said,

"I'm sure the narrator must have been based on Hong, the child of a 'black' family. Her family was persecuted by the Red Guards. Those kids suffered terrible discrimination. They were regarded as 'politically untrustworthy,' with no future in socialist China. Some of them could not help seeing themselves as less than human because they could never become Red Guards."

"Yes, that's why she denounced her parents, I was told."

"I can really relate, because I had a similar experience and harbored secret resentment against my parents," she said in a trembling voice before she controlled herself. "What a poem! It represents the dehumanization of the Cultural Revolution from a child's perspective."

"Yes, the Cultural Revolution caused many tragedies. Even today, there are people who have not been able to move out of its shadow, including Hong, and perhaps Bao too."

"Yang left a novel manuscript, didn't he?"

"It's in English. According to Chief Inspector Chen, it is a novel like *Doctor Zhivago*, about the life of a Chinese intellectual in Mao's years, but Internal Security has already snatched it."

"You could have made a copy."

"We didn't have time. The minute we entered the bureau, Internal Security was there. They already seemed to know about it. And Party Secretary Li was on their side, of course. Chen had read only several pages in the restaurant downstairs—"

"What?"

"He insisted that I conduct the questioning of Bao all by myself—since it was my case—while he read the book in a small restaurant on the first floor. He did not come back until the interrogation was over. I suppose he could have made a copy without my knowledge."

"Has he mentioned anything about the manuscript?"

"No, he hasn't said a word about it."

"He must have his reasons. I am not sure whether you should ask him about it," Peiqin said thoughtfully. "Chen is a clever man. He may try to do something that could be risky."

"You mean he doesn't want to involve me in some risky business—with Internal Security lurking in the background."

"Possibly. I cannot really tell," she said, and changed the subject abruptly. "Oh, we will have a wonderful dinner tonight!" She was mincing shrimp for the tofu stuffing now.

"You don't have to prepare so many dishes. We have no guests today."

"You have proven to the bureau what a capable cop you are. It's an occasion for celebration."

"In fact, I was thinking about quitting the job, Peiqin, that morning at Old Half Place," Yu said. "All these years, I've brought so little home. And you have had to work so hard, at the restaurant and at home. I might earn more for the family, I thought, if I could start some small business like Geng, or like Li Dong."

"Come on, my husband. You have done such a great job as a cop. I'm proud of you," Peiqin said. "Money is something, but not everything. How could you ever have had such an idea?"

"Thank you," he said, without going on to say, *but you once suggested it to me.*

"Now I'm going to fry the ribs. The oil will splash all around. So go back to the courtyard. I'll call you when the dinner is ready."

There was another surprise in store for Yu—an unexpected visitor.

It was Cai, the cricket gambler, who had been released through Yu's intervention. He stood on the threshold, carrying a bottle of Maotai in one hand and a huge live soft-shell turtle in the other.

When he learned that Qinqin had to study for his test, Cai insisted on accompanying Yu out into the courtyard. "Your son is busy with his homework. That's great. That's the most important thing under the sun. If I had had a good education, my business would not have collapsed. Let us talk outside," Cai said, leaving the presents with Peiqin before he clasped his fingers in a gesture of profound gratitude. "Comrade Detective Yu, I thank you."

"I only did what a policeman should do. You do not have to thank me, and you should not have brought me those presents."

"For such a great favor, it's almost meaningless for me to say thanks," Cai said sincerely. "The blue mountain and the green river will long, long remain and I will be forever in your debt."

"Don't overwhelm me with your triad jargon. I'm the policeman responsible for Yin's case. You have nothing to do with the case, so why should you be kept inside?"

"If there were more cops like you, instead of like Old Liang, there would be much less trouble in the world."

"Now that you are out, do something meaningful with your life, Cai. You cannot fight crickets forever. You have to think about your family. Your wife, Xiuzhen, has never wavered in proclaiming your innocence."

"I'll change as thoroughly as if I had washed my heart and replaced my bones. Yes, Xiuzhen is very good to me. She could have dumped me, but she did not. She came to me every day, bringing food made especially for me. I was wrong in believing that she had married me for my money."

"Yes, when you are in trouble, you find out who really cares for you."

"I still have some connections in today's world. I will stage a comeback in the Eastern Mountains."

"I have one question, Cai. When you were taken into custody, why didn't you tell Old Liang about what you really did that morning? As I said, I'm only interested in the Yin murder case. No matter what you tell me, you don't have to worry. It will be between the two of us."

"I trust you, Comrade Detective. I was playing mah-jongg in a bathhouse that night, all night long. Mah-jongg is not gambling, everybody knows that. It's just a game in which you have to put a little money down, otherwise it is no fun.

"But I was sentenced in the early seventies for gambling. So if I told Old Liang about it, he would have made a big fuss. In fact, he threatened to put me back in jail if he ever caught me betting on cricket fights in the lane."

"I see. Mah-jongg or cricket fights, they won't do you any good."

"I give you my word, Comrade Detective Yu. I won't waste this second chance. If my hand ever touches crickets or mah-jongg again, I swear to old heaven, may cancers grow all over my fingers. Believe me."

"Okay. Then I have just one more question for you," Yu said. "While you were in custody, Wan suddenly came forward, taking responsibility for a crime that had nothing to do with him. Do you have any idea why he did that?"

"It beats me. He may have lost his mind, for all I know or care. As a matter of fact, we had a fight not too long ago."

"Was the fight about your family's support?"

"Wan has no idea how much I give Xiuzhen's family each month. And it's none of his business either. That ugly old toad simply dreams of devouring the white swan."

"What do you mean by that, Cai?"

"The way he looks at Lindi speaks volumes. He wants to please

Lindi, but he has utterly lost his mind. He should pee on the ground and see his reflection in the pool."

"Well—" Detective Yu remembered the scene of Wan sitting on a bamboo stool in the courtyard, doing nothing, watching while Lindi cut the spiral shells. "But I still do not see why he claimed that he was the murderer."

"I have no clue," Cai said.

"Mr. Cai, I have just put the turtle into the steamer," Peiqin said in a loud voice from the kitchen area. "It took me a while to clean such a huge one. Please stay for dinner. The turtle will take just a little longer."

"Thank you, Peiqin, but I'm afraid I have to leave. Xiuzhen will be worried if I don't come back for dinner," Cai said. "If there is anything I can do for you, Comrade Detective Yu, let me know. I will do my best, like a horse or a dog."

Yu and Peiqin walked out with Cai to the lane exit.

"We have to wait a little while longer," Peiqin told Yu. "The coal briquettes I made last week do not burn very well. It will take time to steam the turtle." She wiped her hand on her apron, which bore fresh bloodstains.

"Oh, have you cut your hand?"

"No, those spots are turtle blood. Don't worry."

He didn't know how long he would have to wait. He was a bit hungry. He phoned Mr. Ren to thank him sincerely for his tip about Wan, and then mentioned Cai's comment regarding the ex-Mao Zedong Thought Propaganda Worker Team Member.

"I've not heard anything about Wan and Lindi," Mr. Ren said. "People do not talk to me that much. But there's no ripple without a breeze: one evening several months ago, I saw Wan pushing a bulging envelope into her hands."

"Do you think Wan confessed for the sake of Lindi?"

"Well, Cai is the main support of the whole family. If Cai were sentenced and executed, the whole family would be ruined. So it could have been an act of romantic self-sacrifice—a rather twisted notion of it," Mr. Ren said thoughtfully. "But I am not so sure. Wan is a bitterly disappointed old man. All the changes in today's society may be too much for him.

"I can understand. In the early fifties, when my company had been taken away, together with the *shikumen* house, I thought it was the end of the world. I hung on because of my children. Wan is all alone here. For him, this might have seemed to be a good opportunity to end his agony in a politically dignified way, and at the same time make a last noble gesture to Lindi."

"Yes, that makes sense now."

"I'm so pleased with outcome of your investigation, Comrade Detective Yu. The real criminal has been caught. That is what justice is about," Mr. Ren said. "By the way, the sticky rice cake at Peiqin's place, Four Seas, is super. I went there yesterday. You know what, I must have met her father forty years ago. Indeed, in this world of red dust, things may be predestined."

"I'm really glad we met you."

"Next time, I'll bring half a pound of xiao pork to her restaurant. You keep it in the refrigerator. You don't have to go to Old Half Place. But you need good noodles. The pork is best with noodles in hot soup."

"Next time I'll introduce you to my boss, Chief Inspector Chen. Another gourmet. You two will have a lot to talk about."

There did seem to be some mysterious correspondence in this world of red dust, as Mr. Ren had said. Yu still had the phone in his hand when Chen's call came.

"I have talked to the city housing office," Chen said in an urgent voice, "and there is a second-hand room available in the Luwan District. Twenty-four square meters, already partitioned in two. Sure, it's not one of those fancy new apartments, but it is a *shikumen* room, and it's practically in the center of the city."

"Really!"

Yu was confounded by Chen's choosing to talk about a second-hand room he had found listed by the city housing committee rather than about the case. Yu had long passed the stage, however, of being surprised by anything Chief Inspector Chen chose to do.

"I have made several phone calls, and from what I've heard, this is not a bad room."

"A *shikumen* room—" Yu was not sure whether this was an alternative he should jump at. Admittedly, it seemed to be better than the one he now lived in: it was ten square meters bigger, and already partitioned. It would offer some sort of privacy for Qinqin. And Yu would not have to share the entrance with his father, Old Hunter. But there would be no bathroom or kitchen in such a room. And if he took it, he would never be able to get a new apartment from the police bureau.

"You can choose to wait, Detective Yu. As long as I am on the housing committee, I will certainly do my best for you. Next time the bureau gets a new housing quota, you will be at the top of the list, but—"

That part of the speech Yu had heard, many times, especially "*at the top of the list,*" and he knew Chen's emphasis was really on the last word, "but," and on what was not said. No one could tell about the next time, about some "unforeseeable" twist like the events that had supposedly occurred last time. Qinqin was already a big boy. How much longer could Yu afford to wait? After all, it would be a bird in the hand, a real apartment, unlike Party Secretary Li's empty promises.

"Who knows if there will be a next time?" Yu said.

"Exactly. Housing reform may be inevitable in China but," Chen said, quoting a proverb, "*Once you have passed this village, you may not find another hotel.*"

"I'll think about it." Yu said. "I have to discuss it with Peiqin."

"Yes, discuss it with her. I'm thinking of buying a small room in the same area. In my opinion, it is a super area, with a lot of potential. It will be a small room for my mother; we may be neighbors there."

"That would be great."

Yu knew his boss too well. Chen usually had a reason for saying or not saying something, or for saying it in a roundabout way. With his connections, the chief inspector could be full of surprises.

"Let me know your decision as soon as possible."

"I'll call you tomorrow. Thanks, Chief."

Yu stood in the courtyard and lit another cigarette, crumpling the empty pack, as he started thinking about the second-hand room in earnest.

After all, there was one advantage living in a *shikumen* house. The courtyard. If they had moved into an apartment in Tianling New Village, where could he smoke like this?

"Dinner is ready," Peiqin said.

"I'm coming," Yu said.

After dinner, he was going to tell her about that second-hand room. Perhaps he should repeat Chen's comments, word for word. Sometimes Peiqin was quicker than he in reading hidden messages, as in the investigation of Yin's case. He really should be proud of her, he kept telling himself as he opened the door. But first he would enjoy a good dinner. There was a steamed soft-shell turtle on the table.

"Turtle is especially good for a tired, middle-aged man," she whispered in his ear.

It was a huge, monstrous turtle. With its head cut off and its shell strewn with sliced ginger and chopped scallions, it filled the small room with a dreamlike aroma.